THE COCAINE PRINCESS 3

Lock Down Publications and Ca$h
Presents
The Cocaine Princess 3
A Novel by *King Rio*

The Cocaine Princess 3

Lock Down Publications
P.O. Box 944
Stockbridge, Ga 30281
www.lockdownpublications.com

Copyright 2022 by King Rio
The Cocaine Princess 3

Lock Down Publications
Like our page on Facebook: Lock Down Publications @
www.facebook.com/lockdownpublications.ldp
Book interior design by: **Shawn Walker**

King Rio

Stay Connected with Us!

Text **LOCKDOWN** to 22828 to stay up-to-date with new re-
leases, sneak peaks, contests and more…
Thank you!

Submission Guideline.

Submit the first three chapters of your completed manuscript to ldpsubmissions@gmail.com, subject line: Your book's title. The manuscript must be in a .doc file and sent as an attachment. Document should be in Times New Roman, double spaced and in size 12 font. Also, provide your synopsis and full contact information. If sending multiple submissions, they must each be in a separate email.

Have a story but no way to send it electronically? You can still submit to LDP/Ca$h Presents. Send in the first three chapters, written or typed, of your completed manuscript to:

LDP: Submissions Dept
P.O. Box 944
Stockbridge, Ga 30281

DO NOT send original manuscript. Must be a duplicate.

Provide your synopsis and a cover letter containing your full contact information.

Thanks for considering LDP and Ca$h Presents.

King Rio

The Cocaine Princess 3

Part One:

Money, Money, Money, Money, Money Baaaags

King Rio

Prologue
Five Months Prior, November 1, 2011

"Shut the fuck up and listen. Bitch, if you ever wanna see your son again—alive, I mean—I need a billion dollars in cash delivered to Gary, Indiana in exactly seventy-two hours. You understand that?"

"Yes, I understand. Can you let me hear him? I need to know thathe's still.....okay."

"Bitch what the fuck you think this is, Burger King? Didn't I justtell you to shut the fuck up?"

"I'm sorry," Alexus cried.

The deep voiced kidnapper paused for what seemed like an eternity to Alexus Costilla. She was sitting on the right side of her fiancé, Blake King's hospital bed at Chicago's Northwestern Memorial Hospital, rockingback and forth with her iPhone 4S pressed against her ear. Tears were streaming down her breathtaking face. Her hands were trembling as thoughshe was freezing, though the full-length, white fur coat she donned over hersnow white Marchesa dress and five-inch, diamond-encrusted, custom- made Christian Louboutin heels had her feeling rather warm.

"Seventy –two hours," the voice finally said. "I want the cash piled up in the back of a semi-truck, a'ight? No funny shit. If we find any kinda trackin' devices mixed in with the money, I'm blowin' this li'l nigga's headoff. You got that?"

Alexus sniffled, "I understand. Just don't hurt—"The line went dead.

She turned to Enrique Aleman, her black-suited chief of security.

The broad-chested Mexican's eyes were glued to the screen of his own iPhone. Clearing his throat, he looked at Alexus and stated in Spanish, "Thecall came from Gary Indiana, on the corner of Fifth and Madison. Phone was purchased from a gas station in Hammond around six this morning. I'mgoing to head out to Gary, take about twenty men with me."

"I have the address and phone number to where the phone was purchased," Attorney Britney Bostic stated. Seated across from Alexus in an easy chair, clad in a dark blue Valentino pantsuit, the twenty-seven-year- old lawyer rapidly typed on her laptop. Her delectable, pie-shaped chocolate-hued visage was smooth and un-blemished, with a narrow noseand an infectious smile that hardly ever failed to brighten the spirits of everyone she encountered.

But today it was not working. Probably because yesterday, fifty-fivemembers of the Costilla Cartel – Mexico's reigning drug cartel, currently headed by nineteen-year-old Alexus Costilla and her sex-agenarian father, Juan "Papi" Costilla – had been shot to death and torched in Southampton County, Virginia. Also yesterday, Blake King, Alexus' nineteen-year-old fiancé had been shot once in the stomach and once in the shoulder by an ex-lover of his. Alexus had saved his life by putting three .44-caliber bullets through the de-ranged woman's face.

And yesterday, Alexus' four month old son, King Neal Costilla, had been kidnapped.

"I'm composing an email to the gas station manager requesting a copy of the camera footage. I'll wire him five grand and make him sign aconfidentiality agreement," Attorney Bostic told Alexus.

"Let's just give the kidnappers what they're asking for," Alexus said, gazing at the huge twenty-carat white diamond that sparkled prominently on her platinum engagement ring. "I have eight hun-dred and ninety million in hundred-dollar bills stashed in my vault in Matamoros, and I'm sure Papi has four or five times that stashed all throughout Mexico.All I want is my son back."

"What I am interested in knowing is how they got your phone number." Enrique said. "They had to have gotten it from someone close toyou."

"I don't give a damn about any of that right now. Just find my child," Alexus snapped. "Pay that man whatever he wants to get my son back. I want that ransom money loaded onto a Boeing 737 and headed hereby sundown."

Enrique nodded his head and left the room, pulling the door shut behind him. His absence did not worry Alexus. She had sixteen more heavily-armed bodyguards in the hallway, and all of them were trained tokill. Alexus Costilla's current net worth was $57.9 billion. According toForbes, she was the third wealthiest American, right up there with Buffet and Gates. Her paternal grandmother, Vida Costilla, had been a stock market titan for many years, a multi-billionaire for many more, and a Mexican drug cartel leader since her husband Segovia's death. Due to the

U.S. government's insatiable need for "illegal" narcotics to keep their lucrative state and federal prisons filled with drug offenders, Granny Costilla had been able to secure a deal with the Central Intelligence Agency granting her full immunity from any drug-smuggling or trafficking charges. All she had to do was continue to flood the United States with tons of cocaine and heroin via her state-of-the-art drug tunnel, which ran from Matamoros, Mexico to Brownsville, Texas.

Granny Costilla had been poisoned to death back in February, and her will left her then forty-eight-billion-dollar fortune—including a television network, a chain of nineteen lavish restaurants, and a billion dollar hotel resort in Cancun—to Alexus her beautiful, young granddaughter.

Now, seven months later and nearly ten billion dollars wealthier, Alexus found herself wishing Granny Costilla had left her fortune to someone else; having this much money was nothing more than an unprecedented migraine. Especially for a teenager. "Mo' money, mo' problems" as P. Diddy had famously stated, was truer than people realized.

With a despondent sigh, Alexus turned around to study Blake's dark brown face. He was in a drug-induced slumber, his eyes flicking around urgently behind their lids. Alexus touched her fingertips to the two dimple-like gunshot scars on his left cheek. Last Christmas Eve, he'd been shot ten times across the street from his parents' old home in Michigan City, Indiana. Two of the bullets had entered the left side of his face, shattering his jawbones and leaving twin exit wounds in his right cheek.

Miraculously, he survived that shooting and Alexus prayed he would make it through this one as well.

"Where is my sister?" She asked Britney.

"Downstairs with Tasia and Cereniti. I think they're eating breakfast with some of Blake's friends."

"Did you buy her a car yet?"

"No, not yet. I don't know if you should get her one so soon. After all, you two just met yesterday and she's been poor all her life, you know what I mean? Her social circle is full of gangbangers and hood-rats. They'd be all over her if she suddenly pulled up in a quarter-million-dollar car."

Alexus sighed. After a moment of deep contemplation, she sided with Britney. Just two days ago, Alexus had learned of her father's illegitimate eighteen-year-old daughter, Mercedes Costilla. Like Alexus,Mercedes was African American and Mexican, flawlessly-proportioned, and more steatopygic than Buffy the Body. Both of them had long, curly,raven hair, emerald-green eyes, and perfectly sculpted faces. They so closely resembled Nicki Minaj that the two of them could easily have landed gigs as impersonators of the Young Money Superstar.

"On another note," Britney said, "I know you've been looking for anew home here in Chicago. Michael Jordan is putting his Highland Park mansion on the market for twenty-nine million. I stopped by there and checked it out the other day. It's pretty nice, if you ask me—fifteen bedrooms, nine bathrooms, fifty-six thousand square feet. And it even has an eighteen car garage that doubles as a basketball court, so Blake and his friends can—"

"I don't want to hear about it right now," Alexus interrupted.

Still gazing at Blake's serene face and listening to the incessant beep…beep…beep of his heart monitor; Alexus caressed his cheek with herfinger tips, wondering if she would ever hold her son again.

*****

An hour later, Blake was jarred awake by Alexus' elated screams."They found him!" She vociferated, "Enrique found my Baby!"

Chapter One
April 1, 2012

The album was finished.

After months of writing verses, listening to beats, and recording songs, and after signing two more artists to Money Bagz Management, his new record company, Blake King was finally done with his highly anticipated debut album, which he'd named *Bulletface*, a sobriquet he'd gotten from an old girlfriend. Lounging on the long, black, leather sofa outside of the recording booth on his two-million-dollar Newell tour bus, smoking a corpulent blunt of Kush, he nodded his head to the beat of "SolidMob," the first track on his album.

'It's Bulletface...I'm sure you heard, man Rich hood nigga, so my dress code BirdmanShout out to Birdman, and I'm the Birdman
A thousand bricks of thirty-six, I'll send it to yuh curb, man...'

Blake grinned at the sound of his own gruff voice. He wore a LouisVuitton bulletproof vest over a black wife beater, baggy True Religion jeans, and a pair of Jordan sneakers. The four-carat round-cut red diamondsin his platinum necklace glistened as brilliantly as the ten-carat red diamonds in his platinum pinky rings and the small red diamonds in his platinum bracelet and Hublot watch. Due to his grueling two-hour-a-day weightlifting sessions, he was 215 pounds of solid muscle. His left-canted Bulls cap partly exposed his low cut fade, and from the waist up he was covered in tattoos, including four teardrops on the left side of his face and four more on the right.

Money Bagz Management's five other rap artists – Terrance "Streets" King, Blake's older brother, Donte "Young-D" Roscoe, his childhood friend, Demetrius "Lil Meach" Burns, another childhood friend of Blake's, Nakisha "Mocha" Newsome, a sexy, dark-skinned ex-stripper, and Damario "Chucky" Burns, Lil Meach's older (though much shorter) brother—were sitting on the sofa with Blake, vibing to their CEO's album.

Mocha was jotting down lyrics in her rhyme book. The others passedaround blunts and bottles of Ciroc Vodka.

The 45-foot-long mobile palace was parked at the end of the long driveway in front of Blake and Alexus' Highland Park mansion. They had purchased the estate for $27.9 million shortly after

Blake was released fromthe hospital. Alexus had spent another $15 million on renovations. The overhead included five maids, three chefs, a butler, and a nanny.

"Shouldn't we be on our way to the album release party?" Mocha asked as she glanced at her platinum Rolex watch. "It was supposed to startat noon right? Well it's eleven thirty now."

"I know what time it is. We'll get there when we get there", Blake said. He turned and stared out the large, darkly-tinted window behind him. *Where the fuck is Alexus?* He thought. *Her plane landed at Midway over anhour ago. What's taking her so long to get home?*

"R.I.P Trayvon Martin," Lil Meach said, and took a fiery gulp of Ciroc. Like the other MBM rap artists, he was heavily adorned with diamonds and clothed in Louis Vuitton from head to toe. The big red- diamond-encrusted pendant hanging from his necklace read Money Bagz Management. "Fucked up how they let dude get away wit' killin' that li'l nigga. Ain't no way we would've been treated like that. Shit, you see howhard it was for me to get that fifty-five years off my back, and that was forsomethin' I didn't even do."

"I already know bruh", Blake concurred. He pulled a dense, rubber- banded bundle of hundred-dollar bills out of his front right pocket. It was only thirty thousand dollars, pocket change compared to the $428 million inhis Chase Bank account, and the $170 million in drug money he had stashed throughout his four Chicago mansions. "I gotta do somethin' in memory of Trayvon; you know somethin' that'll be remembered for a long time."

"Let's do a song about him," Mocha suggested.

"Yeah bruh," Young-D added. "We can shoot the video before thetour starts. Have everybody wearin' hoodies in the video, wit' bags of skittles and bottles of iced tea."

Nodding his head in agreement, Blake stood up and snatched his iPhone from his hip. "We'll come up wit' somethin'," he said. Blake began to dial Alexus' number. She answered immediately.

"Baby I'm right down the street from our house. Mercedes and herstupid-ass boyfriend met me at the airport, and now they're screaming at each other in the middle of the street."

"What?" Blake frowned.

"I know. Sounds crazy as shit, doesn't it?" Alexus snickered. "Oneminute we were following them up the street, and the next they

14

were leaping out of her car, arguing and shouting."

Blake flicked his eyes around the coach's pricey interior. The walls and cabinetry were Italian maple. All the upward-facing cockpit surfaces— including an eighty-foot long counter top—were swathed in carbon fiber, and the hardwood maple floors were painted a glossy black. His gold-platedKalashnikov AK -47 assault rifle rested atop a cash-filled Louis Vuitton duffle bag on the counter.

He walked to the counter, pushed the AK aside, and unzipped the duffle bag. "That nigga bet' not put his hands on my sista-in-law," Blake said, lifting a gold-plated .50 caliber Desert Eagle handgun out of the bag.

"Just get out here and calm him down before he gets himself killed,"Alexus said. But Blake knew she didn't mean it; the Halloween shootings had taken all of the fight out of her.

"On my way baby." He cocked the pistol and shouted for his driverto start the engine.

Seconds later, the 55,000-pound Newell coach was drifting down the long, circular driveway toward the fifteen-foot wrought iron gates at thefront of Jordan's old home.

Blake was stuffing the thirty grand back into his pocket when his phone rang. The tour bus had not yet reached the gates. He looked at the phone and saw the call was from Kenny-Lord, a Mafia Insane Vice Lord from Gary, Indiana. Since last summer, Blake had been selling kilos of cocaine and heroin and pounds of purple Kush to Kenny-Lord's crew. Overtime they had established a brotherly rapport with one another. This was partly due to their flourishing business relationship, but mostly because Mercedes was cheating on her boyfriend with Kenny. And, in Blake's opinion, Kenny was a better man for Mercedes than her current boyfriend.

"What it is bruh?" Blake answered. He leaned back against the counter and stared at Mocha's ass as she hurried off to the bathroom. She was tall and slender, and her pink denim booty shorts showed off her sexychocolate legs.

"Man bruh," Kenny-Lord said, "you ain't gon' believe what just happened. I called Mercedes to let her know I was on my way over there topick her up, and that nigga answered the phone."

Blake chuckled, "So that's why they're out there arguing now."

"She told me he was supposed to be in Atlanta for two days." "Yeah, but his flight doesn't leave until five. It's not even twelve o'clock yet, bruh. You trippin'."
The gates slowly swung open.
"I wish she would've told me that," Kenny said. "I'm right aroundthe corner from yo' spot now."

"We're on our way to my album release party," Blake said, se-curingthe bulky pistol in his shoulder-holster. "Just follow my tour bus. We'll kickit at Redbone's for a couple hours, throw a few hundred thousand at the strippers, holla at Twista and Ross for a li'l bit, then get the fuck up outta here. I gotta get some rest so I can be ready to perform on *106th and Park* tomorrow."

"A'ight, bruh, I'll be right behind you."

Blake put the iPhone back in its Louis Vuitton clip-on case on his hip. Momentarily, he observed his MGM crew through squinted eyelids. Hewondered if they would be as successful and dominant in the rap game as MMG and YMCMB's artists and if he, himself, would be a legendary CEOlike Diddy and Birdman.

His attention shifted to the cantankerous couple as his driver easedthe tour bus through the driveway entrance.

Mercedes Costilla and her dark-complected boyfriend, who Blake only knew as 'Duke,' were standing face to face in front of her bright, whiteMercedes Maybach convertible. Her hands were planted on her hips. Duke was gesticulating angrily, and both were shouting in each other's faces.

Behind their car, Alexus' snow-white Rolls-Royce Phantom limousine was parked in the middle of the street, followed by three white Tahoes full ofarmed body guards.

Blake told his driver, a thick-browed black man named Joey, to stopthe coach. He stepped outside and perambulated to his sister-in-law's side, fighting the overwhelming urge to sneak a peek at her jaw-dropping derriere. In her black Gucci jacket and snug black leggings, she looked stunning, almost like Mesha Seville.

"Punk ass nigga," Mercedes was shouting, "you shouldn't have fucked my li'l sister! Now you wanna get mad cause I got a friend on theside?! Fuck you, Duke!"

"How many times are you gon' bring that shit up?! I've apolo-gizeda thousand times already! What the fuck do you want me to

16

do?!" Duke raised his hands in frustration. He was six feet tall, the same height as Blake, and his Gucci outfit screamed new money.

Alexus exited the limo and headed toward them, her fur coat shimmering in the cool breeze. Four body guards accompanied her. "Y'all need to chill out," Blake said.

"You," Duke countered, poking a finger at Blake's face, "need tostay the fuck out of my business. This ain't got shit to do with you."

Blake clenched his teeth and scowled at Duke, and Mercedes slapped Duke across the face. *Hard.*

"Bitch!" Duke exclaimed, wrapping his hands around her neck.

Blake shot his fist into Duke's jaw, and Duke went down, unconscious, in the middle of the street.

Mercedes gasped. "Blake! Why'd you hit him?!" She kneeled downbeside Duke and cradled his head in her arms.

Grabbing Blake's hand, Alexus pulled him to the lime-green-paintedtour bus. "You're so fucking stupid," she chastised, snatching him along behind her.

Halfway down the block, Kenny-Lord's black Porsche Panamerawas parked at the curb; Kenny was standing outside of his open driver'sdoor, smiling at Blake and shaking his head.

Blake gave a nod, then boarded the coach behind Alexus.

17

Chapter 2

"That was completely uncalled for."

"No it wasn't. He shouldn't't've put his hands on her." Blake studiedhis fiancée's bellicose expression, easing back on the king-size bed as she stood before him. Her arms were crossed over the chest of her Dolce & Gabbana mini-dress. "Real men don't hit women, punks hit women."

Rolling her eyes, Alexus turned around and cut on the 50-inch LCDtelevision. Her 32D-24-48 measurements strained against the thin fabric of her dress. After nearly two years with her, Blake was still obsessed with ogling her voluminous ass every time she turned her back to him. She tunedthe TV to MTN News, one of her three television networks. Three anchormen were discussing the ramifications of the Trayvon Martin protests.

"He didn't hit her," she said stretching out next to Blake on the bed."Oh, my fault. He *choked* her." Blake scoffed. "Big difference, huh."

Alexus sighed. "What if he decides to press charges? Did you think

about that?"

"You worry too much, give me a kiss." Blake pulled her on top ofhim and grinned up at her.

"Kiss my fat ass, you crazy bastard." She began unstrapping his bullet proof vest. "Aren't you going to ask me how my trip went? I mean Ihave been gone for a week."

Blake chuckled once. "Didn't you tell me to wait until you got backto ask about that?"

"I'm back now. Ask." She was beaming."How did your business trip go, baby?"

"I finally reached a deal with Dubai Investments. They bought my entire chain of restaurants for $2.8 billion, my clothing line for $1.9 billion,and that fledging little construction company for $480 million. Of course, only fifty percent of the money from the clothing company comes to me.

But the rest is all mine... well, ours." She couldn't contain her smile. "Doyou have any idea what this means?"

Blake's eyes were wide and his mouth was ajar. He rested his handson her lower back and waited for her to continue.

"It means I've just taken Hetty Green's spot as the thirty-sixth richest person in history," Alexus said as she removed Blake's vest and holster. "I'm now worth sixty-two point five billion dollars! And I'm noteven twenty yet!"

"Damn... that's nuts," Blake murmured, rubbing his palms downher mammoth derriere. "Sixty-two billion." He emphasized every word. "Who was the number one richest?"

"John D. Rockefeller had three hundred and eighty billion; he's number one. Andrew Carnegie is number two with two hundred and ninety-eight billion." Alexus unbuckled his Louis Vuitton belt, opened his baggy black jeans and tugged them down his ankles. "Kick your shoes off so I canget these pants off."

Blake did as he was told. Seven days without Alexus had been longenough. He snatched off his wife-beater, too.

"What made you sell all those companies?" He asked, pushing up her dress and looking over at the bedroom door to make sure it was locked.His eyes moved quickly back to Alexus as she tossed her dress aside. "Youare the sexiest woman on earth," he added in an honest whisper.

"Awwww." Alexus lowered her mouth to his for a kiss. "My hubbyloves me." She kissed him again before taking off her white lace bra. "Mymom suggested I sell all those businesses so that we can focus on the television and film industry. Too many talented blacks and Latinos are being left out. We need soap operas with Black and Latino cast members. We need a show about a black bachelor. We need—"

"To get to it," Blake interrupted, staring at her reddish-brown breasts. "I know this tour bus"—he sat up and planted a kiss on her stomach

—"is kinda slow, but it ain't *that* slow. We'll be at Redbone's in about thirtyminutes."

Alexus got the hint. She trailed a line of kisses from his heavily muscled chest to his chiseled six-pack, then curled her fingertips around thetop of his boxer-briefs and pulled them down.

His thick eleven-inch-long phallus flopped out, half-erect, and

Alexus licked the crown for a moment before slipping it into her mouth and
forcing it to the back of her throat. Her cheeks dimpled as she applied hersignature vacuum seal, and her lips slowly ascended his shaft. He felt hertongue slathering the tip of his dick, and then it was lodged in her throat again.

Blake's head was spinning from all the Kush and Ciroc. Shutting hiseyes, he relaxed and tried to wrap his mind around marrying a woman worth $62.5 billion. There were definitely more pros than there were cons. For one, he and his family would be set for life; even if he managed to squander away all his millions. For two, he would have the baddest, most steatopygic chick in the game—not to mention the wealthiest woman in human history—by his side for years to come. For three, he would be marrying the love of his life, the one girl who stuck with him through thick and thin, from rags to riches.

But the main thing Blake disliked about his relationship with Alexuswas the international attention. Just about every day, pictures and stories about them surfaced on talk shows and celebrity gossip sites worldwide.

Newscasts, newspapers, magazines—all of them were filled with stories about Blake King and Alexus Costilla, and Blake disdained every publication. He was a 'hood nigga, a devout drug dealer, a gunslinger; thelimelight was not for him.

Still sucking him feverishly, Alexus peeled off her white lace thongand moved into the sixty-nine position over Blake. He opened his eyes, slapped his hands onto her ass, and licked his lips as she lowered her glistening-wet pussy down to his mouth.

An unrelenting tongue-lashing ensued.

He sucked and licked her turgid clitoris until her stunning body tensed and her juice-box gushed. Alexus was a "squirter," and Blake didn'tmind one bit. He loved the taste of her juices.

"Oh, my God," Alexus moaned as she moved forward and positioned her dripping pussy over Blake's saliva-glazed serpent. "If theyhad an Olympic game for cunnilingus, you'd have twenty gold medals bynow."

"Aww yeah?" Blake said with a chuckle. He grabbed her waist and helped guide her down onto his dick, biting the center of his lower lip as he felt her lubricious love tunnel sliding down his shaft. "Let me see *you* earn amedal."

"You're about to do more than see it."

Blake grinned, and Alexus rode him as if she was the star of her own rodeo show. Stopping only after he'd filled her with his viscid cum.

Chapter 3

Redbone's was to Chicago what Magic City was to Atlanta. It was an opulent, upscale gentlemen's club where the Windy City's most prominent socialites, professional athletes, movie stars, entertainers, and other well-off individuals gathered to network, promote their businesses, and throw dollars at sexy pole dancers. It was a place where Black womenwere always dressed to impress and on the hunt for ballers to finance theirdaily expenses; a place where a lot of top-echelon drug dealers came to show off their flashy cars and rotund bankrolls.

But today was different. Blake's album release party was an invitation-only event and he had only invited two hundred and ninety people. Nearly half of them were real niggas and 'hood chicks from all throughout the Midwest. The rest were rappers, R&B stars, record labelexecutives, video models, and a few Chicago Bulls players.

Cheers erupted as Alexus, Blake, and the entire roster of MBM artists walked through the club's rear entrance, flanked by Alexus' burly team of bodyguards. Blake had thrown on a red True Religion sweater overhis bulletproof vest and wedged the Desert Eagle in the waistline of his jeans. The extra-large Louis Vuitton duffle bag he was carrying held three million dollars in bank-new Benjamins.

Fred Douglass, MBM's music manager, was a stern-demeanored brown man with a beard that was almost as dense as his afro. Dressed in adark, conservative business suit, he led Blake and Alexus to a VIP table inthe back of the club. The table was large and circular, and it had a golden stripper pole protruding from its center. There were ten VIP tables in all.

Each one had a cute-faced, big-bootied stripper dancing on its pole.

"I've got good news," Douglass said, standing off to the side as Blake and Alexus sat down. "A hundred and fifteen thousand copies of youralbum have already been sold on iTunes, and that's just the preorders. Morethan likely, we're looking at sales of up to half a million copies in the first week, maybe more."

"We'll sell more than that." Alexus was smiling and waving at RickRoss and Meek Mill, who were seated at the table to the right of her. GucciMane and Waka Flocka occupied the table to her left. She turned and regarded them with the same warm smile, because if not for them exacerbating the popularity of drug dealing through their music, Alexus knew her drug empire would not be as successful as it was now. To Douglass, she added, "I have over 24 million Twitter followers; I'm sure I'llbe able to convince at least a million of them to buy the album."

"The streets gon' buy my music," Blake said, giving a head nod toRoss. "I'm not worried about no album sales anyway. As long as I can puton for the real Midwest niggas and feed my kids, I'm good. I don't give a fuck if I only sell two hundred thousand."

"Let's not kid ourselves," Douglass said. "You're the hottest rapperin the game right now. Everybody's hip to Bulletface. Your mix-tape sold more than eight hundred thousand copies, for Christ's sake. You're on the cover of XXL magazine, and not because you've been shot twelve times."

Shaking her head incredulously and staring up at the talented bootydancer, Alexus said, "Fred, you know how pessimistic he gets at times.

There hasn't been a more prolific gangster-rapper since Young Jeezy and heknows it."

Blake sat the duffle bag on the seat between him and Alexus. "We'llsee. I gotta get out here and shake some hands." He kissed Alexus on the cheek, then got up and headed into the crowd.

"He's a handful, isn't he?" Alexus said, putting on her Gucci sunglasses. "How long is this event scheduled to last? I need to get home tothe kids. Savaria's probably throwing a fit by now."

"It'll be over with before you know it. An hour at the most."

"Good. I don't think I can handle much more than that." Douglass frowned. "What do you mean?"

"I'm supposed to be at church, Fred, praising the Lord and read-ingthe bible. Watching a bunch of slutty women rubbing all over my man wasnot on my agenda."

There were twenty or thirty women encircling Blake as he con-versed with 2 Chainz and DJ Kayslay, and all of them had suggestive smiles on their faces.

"He's a celebrity now, Alexus. You have to get used to women beingoverly attracted to him," Douglass said, turning to look at

Blake. "It's not him they're attracted to; it's his money. They're in-fatuated with Bulletface and the money that Bulletface has. He's worth five hundred and twenty-twomillion dollars. That's seventy-two million more than Jay-Z has and forty- seven more than Diddy's got. Bulletface is the wealthiest rapper alive, to some, he's the *best* rapper alive; and he's engaged to you, the wealthiest woman in history, who also happens to resemble Nicki Minaj with a Heather Bianchi-like body. Every street guy in the country wants to be like him, and every 'hood chick wants to be with him. That's only to be expected."

Sighing, Alexus opened the duffle bag and grabbed a thirty-thousand-dollar bundle of hundreds. "I guess you're right." And with that,she began showering the stripper with cash.

King Rio

Chapter 4

"Nice office," said Trintino "T-Walk" Walkson. Reesie Cup leaned back in his leather swivel chair and interlaced his fingers behind his head. "Haven't seen you in a while, Mr. Hollywood. I thought you were gonna stay in Miami."

"The cast of Brick House wanted to drop by here with Kayslay, so I decided to come along with them." T-Walk strolled over to the window. The parking lot below was packed full of foreign cars. A white Rolls-Royce limousine was parked next to the MBM tour bus beneath a neon-red sign that read, Redbone's, Chicago's #1 Gentleman's Club.

"I wish I would've killed Blake a long time ago," T-Walk said.

"You don't know how many times I've made that exact statement."

T-Walk turned. "Green light?"

"It's not that simple." Reesie Cup pointed a remote control at the flat-screen monitor on the mahogany wall beside his desk. He scanned through several security-camera vantages, located Blake in the downstairs crowd, and zoomed in on him. "You see, since this past October, I've been doing business with his Dub Life crew, and they've proven to be the sweetest drug connect I've ever run across. A thousand kilos of soft for fifteen million. A hundred bricks of heroin for five million. Pounds of Kush for two racks apiece. I got half the city on lock, joe. I need Blake."

Grinding his teeth together, T-Walk stared at the camera monitor for a moment, then said, "Man, fuck that nigga. He tried to kill me over a bitch. That's damn near the fakest shit you can do."

"You had him shot ten times, T-Walk. You're lucky he only put two bullets in you."

T-Walk swept his eyes back over to Reesie Cup and left them there. In urban lexicon, the two men were often referred to as "high-yellow" niggas, the handsome type that women of all ethnicities drooled over. Both of them were clad in expensive suits; dapper young millionaires in their Sunday's best.

Trintino was the producer, executive producer, director, and creator of television's two most-watched, reality TV shows: *Brick*

House of North Palm Beach and *Brick House of Jupiter Island*. The shows were similar to MTV's Jersey Shore, only the Brick House cast members were black women with pretty faces, slender waistlines, and tons of junk in their trunks. They were Straight Stuntin' Magazine models, rap video vixens, adult film stars, high-paid pole dancers, and they were making T-Walk a lotof money. He owned a high-rise condo in Miami, a Bentley coupe, and a bank account that contained a little over $19 million.

"I know what you're pissed off about." Tyrese pressed some buttons on the remote, and seconds later they were watching Alexus Costilla as she tossed dollars at the dancer on her table. "It's her, isn't it?You're still in love with Alexus."

Following a contemplative pause, T-Walk murmured, "Yeah...Istill love her. I'll always love her. But that's only part of the reason why I'mupset." He crossed the room to the camera monitor. "I tried to do what you did, and I failed."

"You tried to what I did? What are you talking about?" Reesie Cup asked, bunching his thin eyebrows together.

"The kidnapping scheme. I heard about the fifty million dollar ransom you got from kidnapping Blake's daughter, so I had some of my folks help me kidnap Alexus' son. But somehow they found the apartment where we had the baby. We had just left. They killed my li'l guy's girlfriendand his son, got the baby back, and that was that."

Reesie Cup gazed fixedly at T-Walk, and T-Walk kept his eyes on Alexus. Just seeing her flawless face warmed his heart.

"Who said I kidnapped Blake's daughter?" Cup sounded leery. "Does it really matter?"

"Hell yeah, it matters! I spend twenty-four million dollars with Blake every month. If word gets back to him about that kidnapping, I'll lose my connect."

T-Walk shrugged. "He already knows. At least that's what I believe. Why else would he have gunned down those two guys down thestreet from here last year? This is your neighborhood; he knew that."

"All he knows is that his daughter was kidnapped from anapartment on Douglas and Albany. The ransom money went to an untraceable offshore account in Panama, and the police were never even contacted. He may *think* I had something to do with it, but there's no wayhe'll ever really know."

"Come on, now, Cup," T-Walk said, walking to the door. "It's twenty-twelve. Nothing is untraceable."

King Rio

Chapter 5

"Mmm, boy, you are so damn fine." "Thank you. Appreciate the compliment."

"I'm so serious, Bulletface. I never in my wildest dreams thought I'd get to meet you face to face. I have all of your mix-tapes. I havea framed picture of you hanging over my bed. Oh, my God, I'm actually talking to Bulletface!"

With an infectious grin on his face, Blake studied the beautiful young woman standing in front of him. Blonde curls framed her yellowishbrown face. She had on a tight purple dress and sparkly high-heel shoes.

Her breasts were large, her stomach was flat, and her enormous ass was justas fat as Alexus', if not fatter. She began walking beside him as he made hisway back to his table.

"What's your name again?" he asked.

"Nona Malden. I'm originally from Detroit, but I've been living here in Chicago for the past six months, modeling and waitressing at ReesieCup's other club."

"The Visionary Lounge?"

"Yeah. I have a bachelor's degree in biology, but since nobody's really hiring, I went ahead and started working at the club." Nona's voice was soft and melodic, and her perfume was tantalizing. "Where are we going?"

Blake stopped to hug and take a picture with Olivia. Then turned to Nona and cracked another grin. "We? Who said *we* were going anywhere? I'm about to get my wife and go home."

"Bulletface," said Nona, "please don't do me like that. I'm sure you're probably thinking I'm just another bad li'l groupie, but I swear I'm not. I meet celebrities every night at The Visionary Lounge. This past Thursday, Common and Kanye performed at the club, and both of them were trying to get with me all night. It's not that I don't like them, I'm justmore into gangsters like you, gang-sters like Yo Gotti, you know what I'm saying?"

"I got his number in my phone right now. Want me to call him?"

"No." Nona glanced toward Alexus and Blake's table, saw that Alexus' view was obstructed by a phalanx of bodyguards, and then

31

turnedback to Blake with a more lascivious expression on her face. "What I wantyou to do is book me as the lead model in your next video."

"That's it?" Blake was having a hard time keeping his cool. It was not every day that his eyes were blessed with the sight of a woman ascomely and thick as Nona.

"No, that's not it," Nona said, grabbing Blake's iPhone from his waist. She typed in a number with a 313 area code, saved it under NM313, and returned the smartphone to the LV case. "I want you to talk to Kayslay about getting me on the cover of his magazine, talk Alexus into putting me on one of those Brick House shows, and mention my name in a song or two.I'll handle the rest from there."

Blake laughed. "Damn, you got a lot of demands to besomebody I just met," he said.

"Trust me, it'll be worth it. Whenever you feel the need to be compensated for your hard work, hit my number."

"You're gettin' the wrong idea. I'm about to get married, li'l momma."

"Why would you go and do something like that?" Nona shook her head. "You're only nineteen, Bulletface. I'm twenty-six, and I'm not even ready to get married yet. You don't see Soulja Boy getting married, doyou? As a matter of fact, you can't name one young rapper who's married or engaged, can you?"

"Wiz just proposed to Amber, and I proposed to Alexus. So, yeah, I can name two," Blake said, turning to shake up with Kenny-Lord.

"Well…I'd still appreciate the help." Nona's voice lost its note of confidence. "I'm just trying to get my name out there."

Blake pulled two bundles of hundreds from the front pockets of his jeans and handed them to Nona. "That's sixty racks. If you can't get onwith that, I don't know what to tell you. I'll call you in a few weeks to see how you're doing."

He watched her stuff the cash in her Gucci bag, knowing that if he did not delete her number out of his phone in a hurry, he would eventually end up in her bed. Nona was far too pretty, and her ass was waytoo fat.

"Thank you so much, Bulletface." Nona gave him a quick hug. "Sixty thousand dollars—I've *never* had this much money."

"It's nothin', li'l momma. Just make sure you use it wisely. Let me holla at my nigga for a minute."

Blake and Kenny—and about fifty other men—ogled Nona's huge ghetto-booty as she sauntered off toward the bar to join her fellow models, all of whom at one time or another had graced the pages of DJ Kayslay's Straight Stuntin' Magazine.

"Fam, that's a baaaaad bitch," Kenny mused. He was dark-brown like Blake, with muscular arms and bushy eyebrows. His outfit consisted ofloose fitting Pelle Pelle jeans, a matching black tee shirt, and Louis Vuittonsneakers, belt, and hat. His wrist and neck glistened with white diamonds and platinum. "I would've gave her a *hundred* racks, on the fin!" he said.

"She is bad." Blake turned to Kenny. "You see me knock that nigga Duke out? Bitch-ass nigga put his hands on Mercedes. I tried to breakhis muhfuckin' jaw."

"Fuck that clown. I really came out here to talk to you about them bricks of soft. We need two hundred more—"

Kenny was interrupted by Alexus as she rudely bumped past him and halted before Blake, hands resting on the hips of her mini dress. She spoke sharply. "Okay, you've taken pictures with just about everyone,and they've played your album five times already. I'm ready to leave."

"What's up, sis?" Kenny said, grinning."Hey, Kenny," Alexus replied bitterly.

Blake chuckled, turning to shake up with Kenny again. "I'll be at you as soon as I get back from New York tomorrow, bruh."

He returned to his table to grab the duffle; then he, Alexus, and her security team left out the back door. He joined her in the Phantom limousine.

"I'm really not in as much of a hurry as I made it seem." Alexus took off the white fur coat, picked up her iPad, and tapped into Twitter. "I just have something important to discuss with you, and you know I don'ttrust speaking in too many places."

"What is it?" Blake asked, trying vehemently to divorce the memory of Nona Malden from his brain.

"My Aunt Jenny's been released from federal prison. She's being questioned by Pakistani officials right now, but she'll be set free sometime within the next twenty-four hours. Papi's calling a family meetingon his yacht in Mazatlán."

"So you gotta fly to Mexico?"

"No, I'm gonna Skype from the computer in our bedroom. But the rest of my paternal family—Uncle Flako, his kids, and Aunt Jenny's son

—will be there on the yacht."

The revelation of Jennifer Costilla's release shocked Blake. He thought back to when she had emptied a submachine gun into Alexus' Bentley on Interstate 94 and, in the process, murdered several innocent bystanders. Shortly thereafter, she had bombed Alexus' mother's house.

Then, after federal agents had raided Jenny's ranch-style home in Brownsville, Texas, and found over a thousand kilos of cocaine and heroin,she fled the country and joined forces with her old friend Bin Laden in Abbottabad, Pakistan, which resulted in a hijacked Boeing jet being purposely crashed into Alexus' beach house in Miami. Jenny had been captured inside Osama's compound during the Navy SEAL Team Six raid on May 1, 2011, and Blake had assumed that she would be given a life sentence, if not the death penalty.

"I'm sure you're wondering how she got acquitted of all those charges," Alexus correctly surmised. "Apparently, the feds were unable toestablish a connection between Aunt Jenny and any of the Al-Qaeda members who hijacked that plane in Miami; her Texas home was in her boyfriend's name, so she can't be prosecuted for the drugs; and the eyewitnesses to the I-94 shooting have either recanted their statements or vanished."

"Damn," Blake murmured, gazing out his darkly-tinted window as Alexus' chauffeur cruised out of the parking lot behind one of the Tahoes. "You think she's still gonna be tryin' to kill you?"

Removing her sunglasses, Alexus looked over at Blake, a perturbed expression darkening her countenance. "I hope not." She took a deep breath. "Aunt Jenny was only trying to take me out to get Granny Costilla's billions. Killing me now would do her no good. She'll need me toregain her footing in the business world, so I'm not really worried about her. What bothers me is"—another deep breath—"her ties to those terrorist groups. She's still upset over her son's disappearance, and I'm afraid of what she'll do when she finds out that he was last seen with me and Papi."

Blake turned back to the window, absently fingering his four-million-dollar red diamond-filled necklace. The 13-passenger limo passedthe liquor store next to Redbone's, the barbershop across the street, the convenient store on the corner of Sixteenth and Drake. Black pedestrians wandering the recently restored neighborhood stopped and cast excited stares at the stretch Rolls-Royce as it crept up Sixteenth.

"I hope things go smoothly between Aunt Jenny and I," Alexus said, more to herself than anything.

Just as Blake was about to respond, Alexus' iPhone started ringing. She answered the call, and her mother, Rita Mae Bishop, urgentlysaid, "You need to get home immediately."

"Why? Is something wrong?" Alexus asked.

"The director of the CIA is standing in your kitchen, snacking on a bag of Doritos and talking to your attorney. I'd say something is definitely wrong."

King Rio

Chapter 6

They made it back to the Highland Park estate in record time.

Alexus found her mother, her attorney, and a dark-suited white man standing in the foyer, admiring the gold-framed portraits of Dr. Cornel West, Dr. Na'im Akbar, and Michael Eric Dyson that hung on the whitemarble walls. Several more dark suits stood near the front door.

"Hello, Ms. Costilla," said the white man, an obese-featured, gray-haired, fifty-something-year-old. He extended his hand to Alexus for ashake. "I'm CIA Director Newt Bowden."

Alexus nodded. "I met your predecessor. In fact, I was under the impression that he was still in office." She ignored Bowden's offered hand until he produced the proper identification. Then, studying his ID, she asked, "What is this about?"

"Can we go somewhere private?" Bowden glanced at Blakeand Alexus' chief of security.

"Anything you need to say to my daughter," said Rita, a forty-five-year-old Angela Bassett look-alike, "you can say in front of me."

"I got it, Momma." Alexus took off her coat, handed it toBlake, then motioned for Bowden to follow her.

She led him through the grand Victorian-style mega mansion, across heated white marble floors, past massive rooms filled with expensiveItalian-made furniture and plush white Persian rugs, and finally to the hotel-white cabana beside the Olympic-sized indoor swimming pool. Sunlight beamed down from the glass ceiling.

"Please tell me this is not about my Aunt Jenny," Alexus said, sitting down across from the chubby man.

"Unfortunately, it is about Jennifer. It also concerns your tunnel, your drug shipments, and your entire cartel." He paused long enough to let his words sink in.

And sink in they did.

Alexus wondered if her uneasy expression was as palpable as it felt.

"A few weeks before your aunt was arrested, the FBI received a tip from a woman in Tengen-Wiechs, Germany. The woman claimed to have seen Jennifer Costilla leaving a clothing store with a couple of bags in hand. On that same day, eighteen kilograms of highly enriched uranium wasreported stolen from a nuclear research facility in Tengen-Wiechs, and another thirty-seven kilograms of HEU was reported missing from a secondnuclear research facility in Munich, Germany. We have reason to believe that Jennifer was behind those thefts."

"Oh shit. You don't mean nuclear as in…nuclear weapons, do you?"

"That's exactly what I mean. Forty-five kilograms of HEU is all it took to produce Little Boy, the fifteen kiloton uranium bomb that decimated Hiroshima. If an A-bomb of that caliber gets detonated in—let'ssay midtown Manhattan on a typical workday—it could easily kill close toa million people. And that's no exaggeration."

Shocked, Alexus looked away and settled her eyes on the 500-inch flat-screen television that covered most of the wall across the pool from her. Beneath it was a fully-stocked bar and a DJ booth, the latter of which was connected to a concert-worthy sound system.

"We've been investigating this matter for over a year now, and we have yet to recover even an ounce of that uranium," Bowden continued."To say that we are concerned for the safety of this nation would be an extreme understatement. Eight thousand troops are being deployed to the

U.S. / Mexico border as we speak."

"I hope you all don't think *I* have anything to do with—"

"No one's accusing you of being involved with any of this. But we do have to take precautions, starting with the monitoring of your drug shipments. From now on, each shipment must be scanned before entering this country. We're installing a camera system in your drug tunnel that's capable of detecting even the smallest traces of uranium and plutonium.

There will also be a blocker—a seven-inch-thick, solid steel wall—placednear the Texas end of the tunnel that we'll be able to lower and lift whenever we deem it necessary."

"You cannot be serious," Alexus scoffed. She stood up and grabbed her hips. "I supply this country with seventy percent of its cocaine;eighty-eight tons of coke every month. Are you telling me that, every week,you're planning to scan twenty thousand kilos of coke, five thousand kilos of heroin, and twenty thousand pounds of marijuana? Do you know howmuch of a delay that would cause to my distributors? There has to be another way to go about this."

"Trust me, our way is the simplest way. It'll only take four to six weeks to get the cameras and the blocker installed. Then you'll be backin business." Bowden stood to his feet. "Construction begins today. It's inyour best interest to call me if you hear anything about that uranium. My number's the same as the old director's."

And with that, Newt Bowden turned and left.

Alexus fixed her eyes on the rippling blue waters of her swimmingpool. *An atomic bomb?* She thought. *Is Aunt Jenny really that crazy?*

A moment later, Blake perambulated in with King Neal Costilla, their nine-month old son, perched on his hip. Five-year-old Savaria King, Blake's daughter from a previous relationship, was holding her daddy's hand as they approached Alexus.

"Fuck was that about?" Blake asked.

"My Aunt Jenny's a lunatic," Alexus replied, slowly shaking her head and twirling a curlicue of her long raven hair around her forefinger.

"A lunatic with the ingredients to build a nuclear warhead."

King Rio

Chapter 7

Blake got in two hours of intense weightlifting in the indoor gym. Then he showered and put on a pair of Louis Vuitton sweatpants, a matching white tee shirt, LV loafers, and a bevy of white diamond jewelry

—four identical necklaces priced at $928,000 apiece, a $400,000 bracelet, a

$190,000 big face Rolex watch, a pair of 18-carat white diamond and platinum pinky rings worth $4 million apiece, and a pair of glistening,round-cut 10-carat white diamond earrings that he had purchased for

$650,000.

He was standing in front of the tall mirror at the rear of his capacious walk-in closet, checking out his blinging reflection and rolling ablunt of Kush, when Alexus appeared in the doorway behind him. He glanced at her, but did not speak. Judging from her somber expression, Blake concluded that she must still be upset over whatever it was the

CIA   director had told her.

"What are you getting dressed for?" Alexus asked, resting a shoulder against the doorframe. "It's five o'clock. Dinner's ready, and my mom wants to talk to you before she leaves. I think it's about having you asa guest on her talk show."

Blake chuckled and turned an about face, sweeping his eyes over the expansive, white marble-floored closet. To his left were three aisles of designer clothing; three aisles of sneakers were to his right, and infront of him were three glass jewelry cases that looked like they'd been taken right out of a high-end jewelry store.

"Now she wants me on her show?" he said, setting the blunt on the jewelry case. "I thought she said she didn't like rappers."

"She doesn't. But, you know, everyone's calling her the new Oprah, and since O finally managed to have a rapper on her show before itended, I guess Momma feels it's only right to do the same thing. Plus, we are getting married soon. She'll have to deal with you sooner or later."

Blake rounded the jewelry case and walked to Alexus. He

placed his hands on her jutting hips and pressed his lips against hers. His strong black hands slipped beneath her mini-dress, and he squeezed her ample cheeks. Pulling back, he gazed into her soft green eyes. "What's wrong, baby? You still worried over Jenny? 'Cause I'll pop that bitch if youwant me to."

"I don't want my auntie to get *killed*."

"Why not? She tried to kill you. Several times, at that."

Alexus shook her head. "She's still my aunt. I'll never condone the killing of a family member. It's already bad enough that I had to watchPapi blow my cousin Savio's brains out. I'm hoping Jenny doesn't find outabout that. Lord knows she'll lose her mind for real this time."

"That's what got you upset?"

Skating her fingertips across the chunky white diamonds in one of his necklaces, Alexus sighed despondently. "Our route's going to be shutdown for about a month or two, but our cocaine and heroin shipment came through the tunnel last night, so at least we have something to grind with."

The Costilla Cartel's grind was a lot heavier than Blake's. They had forty Mexican Mafia lieutenants spread out across ten Southern states, and each of them received the same weekly drug shipment: 500 kilos of cocaine, 125 kilos of heroin, and 1,100 pounds of high-grade marijuana.

Colombia's North Valley Cartel was only charging the Costilla's $2,000 perkilo of cocaine and $50,000 per kilo of heroin. The Costilla's would then cut every kilogram of the pure heroin into ten kilos—500 into 5,000—and sell them to the Mexican Mafia for $50,000 a Ki. The coke went for $10,000 a Ki, and the marijuana, purchased in bulk from a Mexican farmerfor $800 a kilo, sold for $1,500 a pound. In all, the Costilla's spent eighty-one million dollars every week purchasing their drugs, and they made five hundred and sixteen million—every week.

Blake's little drug ring was nothing in comparison. He was moving two thousand kilos of cocaine, two hundred kilos of heroin, and around four thousand pounds of Kush, and that was per month. Althoughhe was paying the same low prices as the Costilla's, he was still only clearing $40 million a month after paying off his distributors, while the Costilla Cartel was raking in $2 billion a month.

"I still got, like, a thousand bricks of girl and a hundred and fifteen bricks of boy left at the River Forest mansion," Blake said, leaningin for another kiss. "My tour's coming up anyway. I need to start focusin'more on my music and my artists' music. Niggas in the streets keep comparin' me to Big Meech, and that's not the look I want. I ain't trying todo all that time. I gotta be here to raise Vari and King Neal. I gotta be hereto take care of you"—he landed a third kiss—"my sexy-ass wife."

Smiling lightly, Alexus said, "The world is ours, Blake. No one can arrest us. We have the fucking CIA on our side, and they're keeping our whole family off the FBI and DEA's radar. I have ten billion dollars indrug money being processed and washed through the stock market as we speak, and guess what? Nobody's gonna say a word. It'll all be seen as profits from savvy business investments, and we will continue to live like the other thirteen hundred billionaires live—like kings and queens, buying politicians and judges, dousing ourselves in diamonds and pearls, traveling the world in private jets. We're unstoppable." She broke away from his amorous embrace, pulled down her dress. "Let's go eat. I had the chefs whip up your favorite meal. Steak tacos, cheesy baked potatoes, spaghetti, a whole turkey, string beans, corn on the cob, garlic bread, and a few other things. I can't remember them all."

Following Alexus to the dining room, which was located way on the other side of the mansion, Blake could not repress the big smile thatcrossed his face as he thought about how far he'd come in life over the pastcouple of years.

Back in 2010, he had spent the majority of his time standing on the corner or sitting in a crack house with his crew, selling rocks of crack cocaine, playing video games, smoking blunts, drinking Remy Martin, and fucking the young 'hood chicks who chased behind all the drug-dealers. In Michigan City, Indiana, Blake was considered a "head bussa" and a gunslinger. He was known for delivering knockout punches to wannabe tough guys and occasionally shooting them whenever he felt disrespected. He had been a low-echelon dealer, buying one or two ounces of cocaine at atime, cooking them into crack, and selling $10 and $20 rocks.

Then he had met Alexus, and his life hadn't been the same since, especially after she transferred five hundred million dollars into his bank account.

"What are you getting me for my birthday?" Alexus asked, shaking Blake from his reverie.

"You'll find out in twenty days."

"It better be something romantic. I don't want any more cars."

As they entered the dining room, Blake spotted Mercedes and her younger half-sister Porsche sitting at the long, Honduran mahogany dining table with Mercedes's two children—sixteen month old Meyonce' and three year old "Baby Duke." Porsche was tall, dark, and slender, with hardly any lady lumps, but her pretty smile and sassy attitude made up for the lack of curves.

Rita was also present at the table. She and Mercedes glowered at Blake as he took his place at the head of the table. Alexus sat at the opposite end, next to King Neal, who was bouncing up and down in his Versace highchair and reaching for her.

"Speaking of birthdays," Alexus said, "today is Porsche's seventeenth birthday. Her party starts at eight."

"Yeah, and Mercedes li'l dusty butt won't even let me drive her car to the party," Porsche said acidly, rolling her eyes. "Like I didn't just get my license the other week. Her dirty ass wasn't trippin' when I was drivin' that broke down Intrepid she had. That Maybach done blew up her head."

Mercedes flicked her cold stare from Blake to Porsche. "Shut the hell up, Porsche."

"I'd appreciate it if you two watched your language in front of my mother," Alexus scolded as the chefs began covering the table with steaming dishes.

Mercedes and Porsche murmured apologies to Rita, then everyone bowed their heads for prayer.

"Lord," Rita started, "we thank you for this generous meal…" Blake's smartphone vibrated on his hip. Cracking open his eyes,

he glanced around the table and, seeing that no one was watching him, grabbed his phone and checked the new text message. It was from Fly, a childhood friend of his who he'd put in charge of delivering his drugs.

"U n Chicago?!"

Blake frowned at the message, then quickly typed, "Yup. At the crib." He got a reply seconds later.

"Bruh some niggas been ridin' around M. City lookin' for u all afternoon. I think they on bullshit."

Blake replied instantly. "Air 'em out!"

Chapter 8

Squirm-G crept slowly down Willard Avenue in his dark blue Magnum, accessorized with chrome thirty-inch Lexani rims, blue Gucci interior, and a thunderous set of fifteen-inch speakers. A Gary native, he had only ventured out of his city four or five times before, and this was hissecond time visiting Michigan City. His first visit had been to club and party with a clique of fellow Gangster Disciples from his own city.

There would be no partying this time around.

He pulled over next to Bee Kay's, a gray stone convenience store onthe corner of 9th Street. The white Hummer H2 on chrome thirty-two-inch rims that parked beside Squirm-G's Magnum was his also, and it was occupied by three Glock-toting Gangster Disciples.

"So...this is Bulletface's 'hood, huh?" Squirm mean-mugged the eight teenaged dope boys that were standing on the corner in front of the store's door. Then he turned and looked at the throng of young black hustlers who were standing in clusters on 9th, and on Patrick Street, as wellas in the alley that separated the two blocks. Lime-green 70's-model Chevy Caprice convertibles on large chrome rims lined both streets. Squirm counted fourteen of them.

"Ain't no way in hell these niggas done bought all these whips wit' drug money," said Lil' Ant, the man seated next to Squirm. He had six thickbraids running from his hairline to the nape of his neck, as did Squirm-G. Ant was a short, dark-complected GD from Miller Projects in Gary. He wasdressed in a blue leather Pelle Pelle jacket over baggy Girbaud jeans and a fresh pair of white-and-blue Jordans.

Squirm-G was brown-skinned, 5'11", and shaped like Bruce Lee. He had on a black Gucci jacket, a Gucci skullcap, Pelle Pelle jeans with a Gucci belt, and Gucci sneakers. An eighty-thousand-dollar platinumnecklace, full of blue diamonds, hung from his neck. Attached to it was a blue diamond-encrusted six-point star with the letters GDN embossed across it in tiny black diamonds.

Last August, Squirm-G, Lil' Ant, and two others had gotten seven hundred and fifty thousand dollars apiece for shooting a man to death, a man who'd been scheduled to testify against Bulletface in a caseinvolving numerous murders.

But now T-Walk, a close friend of Squirm's, had a milliondollars on Bulletface's head, and Squirm-G was thirsty for more cash.

"Folks, on the BOS," Squirm-G said, opening and raising his Lamborghini-style driver's door, "if I see that nigga Bulletface, I'ma put sixbullets *in* his face. All y'all gotta do is murk these otha niggas. I'm finna goin here and grab some blunts, see if I can find out where dude stay at."

"Man, G, we ain't gon' find that nigga out here. Wit' all that money he got, that nigga in Hollywood some muhfuckin' where." Lil' Antopened his door. "You know what it is, though. We catch that nigga, we wet that nigga."

"On GDN," Squirm-G said, chuckling diabolically as they stepped out of the car.

Chapter 9

Tall and lean, with a Drake-like complexion and green eyes, Fly was sitting on the trunk of his lime-green 1973 Caprice convertible, taking sips from a bottle of Mountain Dew and staring coldly at the two strangers who were getting out of a blue Magnum.

A sexy twenty-year-old redbone name Tiff-Tiff was sitting beside Fly. She turned to him and said, "That is them niggas right there. They been askin' where they can find Blake. That dark-skinned boy offered me and Danielle five hundred apiece to tell him where Blake stay at."

There were four young goons standing near a row of bushes a few feet away from Fly's Chevy. All he had to do was give the word and they would grab their AR-15 assault rifles from the bushes and open fire.

Hopping down from the trunk of his Donk, Fly shouted to the two women before they could enter the store.

"Ay, what the fuck y'all niggas want?" What transpired next surprised Fly.

The guy in the black jacket looked at Fly, then draw two chrome semiautomatic .45-caliber pistols from inside his jacket and, aiming one gun at the group of teens on the corner before him and the other at Fly, opened fire.

More gunfire erupted as Fly dropped flat to the ground. Heart racing, he scrambled for cover on the other side of his Chevy. He wasn't sure, but he thought he heard numerous guns blazing simultaneously. A shower of jagged glass shards cascaded down onto his head and the shoulders of his 8732 sweater. Hood chicks screamed; unarmed dope boys fled. Somebody shouted, "Shit, they shootin' from that Hummer, too! Get the choppas!"

Fly pulled his .357 and rose up shooting, just as his goons began squeezing off shots from their AR-15s.

But the two men were already back in the Magnum, and they, along with the Hummer, were gone a few seconds later.

Jogging across the street, Fly fixed his eyes on the four wounded teenagers that were stretched out on the sidewalk in front of the store. His stomach tightened when he realized that Lil Mike, a close friend of his and Blake's right-hand man, was lying dead in a pool of blood, with three dime-sized holes in his face.

Chapter 10

"Don't you dare answer that call," Rita Mae Bishop said, wiping her mouth with a napkin. "In fact, why don't you do us all a favorand shut it off until we're finished eating dinner."

Future's "Tony Montana" ringtone was blaring from Blake's iPhone.

He grabbed it from his waist and turned it off without even looking to seewho the caller was. "My bad, Momma. Forgot it was on."

It was then that Rita decided she'd had enough of her chicken salad.She pushed the bowl aside and addressed Blake in her usual gentle tone. "I need to ask you a very serious question, and I need an honest answer. We clear so far?"

Blake grinned at his mother-in-law. "Absolutely.""Do you love my daughter?"

"Yes, I do. I love her with all my heart, more than anything or anyone I've ever loved in my whole life." Blake didn't hesitate to speak thetruth. He felt the eyes of everyone at the table sliding across his face like butter in a hot pan. Turning to Alexus, he added, "And I'm pretty sure she loves me the same way."

"Does her money factor in anywhere?" Rita added.

Alexus sucked her teeth. "You don't have to interrogate him, Momma."

"I got this," Blake said, and shifted his eyes back to Rita's coal-huedvisage. "If you remember correctly, I was with your daughter when the fedshad taken everything y'all owned. I was with her when she was still wearing blue jeans and gym shoes, so you know it's not the money. I'm glad she's wealthy, but I'd still be with her if she was broke. I'll be with her'til I'm dead."

"Hmm." Rita was nursing a glass of ice water through a straw. Flicking her hazel brown eyes from Blake to Alexus and then back to Blakeagain, she seemed to be pondering what to say next. Finally, she said, "I listened to your album earlier today. Believe it or not, I actually liked a fewsongs. I'm not a fan of anything outside of the gospel genre, but I must admit that you're one of the most talented rap artists I've ever heard. I'd like you to be a guest on my show this Wednesday."

"My manager already has me on a tight schedule. I'll be on a nationwide promo tour for most of this month. Wednesday I'll be in NorthCarolina, South Carolina, and Georgia."

Porsche's eyebrows shot skyward. "All in one day?!"

"Yup," Blake said as his daughter slid down from her chair, ambledaround to him, and leaped onto his lap. "We got a Boeing 747, so I'm ableto take my tour bus and up to fourteen cars with me everywhere I go." He didn't mention that Alexus had paid $60 million for the 747; Rita would have lost her mind.

"So," Rita asked, "did Douglass get your concert tour rescheduled?"Nodding his head yes and checking his icy Rolex for the time—5:48

—Blake replied, "We gotta work around the NBA games for the next fewmonths, but yeah, we got it all worked out. Tickets'll be on sale next Friday."

"Excuse me, Ms. Bishop," Mercedes interjected. "There's something I've been dying to know for a while now: Were you and Papitogether when he got my mother pregnant?"

'Uh-oh,' Blake thought.

Rita took another sip of water. "Papi and I were married. Your momwas my hairstylist. I didn't learn of their affair until last year when you came along. I do remember Whitney being pregnant before she moved hereto Chicago, but I had no idea who the father was. We never did talk much. Iwas always so busy taking care of Alexus back then."

"Is it true what they say about Papi being a Mexican drug cartel leader? I've asked him a couple of times, and he keeps denying it. I justwant to know the truth, in case it has something to do with my mom's murder."

Rita sighed. "Some lunatic went crazy and killed seven women named Whitney on the same night. No one has come forth with any information on the Whitney killings, but I'm sure Papi was not involved. Toanswer your question, though, Papi was the *alleged* leader of a drug cartel in northern Mexico. I believe his father founded the cartel. As far as I know,that cartel's been disbanded."

Taking a bite out of her steak taco, Alexus regarded Blake with a please-keep-your-mouth-shut look. Rita was completely unaware that the Costilla cartel was still in business, and that her own daughter was its leader. And Mercedes didn't know that Alexus had sent a team of hit men to find and kill a woman Blake had admitted to cheating on her with; a woman whose name he said was Whitney. Blake knew how horrible Alexus felt about both devastating secrets, so he kept quiet and fed Savaria a piece of cake.

When dinner was officially over, they all followed Rita out to her pitch black Maybach 57-S. The evening was cool and breezy. Blake stood off to the side while the others spoke to Rita. He couldn't stop thinking about the text messages he'd received from Fly.

"Daddy," Savaria said, tugging on Blake's tee shirt. "Is you goin' to take me to Grandma Carolynn house? Cause, um, I don't wanna go there yet. I can go there the after day."

Blake squatted down in front of his little girl. "Don't say 'the afterday'; say the next day okay? Now...tell me why you don't wanna go to your grandma's house?"

"Cause I wanna go to my cousin Tiffany house and... and to my cousin Danielle house in Imbiana."

"You wanna go to Indiana and visit Tiff-Tiff and Danielle?"

"Mm-hmm." Vari nodded her head, and the four-carat yellow diamond earrings in her lobes jounced lightly. "Cause I, um, I miss them, Daddy. I miss my cousins."

Chuckling aloud, Blake said, "I got you, baby girl. I'll have Alexus take you out there first thing in the morning." He stood up, walked over to Rita, and gave her a hug good-bye. Then he stepped back as she slipped into the open rear passenger's side door of the Maybach. Her driver pushed the door shut and she was gone a moment later.

Mercedes spun quickly around to confront Blake. "I hope you know my boyfriend's in the hospital with a fuckin' concussion you retard!" she ranted.

"A man should never put his hands on a woman in a violent manner; my pops always told me that. I couldn't stand there and watch him choke you out," Blake replied.

Just as Mercedes was opening her mouth to speak, a pink-colored Bentley Continental GT with a red ribbon tied around its middle came rolling around the side of the mega mansion and stopped beside Alexus and Porsche. Even the rims—24 inch Asantis—were painted pink.

"Happy birthday, Porsche," Alexus said, smiling.

Chapter 11

Twenty minutes later, Alexus entered the family room with a bowl of lightly buttered popcorn in her hand. "Finally...some family time," she said, handing Blake the bowl and plopping down next to him on the long, white leather sofa. She grabbed the remote control, aimed it at the 500-inchSony flat-screen, and pressed PLAY. The movie *Think Like A Man* started playing. "Does my mom get on your nerves with all those silly questions? Ican get her to stop if it bothers you. I think she's just worried about us getting married too soon." She looked over at Blake, then at Savaria, who was curled up on the other side of him, her head nestled beneath his arm, her eyes struggling to stay open.

"She ain't got nothin' to worry about," Blake said. "You in good hands wit' me."

"I know." Alexus paused and glanced down at her seven million dollar engagement ring. "Does being engaged to a billionaire make you atall uncomfortable?" she asked suddenly.

"It did a little, at first," he admitted. "I'm cool with it now." "Good; it's a materialistic distraction and I don't want any distractions in our relationship."

"The only think distractin' me from focusin' on you is Papi's old ass. I'll never forget the day he showed up at my Miami mansion carryin' abackpack wit a severed head in it. That crazy muhfucka dumped it on my floor and kicked it at me, like it was a soccer ball. And I bet you he's the one that lynched Rita's fiancée while I was in the hospital; nobody else could've done that shit."

"Nat Turner was found hanging from that tree in Southampton, Virginia on the eleventh of November. Papi was in Italy that week."

Blake shrugged and stuffed a handful of popcorn in his mouth. "Well he had somebody do it. He's still crazy. Niggas in my 'hood don'tchop off heads. That's some wild shit."

"Beheadings have always been popular among Mexican drug cartels. The Colombians sometimes do it, too. It humbles friends and frightens enemies. Whenever you're dealing with billions of dollars in drug money, war is an inevitable factor, and usually the most violent cartels reign supreme. Papi's only doing what's necessary to sustain the familybusiness."

The two of them went silent for a couple of minutes, eating pop-cornand watching the movie. Alexus wondered why Papi had not yet phoned her about the meeting, and why the U.S. Government had released Aunt Jenny from federal prison.

Switching topics, she asked, "Why'd you turn down my mom's offer? Eight million viewers tune in to her show every weekday. You could've utilized that as an opportunity to promote your album."

"The promo tour will be enough to get a bunch of albums sold. AndI'm plannin' on bettin' forty or fifty million on that Mayweather and Cottofight next month anyway. That's guaranteed money."

"I'm not letting you bet that much money on a fight, Blake." "Why not? Mayweather gon' beat the skin off that boy. I might as well make that li'l twenty seven million off the—"

"Are you serious?" Alexus scoffed laughingly. "Cotto is going toparalyze Floyd."

"You're only sayin' that 'cause he's a Mexican."

"I'm just as much black as I am Mexican. Race has nothing to do with it.Cotto's a better fighter, that's all. I'll put fifty million on Cotto any day."

Blake turned to her, a conspiratorial smile burgeoning on his face."Bet," he challenged.

"Nuh-uh," Alexus said, shaking her head and showing a recip-rocalsmile. "You are not about to talk me into a fifty million dollar bet."

"You're the one that said it." He leaned toward Alexus and kissed her on the cheek. "We don't have to bet money though. I can think of a fewother things we can bet." He pushed a hand between her thighs, slid it up beneath her mini dress, and dipped a finger into her naked pussy. "Nanny put the baby to sleep yet?"

"She's doing it now," Alexus murmured, feeling her nipples stiffenin response to Blake's touch. "Mmm...boy, don't start nothing you can't finish."

He stood up slowly so as not to awaken Savaria. His white tee shirt,with its gray, overlapping LV logos, stretched across his broad chest and complimented his four white-diamond necklaces; his gray, loose-fitting sweatpants fit him perfectly. Alexus spent a brief

56

moment studying the longmuscles and corded veins standing out in his arms. Then she lifted her eyesto his handsome face as she got up and stood face to face with him.

"You think you're so cute." She hopped up and wrapped her legs around his waist, and his powerful hands moved swiftly to her ass. "Wheredo we go this time? We've broken in just about every room."

"I know a spot we ain't hit up yet.""Yeah? Where?" She asked.

"The safe." He kissed her all over her mouth and neck as he walkedout of the family room, past the elevator, down a long hallway, and finally to the solid steel door of their safe. After pressing his thumb down on the fingerprint scanner, he typed in a set of numbers—12-12-11-14—and the ten inch thick steel door popped open.

But before he could open the door, one of the maids came running up the hallway toward them with a cordless phone in her hand. "Mr. King,"she said, extending the phone to Blake, "you have a phone call. They say it's an emergency. And"—she looked at Alexus—"Enrique's video chattingwith Papi in your office. Papi wants to speak with you."

Alexus lowered her feet to the heated white marble floor and tuggedher snow-white mini-dress down over her thick bottom, knowing then that her night would not end the way she had intended it to.

King Rio

Chapter 12

"Bruh, I've been tryna call you for the last couple of hours," Flyhad said as Blake was standing in front of the safe. "It's about Lil Mike andTerry. They got shot up. Blub and Moe got hit, too, but they'll be alright.

Mike and Terry didn't make it."

"I'm on the way," had been Blake's concise reply.

Now he was lancing his lime-green Bugatti Veyron 16.4 Super Sportdown Interstate 94, weaving the two-million-dollar car in and out of traffic and smoking an obese blunt of Purple Kush. He was brimming with anger. Some fuck-nigga had the audacity to murder one of his closest friends, and he wasn't about to let Lil Mike's death go un-avenged.

Before leaving home, Blake had put on his Teflon vest under the teeshirt, a gray Louis Vuitton hoody over the tee, and a matching gray skull cap that was leaned to the left in honor of his steadfast alliance with the Traveling Vice Lords, one of Chicago's most notorious criminal organizations.

He turned on his iPhone—it had been off since dinner—and discovered thirty one new text messages and seventeen new voicemails. Every message pertained to the shooting. Blake wanted to call and talk tosomebody, but he didn't want to risk discussing the shooting over the phone.

Scrolling down his phone's list of contacts, he stopped at NM313."Fuck it," he grumbled. Then he pressed SEND.

The phone rang thrice before Nona's cotton voice whelmed the line."Hello?" She answered.

Blake sucked in a mouthful of Kush smoke and turned down the volume on Rick Ross's "Yella Diamonds." He coughed a couple of times,then muttered, "You spend that sixty racks already?"

A shocked gasp blew from the phone. "Bulletface?!"

"Yeah, it's me. I'm on the highway, needed somebody to talk to. Ihope I didn't catch you at a bad time."

"No, no, no, no, no. I'm just lying here in bed, watching last week'sepisode of Khloé and Lamar." She released a light giggle. "To answer yourquestion, no, I didn't spend it all, but I did blow about twenty-five thousand in that Louis Vuitton store on Michigan Avenue. And I spent ten more on abrand-new flat screen TV and some other stuff I needed for the house. I'm thinking about putting the rest toward paying off the mortgage. All I'll oweafter that is— am I talking too much?"

"Nah, you good. I'm listening," Blake said, steering the Bugatti around an eighteen wheeler.

"You sound so...depressed," Nona said. "Are you okay?" Before hecould reply she sailed on. "I know I'd be okay if I were you. The caption rolling across the bottom of my TV just said something about Alexus Costilla made billions off a business deal with some investment company inDubai. That is just *too* much money."

"Ain't no such thing as too much money. Right now, Forbes got medown as having a net worth of five hundred and forty million. I wanna double that within the next couple of years. Shit, you ever heard of the Rockefeller Family? Them muhfuckas had over three hundred billion. If they can do it, I *know* I can do it."

"I suggest you take Machiavelli's advice, then. 'Men walk almost always in the paths trodden by others, proceeding in their actions by imitation. Not being always able to follow others exactly, nor attain to the excellence of those he imitates, a prudent man should always follow in the path trodden by great men and imitate those who are most excellent, so thatif he does not attain to their greatness, at any rate he will get some tinge of it.' That's one of the most thought provoking statements I've ever read.

Whenever I'm feeling pessimistic about my modeling career, I pick up *Machiavelli The Prince* and read that paragraph, and it always galvanizesme. I start saying to myself, 'If Buffie and Maliah can become legends in the urban modeling game, then I can definitely do it. I just have to followin their footsteps.'"

"So what you're saying is I should be a follower." "Everybody's a follower in one way or another. I went out and

bought all this Louis Vuitton because you're my favorite rapper and you'realways wearing Louis Vuitton. You wear it because our society has made itpopular for people who have money. It's a status symbol that the majority of us want, but we only want it because everyone else wants it. We're following the trends. If you want to be successful, you have to follow the path trodden by successful men."

Blake mulled over Nona's wise words for a long moment as he came upon an open stretch of highway and accelerated up from eighty to a hundred and seventy miles-per-hour. Then he slowed down and turned ontoan off-ramp that led him into his hometown— Michigan City, Indiana; the city where he had met and fell in love with not only the dope game, but alsoAlexus Costilla.

"You got a sexy-ass voice, you know that?" He said, flicking the blunt out his window.

"I know," Nona cockily retorted. "I got some sexy faces, too."

"Sexy faces?"

"Sex faces. And I can do magic with this pussy."

Blake chuckled. "I'll holla atchoo later, li'l momma," he said, andhung up.

King Rio

Chapter 13

Six Costilla's were seated around the long oak conference table. Juan "Papi" Costilla; his younger brother, Flako Costilla; Flako's three adult children, Antoney, Pedro and Isabella; and Santiago Costilla, the son of soon-to-be-released Jennifer Costilla. All of them were clad like elite Wall Street bankers, in expensive navy blue suits. They were in a conference room on Papi's six-hundred-million-dollar yacht in Mazatlán, Mexico. Their eyes were glued to a seventy-inch, wall-mounted computer monitor that showed Alexus from the neck up as she sat in front of her owncomputer inside her Chicago home.

Papi leaned forward and asked Alexus, "How do you feel about the Zeta and Sinaloa cartels encroaching on our territory?"

"I didn't know they were," she replied, signaling for a Mexican butler to fetch her a bottle of water. "However, if either of them are found tohave soldiers in Matamoras, I say we take out as many of their head guys asphysically possible."

"Get to that later," said Flako. Like his three children, he was short and corpulent. Alexus always said he looked like an overweight George Lopez. Taking a puff from his Cuban cigar, he added, "We shouldbe talking about that missing uranium and what that could mean to our entire operation. The CIA's already shut down our tunnel. We're lucky itwasn't the FBI, or else we'd all be in prison by now."

"Jenny didn't steal that uranium," Papi said. "She has no knowledge of how to build a nuclear weapon, and we would know if shehad paid a scientist or a nuclear physicist to build one for her. The only reason she was in Germany is because she was on the FBI's top-ten mostwanted list in the States."

Alexus tossed her head back and laughed. "Papi, you cannot be serious. Aunt Jenny was involved with the world's most dangerous terroristgroup, for Christ's sake."

"And what's that supposed to mean?" Santiago snapped; jumping to his mother's defense. He was also short and chubby, though nowhere near as heavy as Flako and his children.

"You know exactly what it means," Alexus shot back. "She had

63

those al Qaeda militants hijack that plane in Miami and crash it into my beach house, had the whole country on high alert. Then she was captured inside the compound of the world's most wanted terrorist. That gives us good reason to be concerned about that uranium. She's already tried to kill me and my mother several times; she set up Papi and Uncle Flako and had them sent to federal prison; and I'm pretty sure she had the waitress at that downtown restaurant poison my drink, the same drink that killed Granny Costilla. With that being said"—she rolled her white leather swivel chair closer to her white marble desk—"I believe we can all agree that she cannotbe trusted."

When no one spoke up, Papi lifted his razor-sharp, goldenmachete from beside his chair and laid it on the table next to his open briefcase. "Any of you familiar with the Yakuza?"

Pedro said, "Isn't that, like, the Japanese mafia?"

"I guess you could say that," said Papi. "The Yamaguchi-gumi branch of Yakuza is looking to purchase twenty-five hundred kilos of cocaine. They want it delivered to an airport in Kyoto, Japan. I'm chargingthem twenty grand a kilo. We also have shipment requests from other organizations in Iceland, the United Kingdom, France, Spain, and the Netherlands."

Alexus was already shaking her head in disagreement. "They're all NATO members. Granny Costilla didn't do business with them for that very reason. We don't need to become an international drug cartel."

"I've already cleared it through the CIA Director Bowden, and the governments in all those countries can't wait for the first shipment to arrive. Our monthly revenue will go up to eight or nine billion. We'll be asrich as the Walton Family in no time."

"Question," Antoney said, raising his hand. "Why would those governments want illegal drugs in their countries? That doesn't make any sense to me."

The Mexican butler returned with two bottles of ice-cold water on a solid gold serving tray. Alexus grabbed one of the bottles, opened it, and gulped down half of it while Papi answered Antoney's inquiry.

"You see," Papi began, "the governments of First World countries are steadfast capitalists. They capitalize off just about every human in their countries. Now, since slavery is generally looked down on these days, the only way to pay men and women twenty cents an hour for strenuous labor is to imprison them and strip them of their rights. So they entice their prey with drugs, arrest them for dealing the drugs, then put themto work, paying their victims slave wages for producing products for

billion-dollar companies. Strategic capitalism at its best."

'I don't know about this,' Alexus thought. She was gazing at Papi'sshiny gold machete and wondering why he'd brought it to the meeting. He usually left it at home.

"But let's get back to the Zeta and Sinaloa cartels," Papi said, turning back to Alexus. His gelid green eyes seemed to penetrate her computer screen. "Bring them in!" He shouted.

Seconds later, a dozen AK-47-toting Costilla cartel members in black suits escorted a bunch of naked, blindfolded Mexican men and women into the room behind Papi. The captives were handcuffed and shackled. Deep lacerations marred their blood-laden bodies.

Papi clamped an age-spotted old hand around the handle of his machete and stood up. "These fools were bold enough to enter Matamoros on behalf of the Zeta and Sinaloa cartels. Apparently, their main tunnels have been compromised, and they're in search of a new route into the States." He grabbed a female captive's ponytail, and she only had a second to scream before the machete hacked through the front of her neck and out the back. Her body dropped to the floor in a spray of crimson. Holding the woman's dripping head by its ponytail, Papi added, "Forty-nine of these filthy vagrants wandered onto our land, Alexus. Forty-nine of them! And they all work for the Zeta and Sinaloa cartels. Now, my dear princess,"—hesmiled at Alexus—"I will show you how to properly dispose of these rodents."

What Alexus wanted to say was, "Please...no more killing." Butinstead she showed a timorous smile and said, "This ought to teach them not to fuck with the Costilla cartel."

She watched in shock as Papi beheaded nine more rival cartel members. Then she shut off the computer, kneeled down in front of the goldtrashcan beside her desk, and vomited.

Chapter 14

There were droves of young African Americans meandering on the corner of 9ᵗʰ and Willard when Blake made it to his old neighborhood on the west side of Michigan City, Indiana. An urban ghetto, the area was mostly replete with ramshackle clapboard houses, a few black-owned churches, three parks, an old redbrick community center that hardly anyone used, a liquor store, and Blake's convenience store, which is where everyone was gathered.

Blake parked the Bugatti in the alley next to the redbrick church across the street from his store. He grabbed his extra-large Louis Vuitton duffle bag from the passenger's seat, got out of the car, and crossed the street to where Fly was standing with the rest of their Dub Life crew. He paused to study the flickering candles that were bunched together alongside the store and the 'R.I.P. LIL MIKE' that had been spray-painted on the sidewalk. All around him people were crying, distraught at having lost a loved one.

"I should've listened to you, bruh," Fly said, pouring a whole bottle of Ciroc onto the sidewalk. "I should've just started bussin' at them niggas when they first pulled up."

As Fly began telling Blake how the shooting had transpired, Blake turned his back to the store and cautiously fluctuated his eyes around the dark avenue. Lined up side by side before him were five lime green 1973 Caprices on chrome thirty-inch Lexani rims. Other cars and trucks were parked on both sides of the two-way street, and the majority of them were candy-painted in the same shade of green as the five Chevy convertibles. Blake had popularized the color last year when he'd had his entire Fleet of luxury cars painted lime-green, and everyone in his old neighborhood had followed suit.

Of the thirty or forty black women standing on the corner, sobbing and drinking cups of hard liquor most of them kept settling their eyes on Blake every few seconds or so. He couldn't blame them. Their money-hungry looks were understandable. A couple of years ago, he had been a low-level crack dealer like all the other young 'hood niggas, and these same girls had been too busy chasing behind the ballers to pay him any attention; now he was worth more money than every dope boy in the country—his pinky rings alone cost $4 million apiece—and they, like mostly every other woman he'd met since becoming a multimillionaire,were all too eager to get to know him a little bit better.

"That was a dumb ass move," he said when Fly finished revealing how the shooting had taken place. "I *told* you to air 'em out. Fuck was you thinkin'?" He sat the duffle bag on the hood of Fly's Caprice, unzipped it, took out three thirty-thousand-dollar bundles of hundred-dollar bills, stuffedtwo of them into the side pockets of his sweatpants, and then peeled the rubber band off the third one. "You talked to Lil Mike's people?"

"I talked to his momma, she was cryin' an' shit, real fucked up,"Fly said.

"Was she at home?"

"Yeah, man. I think his whole family was there. I sent my bitch over there wit' fifty racks to give to his momma."

"Fifty thousand?" Blake made an indignant face. "Call and tell her I got a million for her."

While Fly made the call, Blake counted out two thousand dollars in hundreds and waved over a slender yellow-bone named Tootie.She was a cute, long-haired twenty-five-year old with a petite body and ahistory of fucking and sucking the life out of every man she dealt with.

Blake glanced at the crotch of her tight blue jeans as she walked towardhim, wondering if that pussy was as fat and wet as everyone said it was.

"You do me a favor?" He said, handing her the two racks. "Go down there to the 'L' and grab me twenty bottles of Ciroc. You can keep thechange."

"I'll go and do that now." Tootie folded the cash, strolled quickly across the street to her dark gray Durango, got in, and drove downWillard to the liquor store two blocks away.

Still holding the thick pile of hundreds in his left hand, Blake moved through the crowd of familiar faces, shaking hands with the real niggas, hugging the 'hood chicks, ignoring the lames and fakes. For the most part, everyone was silent, with only a few susurrant voices here andthere. A lot of them were wearing black hoodies with MBM GANG stretched across the chests in big gold letters.

"Y'all need to lighten up a li'l bit," Blake said loudly. "Lil Mike wouldn't want us out here lookin' all sad. Celebrate his life. We finna get fucked up and kick it like we always do, and when I find out who did this shit, y'all know what it is. Make sure they know, hundred-thousand for anybody that can tell me who did it."

Everyone started chatting and drinking and reminiscing on the fun times they'd shared with Michael "Lil' Mike" Lane and Terry Morehouse. Blake had not really known Terry that well—they'd always runin different circles—but he always heard good things about the young nigga, so he decided right then to pay for Terry's funeral expenses as well.

The crowd moved to Blake's newly-built four bedroom house on the corner of Patrick Street. He owned two other houses on 7th and Lincoln,but this one was his kick it spot, which he'd had built for the measly price of $256,000. Since his Bugatti was already parked in the alley out back, heleft it there and preceded everyone into the house via the back door, his cash-filled duffle in one hand, a blunt of Kush he'd gotten from Fly in the other.

The house was fully furnished, thanks to his interior decorator. Hardwood floors rambled throughout the first floor, from the kitchen, to thedining room, and into the living room. But no one was granted access to thefirst and second floors; Blake opened the basement door and led the mob down stairs, to the place he'd dubbed the "LV Room."

A long, U-shaped, brown leather Louis Vuitton sofa wrapped around half the room, the carpet was also brown Louis Vuitton. There werefour stripper poles in the middle of the floor, an equal number of eighteen- inch speakers fit into all four corners of the ceiling, and the walls were linedwith 55-inch flat screen televisions, two on each wall.

"Y'all niggas bet' not start spillin' drank all over my carpet," Blake warned as he sat down on the sofa, taking a deep drag on the bluntand dropping the heavy duffle onto the carpeted floor between his LV loafers. Fly sat beside him, already rolling another Swisher full of Kush.

A minute later, Rick Ross' "Rich Forever" mix-tape was blasting from the overhead speakers, and the movie Scarface was playing on the televisions.

Blake took a pair of gold-framed Louis Vuitton sunglasses from his hoody's belly pocket and put them on; he didn't want anyone seeing theintense pain in his eyes as he thought about his murdered friend.

"Lil Mike can't be dead," he murmured, more to himself than anything. "Not my li'l nigga." He couldn't help but think of all the men hehimself had gunned down. Was Lil Mike's death a simple case of karma?

The mere notion made him shudder.

"I wonder what they was lookin' for you for," Fly said curiously. Like a lot of urbanites, he was completely unaware of how broken his English was, and Blake was in no mood to correct him.

"T-Walk had somethin' to do with it," surmised Blake."Why you say that?"

"Cause…I just know. That's how he is. He had me shot ten times, and he *sent* some niggas to do it. Anybody else would've come through andlooked for me themselves." Blake was watching Tootie saunter toward himwith four bags full of boxed Ciroc; three girls were walking with her, holding more bags, chattering excitedly, and smiling wantonly at Blake.

Tootie and her friends sat the bags on one of the four shortmahogany tables (each one covered with a brown Louis Vuitton tablecloth).

"I bought forty bottles of Ciroc instead of twenty," Tootie said stepping forward and mounting Blake on the sofa. He was not surprised to see that she was wearing a halter with his album cover—a picture of him standing on the hood of his Bugatti Veyron SS, iced out, counting through apile of hundreds—airbrushed on the front of it. "I hope you know how hardit was carrying all that Ciroc down here."

"What's that supposed to mean?" He rubbed her thighs, her ass, her back. "I owe you for the trip?"

"You damn right. And you can take me upstairs to one of those bedrooms and pay me right now."

He was contemplating paying her in full when suddenly his iPhone's "Kiss Me Through the Phone" ringtone started playing. He had assigned the ringtone to the phone line in his and Alexus's bedroom, so heknew who was calling. Tootie moved to sit beside him.

"I gotta take this call," he said, getting up. He grabbed his duffle and cut through the crowd of admiring eyes. Looking back, he saw that two of his guys—Fly and Lil Chris—and Tootie were trailing close behind him.

As soon as they made it up the stairs and into the kitchen, Blake answered the phone.

"What's up, baby?" He asked glumly.

"Are you"—Alexus sniffled—"coming home tonight? I need you to hold me...make me feel loved."

Blake frowned. "What's wrong with you?"

"It's Papi," she cried. "How can a sixty-one-year-old man be so *evil*?! He treats human beings like a farmer treats chickens, so quick to takeoff their heads." She sniffled again. "I just watched him decapitate *ten people*. And two of them were *women!*"

"Watch what you say over this phone, baby." He walked to the living room, cut on the 72-inch widescreen TV, turned to ESPN, and took aseat on the black Italian leather sofa, placing the duffle beside him.

"Our telephone lines are secure. I've told you that a billion times already," Alexus said, still sobbing. She waited a moment, then added, "I'm sorry. I know you're dealing with what happened to Lil Mike. It's just...driving me crazy how heartless my father is. He's worse than that

D.C. sniper was."

Snuffing out the butt of his blunt in an ashtray on the glass-topped coffee table, Blake looked at Tootie and told her to go back downstairs, grab four bottles of Ciroc, and tell everyone they could drinkthe other bottles.

Fly added, "And pick out the five thickest hoes down there to bring back with you. Make sure you get Marketa and Jessica, too."

"What the hell did he just say?" Alexus asked, her perturbed tone shifting to one of anger.

"That ain't got nothin' to do with me," Blake assured her. "I'm here to fuck wit' my niggas and celebrate Lil Mike's life. I'll be home by"—he checked his Rolex and saw that it was 8:55 p.m.— "midnight, alright?"

"Don't make me fuck you up, Blake. I'm serious."

He chuckled sullenly. "What did I tell you about all that worrying? The keyword in faithful is faith. And besides, what could I possibly get from a bitch in the ghetto that I can't get from you?"

"An STD," she retorted.

Lying back in a black leather recliner across the room from Blake, Fly mumbled, "Some brand-new pussy."

"Like I said," Blake reiterated to Alexus, "I'll be home by midnight. I might have to pay somebody to drive me home, but I'll get there."

"Okay well…I'm going over to Porsche's party with Tasia and Cereniti. I spent almost two hundred grand to get the OMG Girls and Mindless Behavior to perform for her, and I want to be there to see it. I really wanted to get an MBM or a YMCMB artist to perform, but I know your crew had a show at Adrianna's tonight, and Young Money's booked."

"She'll be a'ight. I'll bring her onstage at my next show." Blake's eyes went wide as Tootie returned with a round faced brown skinned girl in a tight-fitted denim Apple Bottom cat-suit. The girl was shaped like Kim Kardashian, and she was just as beautiful. "I…uh…loveyou, baby." Blake stuttered into the smartphone as three other women entered the living room. "I'll call when I'm on my way home."

Alexus let out a resigned sigh. "I love you, too," she muttered before hanging up.

Easing back on the sofa, Blake put the phone back on his hip and continued to ogle the dime piece from behind his shades. Tootie took her place on his lap again, this time facing away from him, and opened oneof the bottles of Ciroc. She handed him the bottle.

"What's her name?" He asked, pointing an index finger at the bad bitch.

"That's my girl Tameka," Tootie told him. "She's from St. Louis, moved here a couple of weeks ago."

Blake turned up the bottle and swallowed down four flaming gulps of vodka, wincing as the conflagration worked its way down his throat. He was trying to drink himself into cheating on Alexus, but he knew that he wouldn't actually go through with it. Not after all Alexus had donefor him.

A pair of headlights suddenly swept across the wide picturewindow behind Blake as a vehicle turned onto Patrick Street. Then the window lit up again—a second vehicle.

He twisted around, pushed the black curtain aside, and fingered down the venetian blinds.

A clean black GMC pickup and a green '70's model Chevelle were idling in the middle of the street, lights off, engines running.

Blake rose quickly—forcing Tootie to rise with him—and snatched the couch away from the wall. He grabbed the two AK-47s he hadstashed behind the couch and tossed one to Fly. "You know anybody with ablack pickup truck or a green Chevelle?" He yanked back the slide on the K, chambering a round from the fifty-round banana clip.

"Hell naw," Fly answered.

"Ay, y'all go upstairs right quick," Lil Chris said to the girls as he drew a nine millimeter Ruger from under his long white tee shirt. He wasslim and brown and ready to start shooting.

Once the girls were gone, Blake unlocked the front door. "Aim at 'em, but don't start bussin' unless they get stupid," he murmured authoritatively. His heart was throwing Tyson jabs at his ribcage. His adrenal glands were convulsing with activity.

He flung open the door, and the three of them rushed out onto the porch. The porch's proximity light popped on, which seemed to shockthe two men strolling up the cobblestone walkway more than the sight of the AK-47s that were trained on their faces. They threw their hands to the sky in surrender.

"Whoa, whoa, whoa," said the shorter, slightly overweight light-skinned nigga. "Hold on, my guy. My li'l nigga Lil Lord sent us out this way to cop some work. We was in the joint with the li'l nigga. You can call and ask him yo'self, my guy. Tell him it's Lil Lew from Nap."

"And Smoke from Anderson," the second guy said. Tall and light-completed, he was clad like a professional dope boy: True Religionoutfit and Jordans.

Reluctantly, Blake lowered the assault rifle, keeping a wary eye on the two men. He lifted his iPhone and told Siri, the computerized smartphone assistant, to call Lil Lord, who was currently serving time for murder in Indiana State Prison. The prison was located four blocks south ofwhere they were now standing.

Lil Lord had been a straight goon before he was arrested back in '05. He had introduced Blake to the Traveling Vice Lords in

Chicago, his hometown; he had taught Blake to handle enemies in the streets in the samemanner that the U.S. government handled theirs—shoot them to death; and he'd also instilled in Blake the code of the streets, explicating why snitchingwas so cowardly and why it was so important that real niggas unite and prosper.

"What's the thought, li'l bruh?" Lil Lord answered, his voice flowing crisply through the speakerphone.

"Ay, you know a nigga named Lil Lew from Nap and another nigga named Smoke from Anderson?" Blake asked.

"Yeah, I fuck wit' them niggas. I talked to Lil Mike earlier and told him they'd be comin' through. What happened, they got on some bullshit?"

Blake motioned for Chris and Fly to lower their weapons. "Nah, they ain't on that. I was just checkin'." He informed Lil Lord of what had happened to Lil Mike and Terry. Then he hung up and passed the AK-47 toChris.

"Sorry to hear 'bout cha li'l guys gettin' offed," Lew said. He wore Akoo from head to toe, and gold teeth were shining in his mouth. "I'mjust out here tryna get a bankroll, my nigga. We been payin' twenty-eight abrick down our way, and a lotta times we can only get one or two of 'em.

I'm tryna get a plug that can give me as much as I can buy, you feel me? I'llhit the highway e'ry month and get the shit myself."

"Straight up," Smoke concurred. "I got ninety racks in the Chevy right now."

"And I got sixty," Lew said.

Blake stepped closer to Fly and whispered, "How many you got left?"

buy."

"Thirty-eight."

"A'ight, charge 'em twenty a brick and front 'em what they

"So that's six for Lew and nine for Smoke."

"Yup." Blake turned to the two men. "As long as you niggas stay solid, y'all gon' stay flooded. Kush, boy, girl—whatever. My niggasgon' have it for you."

Smoke said, "Man, you's a rap superstar. You got that Diddy bread, and yo' girl is a fuckin' billionaire, Bulletface. What the fuck are youdoin' out here uppin' Ks on niggas? Shit, if I had that kinda bread, I'd be the last muhfucka pullin' a choppa on a nigga. You can pay some niggas fordat."

"I wouldn't leave Alexus *nowhere* alone, either," Lew chuckled. "Every man in the world wanna crash her."

Blake nodded his head, acknowledging the truth in their opinions. But he was still too upset over Lil Mike's death to converse withanyone, let alone two strangers.

"Y'all stay up. One hun'ed," he said, turning around and heading back inside. He picked up his heavy duffle bag and left out the back door, forcing himself to remain faithful to his fiancée.

Minutes later, he was back on Interstate 94, racing the Bugatti toward the Windy City.

King Rio

Chapter 15

Alexus Costilla looked up as Cereniti Stingley and Tasia Olsen came into the dressing room. She smiled, a half-nostalgic smile, because thetwo ex-strippers had been her friends for almost two years now, and she hadnot seen them since the day before she left for Dubai.

She was sitting in front of the six foot wide mirror at the dressing room table, putting on her makeup and listening to her favorite song on Blake's album.

"Ugh," Cereniti groaned as she reached out and pinched the white fur that covered Alexus's easy chair. "Why are you so obsessed withthis color? Your cars are white, your clothes are white, and everything in your house is white. I don't get it."

"Maybe it's not for you to get. Ever considered that?" Tasia muttered condescendingly.

Alexus smiled at their reflections. Bow-legged, thick-thighed and steatopygic, with smooth, yellowish-brown skin and short, red-streakedblack hair, Tasia was dressed in a skin-tight red Valentino cocktail dress over five-inch Louboutin heels. A black Birkin bag hung from her shoulder.She had the kind of flawless face that made men and stare, and the kind of ass that made everyone stare.

On the other hand, Cereniti was decked out in a fuchsia Chanel jump suit with a matching fedora and Zanotti heels. She looked like AliciaKeys from the neck up and LaLa Anthony from the neck down, with a diamond Movado watch, two diamond bracelets, and a pair of diamond- encrusted hoop earrings dangling among a bevy of shoulder-length dreads.

"Truthfully," Alexus said as she applied her mascara, "I began wearing white because it symbolizes purity. But then I inherited my grandmother's fortune, and I figured I'd stick out more in the corporate world if I stuck to that same unorthodox dress code."

"Fuck all that, yo," Tasia said, planting a hand on her hip. "You just made four billion, two hundred and thirty million dollars in Dubai. I know I'm good for one of those Phantoms you got stashed away in that bigass garage."

"Begging already?" Alexus narrowed her eyes at Tasia's

reflection. "It usually takes you twenty to thirty minutes before you turninto Sister Gimmy."

"Ha ha ha," Tasia retorted sarcastically. "Real funny, bitch."

They shared a laugh, a welcoming, I-miss-you sort of laugh, and then the quotidian topics began. Tasia and her boyfriend Bookie— Alexus's first cousin on her mother's side—had broken up again after Tasia caught him sexting with another woman; Cereniti was still single and in search of anew lesbian lover; she and Tasia had finally decided on a plan to host their own stripper based reality show, which Tasia had already named "Down thePole."

"Who do we pitch the show idea to?" Cereniti asked. "And please don't say T-Walk. He already thinks he's the black version of RyanSeacrest." She sucked her teeth. "Ol' bougie-ass nigga been wearin' suitsever since they put him on the cover of GQ Magazine."

"Why you always hatin' on my brother?" Tasia snapped. She called him brother because he and Bookie were best friends.

Rolling her eyes, Alexus stood and adjusted her strapless white Marchesa dress. "Submit your idea to T-Walk. I'll tell him to work out thekinks and get it to the MTN board of executives."

"Will they approve it?" Tasia sounded anxious.

"*I'll* approve it," Alexus said. She started out of the dressing room,which connected her massive bathroom and her and Blake's master bedroom suite; the clicking of her six inch, pearl white Christian Louboutins on the white Carrera marble floor muted as she reached the snow white faux fur carpet in the bedroom. "I'm having lunch in New York with Beyoncé' and Serena tomorrow while Blake's on 106th and Park, and Ican't think of a damned thing to say."

"Ask her about the baby," Cereniti suggested "You two are probably the only black celebs who have babies with two names. And bothof you are in relationships with rappers."

"Serena used to date a rapper, too," Tasia pointed out.

Alexus shrugged, picking up her iPhone from its charging pad. "I guess so." She grabbed her white Himalayan crocodile skin Birkin bag off the dresser, and the three of them left the bedroom.

Enrique and seven other bodyguards were waiting in the foyer, along with the butler, who had Alexus's white fur coat draped over his arm,and two house maids holding Tasia and Cereniti's gray-black chinchilla coats. The butler helped Alexus into her coat, while she gazed emptily at the gold-framed portrait of Michael Eric Dyson and wondered what Blake was up to. She hoped he wasn't somewhere cheating on her. She'd already been forced to shoot dead Janautica Spalding, the last woman he'd cheated with, and she had vowed that day to leave him for good if he ever cheated again.

As she was walking out the front door, checking her Twitterpage on the iPhone, something occurred to her belatedly.

"Enrique," she said. "About that…international business venture. How are we going to acquire that much product?" She stopped next to him.

The Rolls Royce limo was parked a couple of feet ahead of them in the circular driveway, a chauffeur waiting beside its open rear door.Enrique waited 'til Tasia and Cereniti were inside the limo to reply.

"You'd have to start purchasing Kilos from Peru's Lima cartel, Bolivia's Santa Cruz and La Paz cartels, and Colombia's Medellin and Cali cartels. You might also need to have the North Valley cartel in Colombia double the shipments you're getting from them now. Papi's working on getting the bosses of all those cartels together for a meeting on his yacht some time before next month's NATO summit. Of course, you'll need to bepresent as well." A pronounced grin brightened his usually stern expression."All of them refer to you as the 'boss of all bosses'." He shook his head, incredulous.

Alexus frowned at him. "What are you smiling about?" she asked.

"Oh, it's nothing derogatory. I'm just…impressed, that's all.

The CIA offered that same international cartel deal to your grandmother when you were nine or ten, and she turned it down. Said she wasn't interested in digging herself any deeper into the Illuminati than she alreadyhad. If she had taken that offer in '02, I'm almost certain she would have been worth at least two hundred and fifty billion when she died."

Illuminati." birthday."

"The Illuminati? She never said anything to me about the"You aren't supposed to find out until your twenty-first

"Well, what if I don't wanna wait?" Alexus turned and studied the other four vehicles in her driveway—the two white Tahoe's that sandwiched her limo, Cereniti's even whiter Lamborghini Aventader, andTasia's same colored Panamera Turbo.

"Enjoy your youth," Enrique advised wisely. "All you've got is a year and twenty days left before you become one of them." He placed a hand on the back of her coat and urged her toward the supremely ostentatious limousine.Chapter 16

Tasia and Cereniti were chattering about how exciting it had been to sit courtside with Pippen at a recent Bulls game when Alexus climbed into the limo. She was grateful that they were so enveloped in conversation. It gave her time to ponder the ominous question that was bouncing around in her head.

'Am I a member of the Illuminati?'

'No,' she told herself. 'There is no possible way that I can be an Illuminati member without knowing it. And I'll be damned if I ever join them.'

In an effort to rid her mind of troubling thoughts, she turned on the compact disc player, flipped through a bunch of MMG, YMCMB and MBM albums and mix-tapes until she reached Blake's new album, went to track number eight—"King of the Midwest," her favorite song on the entirealbum—and hit PLAY. Then she shut her eyes, eased back on the sumptuous white leather seat, and listened.

'Born a King, guess that's how I got my last name.Al Einstein when it comes down to this cash game.

Blew a couple million, hurt yo' feelings? Oh, my bad, lame Five-hundred-million-dolla nigga, Money Bagz Gang

All throughout Indiana over to Illinois

You think you Larry Hoover? I think I'm Willie LloydShout out to Larry Hoover, Willie Lloyd, T-Fly

On King Neal, I'm stickin' to the code 'til I die (yup)I'm Kush-high, I smoke until my ears pop…

Real nigga, real mothafuckin' teardropsGold-plated AK for all you fuck-niggas

Get on some bullshit, you'll be shit outta luck, niggaSolid Travelin' Vice Lord, yeah I'm plugged, nigga So I only kick it wit' gang members and drug dealasA thousand kilograms of the white powder

And you can come and get 'em for Dwight Howard...'

"You know what, Lexi?" Tasia said. "I might not like Blake as aperson, but he went ham on this whole album. He killed 'em with that Dwight Howard line."

Alexus opened her eyes and scowled at Tasia. "Would you still hatemy man as much as you do now if he hadn't shot Bookie?"

"Probably not," Tasia shamelessly admitted. "I'm still trying to figure out why *you* haven't gotten upset over it yet. I mean, Bookie is yourcousin. I'd be *mad* angry if somebody shot *my* cousin."

"Word is bond," Cereniti agreed. She and Tasia had been born andraised in the same Harlem neighborhood, and sometimes their alien dialectirritated Alexus.

This was one of those times.

Rolling her eyes and sucking her teeth indignantly, Alexus calmlysaid, "I love my cousin and I love Blake. That's all there is to it."

"Bet you still love T-Walk, too, huh?" Tasia grinned.

"I love the work he's doing for my television network. I love the way he presents himself to the media, like he isn't the same Gangster Disciple that was selling kilos with us not even two years ago. I love that he's created an outlet for women shaped like us to make money and becomefamous. I love that he's kind and—"

"Bitch, please," Tasia remarked with a derisive chuckle. "You knowwhat the hell I meant. Do you still love him the way you did when he was fucking you?"

Alexus sighed and turned to look at her darkly tinted bulletproof window as the limousine streaked past other sprawling Highland Park mansions. Too long ago to vividly remember, she had been in love with Trintino Walkson. But he'd left her when she was pregnant with King Neal

—she still didn't know whether he or Blake was the baby's father—and shehappily went back to Blake, who she'd been with ever since...well, there was the one time she'd had sex with T-Walk last year, but that was only after she caught Blake cheating on her with a Barbadian pop star at one of his concerts. Although she often found herself wondering how her life might be had she stayed with T-Walk, she never considered going back to him.

"No," she finally said. "I'm in love with Blake and only Blake."

Shechanged the subject. "I'm thinking about just flying out to Vegas and marrying Blake tomorrow…or the day after. I wanna do it before he starts touring all over the country." She glanced at her friends, half expecting them to be glaring incredulously at her. But both of them were fiddling withtheir iPhones.

"Why would you wanna do that?" Tasia asked without looking up."Yeah," Cereniti said. "I thought you said you wanted one of those

big, expensive weddings like Kim K. had, with all the cameras andcelebrities. You don't remember saying that?"

"I know," Alexus sighed, tucking a strand of long black hair behindone ear. "It's just that…he is going to have all kinds of slutty little groupiestrying to suck his dick after every show, and I don't want to compete with them. I'd rather us get married now."

"That has got to be the most ignorant thing I've ever heard come outof your mouth," Cereniti commented, flicking her eyes over at Alexus before returning them to her phone. "No one can compete with you, Lexi.

You're beautiful, you're rich, you're faithful and honest, and you're a great mother—who's Blake gonna find that can top you? If he fucks another bitchit's because he either has a sex addiction or you're not giving him as much sex as he wants. Marrying him won't change that, girl." She put down the smartphone and looked at Alexus. "There is no competition. You're the fuckin' truth, yo. The epitome of bad bitch. Word is bond."

"Yeah, yeah, yeah," Alexus muttered, a dim smile crossing her faceas she dug in her Birkin bag for a stick of Big Red chewing gum. "Who were you texting? Looked like your skin was glowing."

"Sexy li'l cheerleader I met at the Bulls game the other night. She's Puerto Rican and Brazilian, kinda resembles Rosa Acosta. Crazy thing is"—she laughed jubilantly—"I actually got her by talking about Blake. Shewanted to know if I ever hung around Bulletface, if I'd ever watched him record in the studio, if all that jewelry was really his, if"—another snicker

—"his dick was as big as they say it is."

"Don't get that bitch fucked up," Alexus warned, glowering at herlesbian friend. "She'll end up like those Whitney bitches in Indiana."

The Cocaine Princess 3

Tasia and Cereniti gasped in unison, and Alexus instantly regretted her words. Up until now, no one aside from Blake and a couple of Costilla cartel members had known about Alexus's direct involvement in the now infamous Whitney murders. She quickly thought up an explanatory spiel.

"Not that I had anything to do with that, but…I'm sure I can pay somebody to do it," she muttered unconvincingly.

"O…M…G," Tasia said, emphasizing each letter. "Please tell me you did not have your sister's mother killed."

"No! No, I didn't have Mercedes' mom killed. I didn't even know I had a sister when those women were killed."

"Hmm," Tasia grunted dubiously, and went back to perusing her phone screen. "Sure didn't sound like that."

Alexus was contemplating cussing Tasia's ass out, but the ringing of her phone interrupted her thoughts.

Chapter 16

"I'll be home in about five minutes," Blake said as soon as Alexus answered her phone. He was speaking into his Bluetooth earpiece, traversing the dark Chicago streets in the world's fastest production car. Hehad taken the gold-plated .50 caliber out of the Louis Vuitton shoulder- holster under his hoody and laid it on his lap shortly before he got off the highway; one could never be too cautious in this city.

"I'm already on my way to the party with Tee-Tee and Tasia," Alexus told him. "What are you doing home so early anyway? I thought you were staying out till midnight."

"I changed my mind. Turn around and come back home."She scoffed in disbelief. "Blake, are you serious?" She murmured.

"I'm always serious—even when I'm laughin'. Now I know you got two or three Tahoe's followin' you. Hop in one of 'em and comehome. And tell Tasia to let T-Walk know, if I find out he was behind thisshit that just happened to my li'l nigga, I'm at his head."

"Calm yourself down, boy. Don't go jumping to conclusions. With all the people you've shot and killed, there's no telling who—"

"How many times do I have to tell you to stop sayin' that over the phone?" Blake fustigated. "I don't care how secure you think these lines are." He paused, ashing the pinguid blunt he was smoking. "I ain't never killed nobody anyway."

"I was only kidding. Hold on a second." Alexus shouted forher driver to return to the mansion. Then she was back on the phone. "I hope you aren't drunk driving."

"Nah, I'm good. I only had a few sips of Ciroc before I left. I'm on my fifth blunt, though." He coughed several times. "I'll see you ina minute, baby. Love you."

"I love you, too."

Taking in the scenery through stringently squinted red eyes, Blake was, like always, amazed by the affluence of his Highland Park neighborhood. Parked along the curbs were Benzes, Jaguars,

Range Rovers, Porsches, and few Bentleys and Rolls-Royces. The mansions were large, their rolling lawns impeccably landscaped. Everything was perfect.

"How in the hell did these white muhfuckas get all this money?" He muttered aloud to himself. His phone beeped before he could ponder the profound question.

It was a text message from Nona Malden:'Made a vid 4 u. Can I send it?'

Blake waited 'til he was at the looming wrought iron gates in front of his home to reply.

'U can't be textin' me like that li'l mama. I'm about to getmarried. I'll plug u wit' 1 of my niggas, though.'

He sent the message, then reached up to the small rectangular remote clipped to the overhead visor and pressed its single button; the gatesopened.

Driving up the quarter-mile-long driveway, finishing off the blunt and wishing he was single so he could pay Nona a visit without feeling fakeabout it, he glanced around the expansive lawn at the dozen or so dark suited Costilla cartel bodyguards. They were armed with FN P90 machine guns, dressed like they were auditioning for the newest *Men In Black* movie.

By the time he made it to the circular drive in front of the mansion Alexus' limo and her security's two Tahoes were rolling toward him. He re-holstered the golden Desert Eagle, grabbed the duffle bag, and stepped out of the car, taking in a deep inhalation of the cool night air. He thought of his parents, who were now residing in California's posh suburban Brentwood area, and wondered if their nights were ever this cool.

Alexus was at his side a moment later. "Mind if they"—she canted her head toward Tasia and Tee-Tee, who were standing beside thelimo—"stay over for the night? They won't bother you, I swear."

"I ain't trippin'. Long as Tee-Tee don't go on another stealin' spree."

Last year, Cereniti had stolen close to $5 million in drug money from Alexus, and although Alexus had forgiven the thieving bitch, thetreacherous act still did not sit well with Blake.

He trailed them into the mansion and smiled when they took off their fur coats; thick derrieres never failed to put a smile on his face, and three fat asses were infinitely better than one.

They ended up at one of the umbrella-shaded octagonal tables that sat next to the indoor swimming pool. Alexus sent a housemaid to fetch a deck of playing cards and the "Think Like a Man" DVD, while Tasia and Tee-Tee walked over to the bar to get themselves some drinks.

Regarding Tasia with an accusing stare, Blake murmured: "I think you should have had Enrique to find out exactly who kidnapped our son, baby." He retrieved a fresh box of White Owl cigars and a sandwich bag containing about a half ounce of Purple Kush from his hoody pocket. "I understand why the kidnappers killed the four bodyguards, and why theymade that jewelry store owner give up the security footage...but what I don't understand is why they didn't touch Tasia."

"Believe it or not, a lot of American men are against hurting women," Alexus said. She was gazing at him from across the table. "And Ireally didn't want to go searching for answers. All that matters is that we got our son back. Enrique killed the woman whose apartment it was, and her son, but he didn't ask any questions. There was really no need to try and figure out who the kidnappers were. It just taught me to heighten our security and to never let anyone who isn't family leave with our kids."

Blake shifted his eyes from Tasia to Alexus, and suddenly all the grief he was feeling over his friend's murder evaporated. Her perfect face held him spellbound. Without the makeup she was still beautiful, butwith it she was even more stunning. Her long, straight black hair, parted down the middle, framed her angelic visage. The alluring scent of her perfume overwhelmed his senses.

Instinctively, he leaned toward her, planting his elbows on the table. She copied his movements, and their lips connected. Electricity sparked through him as he tasted her sweet breath. She closed her eyes, anda cavernous moan sounded in the back of her throat. Then she pulled back, glowering weakly as he split open a cigar and dumped the tobacco in the ashtray.

"Why are you mean-muggin' me?" He asked, grinning.

"Because you always do this," she complained. "You get my pussy all wet, and then you sit back and roll up your Kush like everything'sfine. Got me sitting over here—"

"Would you two please get a room?" Cereniti said as she and Tasia returned to the table, holding a bottle of Remy Martin and two crystal-stemmed glasses.

"Take that shit back and get some Ciroc," Blake demanded calmly. He was halfway upset that his moment with Alexus had been spoiled.

Tasia rolled her eyes and sat down in the chair to the right of him, but Cereniti headed back over to the bar and grabbed two bottles of Ciroc vodka. By the time she made it back to the table, the housemaid wasstrolling in with the playing cards and the movie, and Blake was splitting open a second cigar after having already rolled the first blunt.

"What's with you and the Ciroc?" Cereniti asked, handing Blake both bottles. "Is it because you like the taste, or are you just supporting Diddy? 'Cause that niggas already filthy rich." She took a seatto the left of him and started shuffling the cards.

"I'd rather put some money in a black man's pocket than anybody else's," Blake said. "I'm about to start wearin' that new clothin' line Tunechi just dropped. I dig those Trukfit hats." He broke up the bud ofKush and spread it across the empty cigar wrapper. Then he rolled it up, saliva-sealed it shut, and used his gold Zippo lighter to dry it.

Alexus was shaking her head at him. "You smoke more weed than anybody I've ever met," she muttered.

Ignoring her observation, Blake fixed his gaze on the blunt as heput fire to the end of it. A wave of frustration abruptly washed over him.

Someone had come looking for him, and it had resulted in the death of hisbest friend, one of the realest niggas he knew.

So who had sent the shooters? The question bounced around in his head like a tennis ball.

"Y'all wanna fuck around with some X-pills?" Cereniti asked, still shuffling the cards. "I got a big bag of 'em in my purse. My cousin gave me a thousand Blue Dolphins for three dollars apiece."

Blake declined the offer, but Cereniti and Tasia each swallowed twoof the pills, and they convinced Alexus to pop one.

The four of them started a spades game. After every hand, the three with the lowest number of books had to take two shots of Ciroc, which led to all of them being rock-star wasted by the end of the second game. They hardly even glanced at "Think Like a Man" as it played on the 500-inch flat-screen television over the bar.

"Is it just me, or is it hot as hell in here?" Alexus peeled off the white Marchesa dress and tossed it to the floor, regarding Blake with an uninhibited, lascivious expression that told him how incredibly freaky she was feeling without having to utter a single word.

"It's not just you," Tasia said. She stood up, pulled off her red dress and high heel shoes, and then dived head first into the heated swimming pool. Alexus and Cereniti, laughing heartily, splashed into the water a moment later.

Grinning his signature grin and smoking the second blunt, Blake rose from his seat and took the smartphone from his waist to take a couple of pictures of the girls in the pool. He had three new text messages from Nona and a text message from his music manager reminding him to be ready for his 106th and Park appearance tomorrow. He ignored Nona's messages; no need in leading her on any further.

"Come on, Blake," Cereniti suggested, waving him over.

He shook his head no. "Nah, I'm good. Y'all get it in," he encouraged, Kush smoke pouring from his nostrils.

Ogling the three sexy women, he began snapping picture after picture especially when their jiggling backsides were visible as they took turns leaping off the diving board. Unintentionally, he studied Alexus and wondered if her measurements—32D-24-48, if his memory served him correctly—were more impressive than Nona's.

Before he could stop himself, he opened Nona's first text message. It was a reply from the one he'd sent.

'I understand you're getting married but you're not married yet, and I at least wanna show you what you'd be missin'. You might want some of this good-good before you get married. I know you like pretty bitches wit' big butts and I'm all that plus some. I'll give you a bachelor party you'll never forget! And, no, I don't want one of your boys, either. I want the CEO of MBM. I want Bulletface.'

Chuckling to himself, Blake moved on to the next text message. 'Just check out the video and tell me what you think. I'm about to send it then I'm going to bed. Mwah.'

"And I'm about to go to bed, too," he mumbled, head spinning. He deleted the two messages he had just read and left the video unopened. Then he picked up his oversized duffle bag and shouted, "I'm goin' to bed,baby."

Alexus didn't respond; she and her two friends were huddled together in one corner of the swimming pool, confabulating in whispers.

With an unbalanced gait, Blake strolled through the spacious white palace, leaving a trail of Kush smoke in his wake. He stopped at Savaria's bedroom door and poked his head in to see if she was asleep. Shewas; her slender brown arms wrapped around one of her many teddy bears. Farther up the hall was King Neal's bedroom, and he, too, was sleeping, lying on his side in the four-hundred thousand dollar gold framed crib.

In his own bedroom, Blake hurriedly stripped down to his boxers, cut off the lights, and got himself comfortable beneath the covers. For a long while, he gazed up at the mirrored ceiling, trying vehemently tothink clearly through the Kush and Ciroc that clouded his brain.

All his thoughts revolved around money, how to make another five hundred million dollars. He considered the notion of buying into a vodka or cognac company and then promoting the liquor in his music to accumulate some more cash. Opening an upscale lounge like Jay-Z didn't sound like a bad idea, either. Maybe he'd start a clothing line. A publishing company. A restaurant franchise. A magazine, like DJ Kayslay.A reality show, like T-Walk.

T-Walk.

The name made Blake's blood boil. He knew T-Walk had to be behind Lil Mike's murder. That shooting had T-Walk written all over it. Afew years ago, back when Blake and his clique had been copping nine ounce blocks of cocaine from Trintino Walkson, Blake had learned how T- Walk handled beef after watching Trintino and another hustler get into a fistfight outside the convenience store that Blake now owned. The other guy had gotten the best of T-Walk, and the following morning he'd paid for it with his life. An 80's model Buick Regal had pulled up alongside him, andsomeone had emptied a Tec 9 submachine gun into his head and chest.

Blake later found out that T-Walk had paid $50,000 for the hit.

Then there was the time when T-Walk sent three ski-masked men to gun Blake down. Blake had managed to return fire and kill one of them before he was shot ten times and left lying on the sidewalk across thestreet from his childhood home. He had lured T-Walk to a park on the northwest side of Chicago several months later and emptied two nine millimeter pistols into T-Walk's Rolls-Royce Ghost, hitting T-Walk twice.

And now Lil Mike was dead, gunned down in the same fashion. "I gotta kill that nigga, T-Walk," Blake muttered acidly as he shut his eyes and rolled onto his side.

He was teetering on the edge of dreamland when he heard Alexus's gentle voice.

"Blake, Blake, are you awake?" She whispered. Her voicegrew closer with every word.

Blake contemplated rolling over and putting Alexus to bed. But his head was spinning at dangerous speeds, so he kept quiet and didn't move, even after she'd shaken his shoulder a few times and murmured his name again.

He felt the covers on the large, custom-designed circular bed shift as she climbed onto it. The palatable scent of her skin invaded his nose.

And then, maybe a minute later, she moaned. An unmistakably sexual moan. Blake forced open his eyes and stared at the glowing red numbers on the digital clock that sat on his bedside table. 10:57, it read.

Alexus moaned twice more, and Blake smiled widely. He presumed she was pleasuring herself with one of her many sex toys—sheowned a plethora of them, dildos, vibrating dildos, lubricants, anal toys —'til he heard Cereniti's distinctive voice whisper, "Quiet down, yo.You're gonna wake him up."

"I'm sorry, I'm sorry," Alexus whispered back.

Blake listened for a while, grinding his teeth at every wet, sucking sound he heard. The fact that Alexus was involved sexually with another woman didn't bother Blake; he actually liked the idea of seeing herhave sex with a woman. What upset him was the sneakiness of the whole situation.

He closed his eyes, took a deep breath, and, reluctantly, drifted off to sleep.

King Rio

Chapter 17

Jennifer Costilla looked excellent for a woman in her mid- forties, like Selma Hayek with a slightly darker complexion. Her long hair tumbled down around her back and shoulders in lustrous black curls. Although she was dressed in the threadbare sweatshirt and jeans that had been given to her before she was released from Guantanamo Bay, she stillmanaged to retain the same regal posture she'd always possessed.

Legs crossed, back straight as an ironing board, she was sitting alone on the Gulfstream VI jet that Papi had sent for her, reading RobertGreene's *The 33 Strategies of War* on a Nook computer tablet.

A million thoughts were running through her mind, the first of which pertained to her missing son, Savio Costilla. She was almost certainthat Papi had murdered Savio in response to her attacks on Alexus and Rita. But she had a remedy for that transgression. She would take from him what he'd taken from her, and since Alexus was the new head of the Costilla cartel, Jenny was left with only one alternative solution.

Mercedes Costilla had to die.

Two other more pressing thoughts bullied their way to the front of Jenny's mind. The first was her fear that the two U.S. Fighter jets that were flying on either side of Papi's jet would shoot her down before she made it into Mexico. The second was her fear that Papi would murder her the moment she stepped off the plane.

A vulpine smile grew on Jenny's face as she envisioned a fifteen kiloton uranium bomb exploding near Alexus's family. If such a thing wereto happen, the Costilla Family fortune would have to be left to either Jenny or Flako—unless Alexus had a written will leaving the fortune to some kindof charity. And, sure, the U.S. government would assassinate Jenny once they learned that she'd actually been behind the HEU thefts, but that didn't matter. As long as Santiago, her second child, inherited at least ten billion dollars, she knew he'd be the next leader of the cartel. And that's all she wanted. No more half blacks running the show.

Jenny set the Nook aside and poured herself a glass of Cristal champagne, wondering where she was going to find a nuclear phys-icist thatwould build the bomb for her without sneaking off to report it to the U.S. government.

She had a remedy for that, too.

Chapter 18
Two Months Later, June, 5, 2012...

Blake's debut album sold a million copies the week it was released, a feat that hadn't transpired since Lil' Wayne's *The Carter III*. The unexpected success of his album—the media attributed it to his relationship with Alexus—galvanized concert-goers nationwide and sent MBM Street King Tour ticket sales through the roof. By the first day of June, Blake's album had sold 2.8 million copies, and he'd performed at twenty-seven soldout venues, mostly stadiums and amphitheaters. Due to him being the CEO of Money Bagz Management, he received seventy four percent of the proceeds from his album sales, which, after fifteen percent in tax deductions, added up to twenty-one million and some change he'd accumulated off the twelve-dollar records, and he was averaging $1.2 million every show after taxes. Not to mention the $4.9 million off the mix-tapes his other artists had dropped and the $62 million he'd made in drug money. Last week's Forbes had named him "Hip-Hop's Six Hundred Million Dollar CEO," completely unaware of his other $232 million.

Today was his off day, and he was sitting courtside at the Celtics and Heat game inside the American Airlines Arena in Miami; clad in a white tee shirt with MBM printed on its chest in big black letters, baggy white Akoo jeans, and, of course, lots of Louis Vuitton, from his white, left leaning skull cap, to his shades, belt, and sneakers. An assortment of white diamond jewelry blinged on his neck, wrists, pinkies and earlobes.

Alexus was seated next to him in a white Roberto Cavalli jumpsuit and white suede Giuseppe Zanotti booties. Birdman of Cash Money Records sat a few seats down from them, dressed in all black with his fitted cap pointing backwards.

"I really don't see what's so exciting about basketball," Alexus said, staring down at her iPad. She was watching the season finale of BET's The Game on the thin computer tablet.

Blake chuckled. "Baby, this is game five of the Eastern Conference Finals. I got a million dollars ridin' on this game."

"So what?" She shrugged her shoulders. "It's still stupid." "You could've stayed home if you didn't wanna come. I told

you that before we left." By 'home' he meant the twenty-million-dollar Miami mansion he'd purchased last year during their
brief split.

Alexus sucked her teeth and then said nothing for the rest of the
game. Her attitude didn't surprise Blake. She'd been speaking flip-
pantly tohim ever since his music manager had phoned them with
the news that his album was certified platinum. Even on the twenty
first of April, when he had rented out the entire Six Flags Great Ad-
venture in Jackson, New Jerseyand spent the day there with Alexus
and a handful of their closest friends, having fun and celebrating her
twentieth birthday, she still had spoken bitterly, arguing with him
over the most frivolous, insignificant things.

And slowly but surely, he was getting fed up with her bullshit.
He was bossed up, sitting on eight hundred and thirty million dollars. Badbitches, movie actresses, sexy models from all over the
world—all of themwere practically begging to give Bulletface some
pussy. Yet here he was, being faithful to a woman that didn't even
appreciate his presence; turningdown hundreds of women at his
shows only to be berated over the phone once he made it back to his
tour bus.

The million dollars he'd bet on the Heat went down the drain,
leaving him mildly upset as he and Alexus stood to leave.

Their twenty person entourage and eight of her bodyguards occupied the seats behind them. Blake's party of eight consisted of
four Mafia Insane Vice Lords out of Gary, Indiana, three Traveling
Vice Lords from Chicago, and his drug distributor, Fly, the only
non-Vice Lord in the group; Fly was a Black Disciple, plugged with
a clique of BDs on Chicago's Low-End. The whole group was thuggishly-comported in baggyjeans with Louis Vuitton and Gucci accessories, and each of them had on atleast a hundred thousand dollars' worth of diamond jewelry.

Alexus had brought along Mercedes, Porsche, Cereniti, Tasia,
and eight more Chicago women who she'd been club-hopping with
for thepast couple of weeks. They were Mercedes and Porsche's
cousins and friends, and Alexus had all of them rocking thirty-thou-
sand dollar designerdresses, Louboutin heels, diamond earrings and
tennis bracelets. They looked more like Hollywood girls than 'hood
chicks.

Flanked by the eight bodyguards, Blake and Alexus headed out of the stadium behind their entourage.

"We're all going over to Club LIV," Alexus said, glancing over at Blake. "Me and the girls are meeting up with Trina to party for a while. If I don't answer my phone, it's probably because I didn't hear it." She shot him another look. "I know you're about to enjoy yourself at King of Diamonds, and I don't have a problem with that. Just try to keep your dick in your pants."

"What?!" Blake scoffed, knitting his brows together. "You getting' on my muhfuckin' nerves wit' all these slick-ass comments. Better fix that attitude."

She sighed, shaking her head and rolling her eyes. "Whatever, Blake. I am not about to argue with you. Go and do whatever you feel like doing. It's not like you really want to marry me, anyway."

Stone faced, Blake stared straight ahead as they tramped down a brightly lit hallway that led into the parking garage where all the NBA players and officials parked. He thought: *'God, why are women so difficult?!'*

He pulled Alexus aside as soon as they entered the garage. "Baby, what the fuck is wrong with you?" He had a firm grip on her elbow.

"You are what's wrong with me!" She hissed furiously, crossing her arms over the ample cleavage displayed in the V-split chest of her jumpsuit. "Why don't you want to marry me?"

"Who said I didn't?"

"You did—the day we went to New York for 106th and Park. I asked you if you wanted to fly out to Vegas and get married, and you said no."

"Because I want my family there when I get married. I want our kids there. Fuck we look like getting married in Las Vegas, wit' nobody there to celebrate wit' us?"

"Kelly Rippa and her husband did it," Alexus pointed out. "So did Ice T and Coco. I don't see why we can't." She reached in her Gucci shoulder bag—white leather, of course—and snatched out her iPhone. Two seconds later she was holding it up in front of Blake's face. "I bet you would have married this bitch."

Blake stared at the picture in shock. It showed Tootie sitting on his lap in the basement of his Michigan City home. She was facing him, and his hands were on her ass.

Someone had taken pictures on the night of Lil Mike's murder. "Mmm-hmm. You fucked her, didn't you?" Alexus sounded calm—the calm before the storm, the eye of Katrina. "Tell me the truth,"she demanded, taking off her Marc Jacobs shades with one hand and ripping Blake's from his face with the other.

"Baby, on King Neal—" he started.

"Don't lie on my son's name," Alexus interrupted.

"Swear to God I'm not lyin'. I didn't fuck that girl. As a matter of fact, I left that night and went back home to you just to keep myself fromcheatin'. That was the same night you and Tee-Tee got on that freak shit inour bed."

Alexus sucked her teeth. "Don't try to turn this on me. We came in there to have a threesome with you, and when I saw that you were asleep, I let her eat my pussy. That's all that happened. And I tried to wakeyou up several times." Her hands moved to her hips. "I've told you before,if you want to fuck with another bitch, we'll do it together. Sneaking around behind each other's backs is not cool." She gave him his shades. "Here, boy. We'll finish this conversation later. Love you."

She pecked her lips against his, squinting dubiously. Then she turned and sauntered to her snow-white 24-passenger H-2 Hummer limousine, her huge ass shaking with every step. Enrique helped her into the limo, and then it was gone, followed by two white Tahoes.

Blake started off toward his triple-black Bugatti Veyron Grand Sport convertible, where his entourage was standing. The cars they'd driven—two Bugatti Veyron Super Sports and three Rolls-Royce Phantom Drophead Coupes—were also triple-black. All six of the cars were Blake's,and he'd had their colors changed from lime-green to black the day after LilMike's funeral.

"Fuck was she talkin' 'bout?" Kenny-Lord inquired. He was leaning back against the trunk of Blake's Bugatti convertible, wearing a white tee with Free K.T. printed across the chest in bold black letters. Theother three MIVLs—Rube and Batman, two lean and dark-skinned men with dreadlocks, and Pat, a brawny, bald-headed, brown-hued ruffian—wore identical tees.

"Nothing important," Blake said. "Check this out, though. I need y'all to seek out all the niggas that look like real dope boys tonight. Pull 'em to the side and holla at 'em. Ask other niggas about 'em. Shit, Birdman and Ross'll be there; ask them about 'em. Find as many real niggas as possible and tell 'em they can get bricks from us for fifteen-a-ki, ten if they cop at least a hundred of 'em. And we got bricks of boy for fifty,pounds of Kush for twenty-eight hundred. Next day delivery, too."

"Man," Fly said, "I done already hollered at some Top Six and Zoe Pound niggas, bruh. All you gotta do is kick back and let me handle this shit. I'm guaranteed to get rid of two or three hundred bricks this week."

"I got seven hundred and fifty thousand for fifty mo' bricks right now," said Bam, a five-star branch elite of the Traveling Vice Lords. He was tall, dark brown, and heavy-set, sitting in the driver seat of the drop-top Phantom that sat in the parking spot to the right of Blake's convertible. Rubbing a hand over his bald head, he added, "And Reesie Cup want a thousand mo'."

The two other TVLs, Sawbuck and Tweet, nodded their heads.

Both of them were tall and brown, but Sawbuck was darker and skinnierthan Tweet. Like everyone else in the group, they were certified bosses,million dollar niggas with droves of young gunslingers working beneaththem, all thanks to Blake and his seemingly endless supply of kilos.

"Let's go on and hit up K.O.D," Blake suggested, opening his driver door and getting in. "I'm ready to make it thunderstorm."

Leaving the American Airlines Arena, Blake dropped the top onhis Bugatti and turned on his CD player. "Donald Goines," the third track on his almost triple platinum debut album, began to blare from the speakers.

'Like Donald Goines, I'm a storyteller of the streetsNo narrative needed, I'm the fella with the heat

It's like his troubled soul done somehow drifted into meGod gave a gift to me to set the realest niggas free

When I'm deceased, the realest street nigga I still'll beNeva snitchin', neva runnin', gutta 'til they finish me Kush replenish me, gives me an omnipotent energy

Feel like I'm rich as Carnegie, 'cause big money befriended me Couple enemies, tell them niggas shoot if they carry it

Buncha frenemies, yeah I'm talkin' Judas IscariotsSo in the

custom Louis duffle I be carryin's

Enough money to have a few of my niggas bury 'emI got a dope house, and an AK house

Publish bestsellers in the booth, Holloway HouseGive me a sick beat, and I promise you I'ma go in

You'll think Big Meech wrote it...wit' Donald Goines...'

The warm Dade County air felt good on Blake's face. He inhaled a deep breath of it. Relished it. He loved the Midwest, always would, but there was no weather like Miami weather. And the scenery—palm trees, scantily clad women baring their curves for all to see, perfectazure waters stretching beyond sandy beaches—it made him want to stayhere forever.

Fly and Sawbuck were trailing him in the two Bugatti coupes, and behind them were the three Phantom convertibles. The fleet of luxurycars had cost Blake $8.5 million altogether, including what he paid to get them bulletproof and equipped with stash boxes, their paint and interior jobs, and the black-painted 24-inch rims on the Rolls-Royces.

Hundreds of awestruck eyes ogled the Veyron's and Phantoms as they zoomed toward North Miami Beach. Thrice, when they were stopped at red lights on Collins Avenue, Bulletface Fans leapt from their vehicles requesting autographs and pictures, and he graciously obligedevery time, signing albums and breasts, smiling for the photos.

'This is the life,' he thought. 'I wish all real niggas could ball like

this.'

Chapter 19
Chicago...

MBM Music Manager Fredrick Douglass steered his brand new 2012 Cadillac XTS down Lake Shore Drive, occasionally glancing over at the dark, rippling waters of Lake Michigan. Intent on impressing his dinnerdate, he had put on his best tuxedo—a black Armani ensemble—before leaving his three million dollar condo at the Trump International Hotel & Tower.

When he made it to Great Aunt Micki's, the upscale soul food restaurant on Michigan Avenue where his date was waiting, he parked behind a coal-black Maybach—hers, he presumed—and took a deep breathto calm the butterflies that were flapping around in his stomach. Then he stepped out of the black XTS, straightening his bow tie, and entered the opulent restaurant holding a dozen red roses in one hand.

Tall, light brown, and well-dressed, with wooly African hair, prudent brown eyes, and a confident gait, Douglass was an intelligent, successful black man from Baltimore, Maryland. A veteran in the music industry, he was accustomed to mingling with some of the wealthiest, mostpowerful people in America.

But never anyone as powerful as Rita Mae Bishop, the top executiveof Costilla Corporation—a corporation that included a newspaper, magazine, and book publishing company, three TV and CATV stations, a film production and distribution company, a billion dollar resort in Cancun,Mexico, and a social networking website.

A female host led Fredrick through the dimly lit restaurant to a doorat the back wall. Two burly black CPD officers stood on either side of it.

The host pushed open the door and preceded Douglass into a privatedining room with red marble floors, red walls, and circular tables covered with red cloths. There were only five tables. Kanye and his girlfriend Kim were seated at one of them, far across the room from Rita Mae's table.

She rose from her seat, smiling vastly, as Fredrick strolled toward her. He handed her the bouquet of roses, hugged her, kissed her on the cheek, and then took a step back to admire her form-fitting, peach-coloredcocktail dress and the beautiful buxom and steatopygic body it concealed.

"Mmm mmm mmm...God is good," Fredrick murmured in his throbbing baritone. He studied her dark brown face as they sat down acrossfrom each other. "You look stunning, Rita. I see where Alexus got her looks."

"Thank you." She sniffed the roses before setting them aside.

"Youlook amazing, as well. I like your little bow tie, too. It's cute."

Fredrick grinned appreciatively. "That dress—it fits you perfectly.""Squeezing my big behind into it was struggle," she sheepishly

admitted, "but I've taken a liking to Dolce & Gabbana's new cocktaildresses. I've been wearing them a lot lately, especially on the show."

"If there is no struggle there is no progress," Douglass said, pickingup a menu. "What are you eating?"

"I've already ordered our meal. Lobster crab cakes and a bottle ofArmand de Brignac."

"No dessert?"

She shook her head no. "I'm on a diet. Alexus and Blake's weddingis coming up soon, and I don't want to bust out of my dress while they're reciting their vows."

They shared a laugh as a slim black waiter arrived with their food.

He popped open the bottle of Ace of Spades and filled their champagneglasses with the costly intoxicant.

"Anything else?" He asked.

"That'll be all," Rita Mae told him, and he walked back out of the

room.

"So," Fredrick asked, "how's your day been? How's the corporate

world treating you?"

"I can't complain. Costilla Corporation is now worth nineteen and ahalf billion dollars, which means we're worth more than Viacom, CBS, andCC Media Holdings. Only entertainment businesses with more revenue than us are Time Warner, Walt Disney, and News Corp. And I don't know how my daughter's stock investors are doing it, but somehow they're gambling her billions in the stock market and winning every time. She's made fourteen billion in the past two months alone."

Fredrick blew a stream of air from between his lips, and his eyebrows ascended to his forehead. "Fourteen billion dollars in two months?"

"I know—sounds impossible, doesn't it? I'm still finding it hard to believe that my daughter is now the wealthiest person on Earth. There is no way one person should have seventy six billion dollars. Definitely not a twenty year old. She's been blowing money on everything she can find. Justyesterday she spent a hundred and twenty five million on a mansion in South Beach simply because it belonged to Versace. And the crazy part about it is she's down in Miami right now, she hasn't even gone and lookedat the place."

Fredrick took a bite of his crab cake. It was warm and tasty. "Well, look at it like this," he reasoned. "The U.S. economy was

built upon the blood of our African ancestors. Up until the nineteen sixties, almost a hundred percent of American capital was owned and controlled bywhites who lynched and robbed our ancestors for fun, and the government has yet to even apologize, let alone compensate our families for all the free labor they got out of us. Alexus deserves every dime of that money, if you ask me. There would be at least one or two hundred black millionaires in America today if we were given our proper share of the pie. Half of Hollywood would be populated with blacks."

"You sure are right about that," Rita Mae said, nodding. "Are you coming to the first annual MTN Music Awards on the tenth? Blake's nominated for album of the year, best new artist, best collaboration for thatsong he did with T.I. and Lil' Wayne, and video of the year for "Lime- Green Bugatti." He's supposed to be performing."

"Of course I'll be there. The whole MBM team will be there. We have two other artists nominated for awards, too. Mocha's up for best female R&B artist, and Lil Meech is nominated for mixtape of the year. Plus, Mary J.'s performing, and there's no way I'd miss that. Blake's also performing at the BET Awards on July first. He's nominated for three BETAwards."

Rita Mae was nodding again, poking her fork at the crab cake.

For along moment she said nothing; then; "You know, I'm actually kind of proudof Blake. I honestly thought his record company would fail miserably, and Iwas certain his album was going to flop. He's doing pretty good, though."

"Yeah. He just signed four more rap artists, a female R&B group, and a pop singer from the UK. And *Heart of a Taurus*, Mocha's sophomorealbum, will be released this Friday. Blake's a phenomenal CEO, Rita.

Truly amazing."

"I see that now," Rita Mae sighed. "I just wish he was more like Trintino Walkson."

"T-Walk?" Fredrick frowned.

"Yeah. Trintino dresses like a businessman is supposed to dress. And he's making a good name for himself in the entertainment industry. He's being compared to industry moguls like Tyler Perry and Ryan Seacrest, and Blake's more like Birdman, or Rick Ross. Always talking about guns, money, drugs, and jewelry. Always hanging around gangsters. Icannot for the life of me understand how a black man with over a half a billion dollars in the bank could still hang out in poor neighborhoods with thugs who'd rather sell poison to their people than go out and find a job."

"Rita, what you need to understand is—""Call me Rita Mae."

"Rita Mae. There are virtually no jobs in poor black communities. Those kids are out there starving. None of their family members are doing well. They're killing each other at the drop of a dime because they're so broke that they no longer care about life. Blake used to be just like them. He's not leaving the ghetto for Hollywood. He's far too real and loyal to hisroots to do that."

"Still, though…he shouldn't be glorifying drug-dealing."

"Do you know how many U.S. companies are selling poison legallyevery single day? Look at how many people die every year from using tobacco products? Isn't that poison? How is it illegal to smoke marijuana,which is perfectly harmless, yet it's okay to smoke another plant that'll probably give you a thousand different kinds of cancers?"

Rita Mae suddenly looked up from her plate and smiled a Colgate smile. She leaned forward, cupping her left hand around her neck. "There isnothing I can say to make you view Blake differently is there?"

"Nope," Fredrick chuckled. "I'm riding this MBM train till the wheels fall off. We're building an empire. Loyalty is the glue that holds empires together."

"Well...there is something else I'd like you to be aware of be-forewe...go any further." Her smile vanished. "Last year, I got en-gaged to anMTN News anchorman named Nat Turner."

He nodded his head knowingly. "I remember. The guy went crazy after his family was found dismembered in their Virginia home. He killed fifty-five Mexicans in Southampton, Virginia. Deadliest shooting since Virginia Tech. They say he hung himself before the authorities could capture him. November eleventh, I be-lieve it was."

"Okay, clearly you've been misinformed. But I'll get to that in a second. The man I was with before Nat—Neal Miller, a homicide detective —is also dead. First he was paralyzed when Jennifer Costilla detonated abomb on my doorstep, then he was killed when she hired a group of al Qaeda members to hijack an airplane and crash it into Alexus' old beachhouse in Miami."

"I remember that, too. Flights were canceled nationwide."

Rita Mae sipped from her champagne flute. Ten silent seconds ticked by.

"So what you're saying is...?" Fredrick asked.

"I'm bad luck. Jennifer's out of prison and laying low some-where inMexico, but she could very easily come after me again. Papi killed Nat because he wants me to stay single if I'm not with him. He doesn't really mind if I'm in a single relationship with someone. Anything more, though —an engagement ring, marriage plans—there's no telling how he'll take it."

"Papi's a killer?" He laughed. "Are you kidding me? He's an oldman, sixty something years old."

It was Rita Mae Bishop's turn to laugh; though hers was not an incredulous one. She sounded nervous.

"You don't know Papi," she said, and downed the remainder of her drink.

King Rio

Chapter 20
Club LIV, Miami, Florida

'How did I know this was going to happen,' Alexus thought. Arms folded, she squinted at Trintino Walkson as he walked into the VIP section where she and her girls were seated. Her annoyance was palpable; she contemplated picking up one of the many bottles of Moscato Rosé from the table in front of her and cracking Tasia over the head with it.

"Tasia, I fucking hate you," she hissed, jamming her right elbow into Tasia's ribcage. "You called and told him I was here, didn't you?"

A guilty snicker burst from Tasia's mouth.

T-Walk was dressed in an expensive light-blue suit. His handsome mulatto face was one big smile. The three men following behind him were also wearing expensive suits, and they all had braids. T-Walk was the only one with short hair, 360-degree waves.

"Daaaaaamn, girl," Mercedes crooned lustfully from Alexus' left side. "Who is that sexy-ass nigga? The one in the baby blue."

"That's T-Walk," was all Alexus had to say. She'd already told her sister about her past relationship with Trintino, and that there was still a fifty-percent chance of him being King Neal's father.

"You didn't tell me he was *that* fine. He got a brother?" Mercedes japed.

Trey Songz and Waka Flocka's "I Don't Really Care" was blasting throughout the club, and T-Walk somehow managed to move to the beat as he swaggered over to Alexus, stopping to personally greet every girl in her section. When he finally made it to Alexus, she reluctantly stood up and hugged him, holding her breath in an effort to keep his enticing cologne from soaking her panties as he pulled her against his hard chest.

"You could've at least sent me an e-mail letting me know you were in town," he muttered, taking a step back and resting his hands on her shoulders. His contagious smile infected her, and she smiled back. "If only you knew what that smile does to me, Lexi."

"Nice to see you, too," Alexus mumbled.

'*Shit,*' she thought. His scent was in her nose; her pussy started topalpitate, her pencil eraser-shaped nipples grew stiff.

Abruptly, she returned to her seat.

"You can't be touching on me like that in public," she said. "Look athow many people are aiming their smartphones over here. Those pics and videos will be on YouTube tonight and TMZ in the morning. They're probably already on Facebook and Twitter."

"Wouldn't want that to happen, huh?" He chuckled

"I'm not trying to piss Blake off. You and I both know how that boyis. He's still upset about what happened to Lil Mike. I don't want the mediaputting any unnecessary pressure on him."

T-Walk dismissed the notion with a flick of his wrist. "That nigga been shot twelve times, Alexus. A little controversy isn't going to kill him."

He began introducing his three friends to the girls. The two dark- hued men were Reggie and Anthony, and the brown-skinned man was Squirm. Alexus noticed Reggie's truculent expression and wondered why he was so angry. Twice, for a few fleeting seconds, she caught him glaringcoldly in her direction. But then T-Walk was talking to her again, and she forgot all about the evil stare.

"Can we go somewhere and talk? I have an idea for a television event, and I'd like to run it by you before I present it to the MTN board of executives," he said. "We can go up to my place. It'll only take a few minutes." He chuckled, cutting a glance at Enrique, who was standing a fewfeet away from them. "Besides, it's not like you'd have to worry about me attacking you the way I used to. Not with all these bodyguards you got hanging around."

"You know I can't do that, T-Walk. Just call me tomorrow and tell me what you have in mind. Better yet, send me an e-mail tonight. I'll phoneyou with my opinion first thing in the morning."

With a concurring nod, he bent forward so that his mouth was next to her ear and said, "Fourteen billion dollars—in two months! What kind ofstock investors are you dealing with? I need that kind of team helping me flip my money." He straightened himself and gazed down at Alexus, waiting on a response.

She showed him an arrogant grin. "There are some secrets that noteven the President is aware of," she said matter-of-factly. "Add into the e-mail the sum of money that you're willing to invest. I'll call you about that,too."

His mouth was at her ear again. He spoke in his old ghetto lexicon. "You still sellin' dope?" Then, as if justifying the question, he added, "I know a coupla niggas tryna grab some bricks."

"I've never sold dope," Alexus replied kindly.

Another chuckle escaped from T-Walk's lips, accompanied by a warm exhalation of sweet-smelling breath that hit Alexus like a ton of bricks. She wanted to press her lips to his, to wrap her legs around his waistand let him carry her to the elevator and up to his suite. But that was the x- pills thinking for her. She'd swallowed two of them not even an hour prior.

She and the girls stood up and took pictures with T-Walk and his three friends before the men departed.

"How the hell did you leave him for Blake?" Mercedes asked. Shewas still angry at Blake for what he had done to Duke, mainly because Duke had left her after the incident.

Tasia said, "I tried to talk some sense into Alexus a long time ago.

She'd rather be with a nigga who runs the streets like Lil Boosie than acorporate-type like Jay-Z."

"First of all," Alexus said, a hundred pounds of attitude weighing down her tone, "I didn't leave T-Walk, okay. He got upset over me giving Blake some money, so he sent my cousin Bookie and two other niggas to kill Blake, and he broke up with me. Now that I'm a billionaire, he wants me back. Fuck that. Blake's been with me since we were all driving aroundwith bricks in the trunk, so he's who I'm marrying. End of story."

And the truth was, Alexus was in a hurry to jump the broom—for a number of reasons. Topping the list was her worry that she would be murdered—by the Zeta cartel, or the Sinaloa cartel, or maybe even by her own cartel—before she and Blake were able to tie the knot. Second was thedaunting thought of Aunt Jenny and the highly enriched uranium the CIA suspected her of harboring. Alexus had gone online and viewed a video of a1946 atomic bomb test in the Pacific Ocean, and she still could not get the image of the massive mushroom cloud out of her head. The CIA was keeping a close eye on Jenny, who'd been staying at the Costilla Resort Hotel in Cancun since her release from the military prison. Director

Bowden claimed that Jenny was doing nothing more than relaxing in thesun, spending thousands, out of the $15 million Alexus had given her, onthe twenty-something-year-old boy toy she was dating. But Alexus was certain that Aunt Jenny was up to something.

Aunt Jenny was always up to something.

Suddenly, the music stopped, and the DJ's voice boomed throughthe club:

"Hold on one second everybody. We have a special, special guest inthe house tonight. She's the woman who's engaged to one of the hottest rappers in the game. She's the woman whose net worth has just surpassed Carlos Slim's, making her the number one richest person in the world. Y'allgive it up for Alexus Costilla!"

Alexus found herself blushing as the applause started, a blush that deepened when her entourage stood and clapped along with everyone else.She took off her sunglasses and mouthed, "Thank you," seven or eight times. Then the DJ put on "Money In The Air," a strip club anthem off Blake's album, and the crowd went ham.

The Cocaine Princess 3

Chapter 21
King of Diamonds Strip Club

'She grabbed her knees and made that ass vibrate…Did it so good she made my eyes dilate

I'll throw a hundred thou now, nigga, why wait Tell 'er give me head till I'm dead, hope I die late

Realest nigga in this bitch, and I'm the richest, tooFranklins in the air, I know you wanna get a few My bitch bad, lookin' like a bag o' billions, true

Three Bugattis in the parkin' lot, it's fuckin' pitiful…'

Blake was standing between Rick Ross and Birdman, throwing fistfuls of hundred-dollar bills at a bad-ass stripper named Chyna and puffing heavily on the chubby blunt of Kush that was stuck between his lips. He had already thrown $200,000 in ones, and now he was working onemptying the $3 million in hundreds out of his duffle bag.

The 35,000-square-foot club was jam-packed, with everyone bouncing their heads to the beat of Bulletface's "Money In The Air," whichwas currently the number one single on the Billboard Hot 100 chart. Thanksto Rozay's gratuitous purchase of three hundred bottles of Ciroc, all the realniggas were drinking and having a good time.

And watching Bulletface as he showered Chyna with millions.

Blake paid them little mind, choosing to only converse with the bosses-Birdman, Ross, Meek Mill, Khaled, Busta and Slim. There was no time to speak with anyone else. The real niggas knew why he was in town.Their guys were negotiating drug deals with his guys. Boss shit.

Besides, there was no way Blake could focus on anything other thanthe professional stripper's booty-dancing skills. The reddish-brown-skinnedparagon was doing moves he'd never before seen, and it was driving him crazy. She made her ass clap, then made it shake like disturbed Jell-O, thenslammed down into a split that made the crowd go wild.

An hour later, when Blake and his crew were leaving K.O.D., Chynawas right behind him, carrying the cash he'd thrown at her in a black garbage bag. She had changed into a cherry-red tube dress

111

and a different pair of Louboutin heels. Her hair, long and black, was pulled back in a modest ponytail. Five more bad bitches were trailing Blake and Chyna, chatting among each other as they all headed into the parking lot. Blake's eyes were on Chyna's sexy, round face, her Meagan Good shaped lips, her exotic-looking eyes.

"You'd better not get me cussed out by Alexus," she said, taking a remote key out of her Gucci bag. "I'll miss out on all types of business opportunities if I fall out with her. She can probably make one phone call and destroy my whole career."

Blake grinned. They were nearing his drop-top Bugatti.

"I'd never let that happen, li'l momma. She wouldn't do that anyway," he said. "Matter of fact, she'll probably open up a thousand doors for you. I'll do whatever I can, too. Just let me know what you're trying to do and I got you."

She pressed a button on the remote key, and the taillights on a dark-colored Maserati convertible that was parked five spaces to the left of Blake's car lit up. Blake opened his trunk and dropped in his empty Louis Vuitton duffle bag.

"I want to be an actress one day," Chyna said. She looked at the garbage bag and added, "Might be able to make my own movie with all this money." She giggled softly.

"How much of that did you give to the club owner?" Blake asked. "About half. Terry didn't ask for that much, but that's what I gave

him. He's always looked out for me." Chyna's cinnamon eyes flitted over the Bugattis and Rolls-Royces lined up to the right of Blake's Veyron. "Are all these yours?"

"Yup. I got a lot of cars. I'm addicted to cars and jewelry." He grabbed the garbage bag from her, tossed it in his trunk. "Leave your car here and ride with me. We'll send somebody to get it later."

Reluctantly, Chyna thumbed down the button on her remote key, re-engaging her car alarm. Blake opened his passenger door and stared at the meaty ass protruding from the back of Chyna's tight dress as she got in. He shut the door, and her angelic face turned up to his.

"I hope you know what you're doing—with your young ass," she
said.

Blake pulled his brows together and took off his shades. Chyna read

his expression correctly.

"That dick; I hope you know what you're doing with it," she explicated. "I am four years older than you."

A witty reply was crawling up Blake's throat when Fly and KennyLord appeared at his side. He told Chyna to hold up a minute, then movedto the rear-end of his Veyron. Fly was the first to speak.

"Baby want five hun'ed of 'em for twelve five apiece. Fat guy wanta hun'ed. The Haitians want twenty bricks of boy, fifty bricks of girl, and ahun'ed pounds of Kush."

"Which Haitians?" Blake asked."Top Six and Zoe Pound."

Kenny-Lord said, "Shit, don't forget about us. Me and Pat need a hun'ed of 'em, and two hun'ed pounds of Kush. Rube need ten mo' bricksof boy. I think Batman need twenty bricks of boy."

"Then," Fly said, "We still gotta take care of the Indianapolis, FortWayne, and Chicago niggas. We'll be sold out in a few days."

"Well"—Blake reached out and shook their hands with one hand,slapped their backs with the other—"everything's a go. Let's get this money" Stepping around the driver's side of his Bugatti, he turned his attention back to Chyna, who was studying her flawless reflection in the visor mirror.

He slid into the driver seat, started the powerful engine, dropped thetop, and then raced out of the parking lot.

"You never answered my question," Chyna reminded him as she flipped the visor shut.

Blake glanced over at her, displaying his idiosyncratic grin. "I knowenough," he replied. "I'm workin' wit' a monster, too. Don't fuck around and get hurt."

Rolling her eyes doubtfully, she smiled. "Yeah right. That's whatthey all say. The last nigga I fucked with swore up and down—"

"I don't wanna hear about the last nigga. And I don't want you tellin' the next nigga about me. You shouldn't even have another nigga afterme—unless it's a muhfucka wit' my kind of bread—but that's really up to you."

"Boy, aren't you about to get married?""Yup."

Chyna hesitated, gazing intently at him, her hair flailing in the

113

warmnight air. "Well," she finally said, "I'll have to see how things work out. I'mnot trying to break up anyone's relationship." She paused for a few long seconds. Then her hands were caressing the perfect musculature of his chest, unbuckling his diamond-encrusted Louis Vuitton belt buckle. "I hopeyou know that I fuck the same way I dance," she informed him.

"I hope so."

She tugged out his eleven-inch-long phallus and gasped, squeezingit with on hand. "Oh, my God," she whispered. "What did you do, use a penis pump or something?"

Blake's signature grin returned. He glanced down and watched as aglob of spit descended from between Chyna's pink-glossed lips and landedon the tip of his hard dick. Then her mouth fell upon it, and she began fellating him, taking in only half of his length at a time, but sucking that portion thoroughly. Blake struggled to keep his eyes on the road as her gripping mouth fluctuated wildly on his pulsating erection.

It was a long, toe-curling blow job. He was pulling into the driveway of his twenty-million-dollar mansion when his scrotum started totingle and tighten up. Alexus' motorcade had not yet arrived, but black- suited members of her security team were situated all around the estate likeSecret Service agents.

Leaning his seat back as far as it could go, Blake said, through clenched teeth, "Ay, don't get that cum on my pants."

Chyna continued sucking and slurping his dick as it spurted and gushed—and spurted and gushed—a thick dose of cum into her mouth.

Somehow, she managed to keep the semen from cascading down his shaft.When his semen finally stopped flowing, she raised her head from his lap, gagging on the mouthful of cum, her expression twisted into a look of disgust. She swallowed it all down in three big gulps, fanning her stringentface as she did it.

"What was that, two months' worth of cum?" She asked softly, thumbing a globule of semen from her lower lip and into her mouth. "Feelslike I just drank a milkshake."

Simultaneously, Blake chuckled and sighed, putting away his now flaccid penis. He looked past Chyna and saw that his guys and the five girls they'd acquired from King of Diamonds were disappearing around the side of the mansion, presumably on their way to the swimming pool. While Chyna applied a fresh coating of MAC lip gloss to her pillowy kissers, Blake grabbed his iPhone to call Alexus. But it was ringing before he reached her number. The call was from his music manager. He put his Bluetooth in his ear and answered.

"What it look like, old man?"

"Looking good," Douglass said. "Everything's set for your shows at the Bankers Life Field house in Indianapolis and the Genesis Center in Gary tomorrow. Then Thursday we have the Hot 97 Summer Jam at Meadowlands Sports Complex in East Rutherford, New Jersey and the MBM Meets YMCMB Showcase at the Nassau Veterans Memorial Coliseum in Uniondale, New York. Friday you'll have two more sold out shows, one at Madison Square Garden and another at the Best Buy Theater in Times Square. Two more shows Saturday at the Sleep Train Amphitheater in Wheatland, California and the Hollywood & Highland Center in Hollywood. Then we have the MTN Music Awards at the Shrine Auditorium in L.A. on Sunday."

Blake rubbed his palms together in anticipation of the cash he'd make off the upcoming shows. "Now *that's* the kind of news I like to hear. Racks on racks on mothafuckin' racks."

"Mocha's show at the Regency Ballroom in San Francisco just ended about an hour ago," Douglass continued. "Everyone else is at the Chicago studio recording. I'll have your money from Mocha's show deposited into your account by daybreak."

"Did you go on that date wit' Rita?" Blake inquired.

"Yes I did. I had no idea that woman was so beautiful. We had dinner at a fancy little black-owned soul food restaurant in downtown Chicago. Spent some time getting to know each other a little better. Then we came back here to my place, and we discussed Africa's AIDS epidemic and why the World Health Organization injected over a hundred million Africans with an AIDS-laced smallpox vaccine in nineteen seventy-seven."

"Damn they did?" This was new to Blake.

"Of course they did. They also injected an AIDS-laced hepatitis B vaccine into over two thousand white male homosexuals the next year through the Centers for Disease Control/New York Blood

Center. The United States Defense Department received ten million dollars to create theAIDS virus in nineteen sixty-nine. World leaders were concerned that overpopulation might soon lead to the collapse of our species. So they decided to decimate the elements of society that they felt were undesirable to society as a whole—blacks and homosexuals. The entire black population of Africa was expected to be dead within fifteen years after theywere infected."

Blake wanted to hear more, but the bad redbone sitting next to himwas pushing open her door, and Alexus' motorcade was pulling into the drive way. He told Douglass he'd see him in Chicago in the a.m., then ended the poignant call and stepped out of the car.

"Is that Alexus?" Chyna asked, her tone replete with awe as the longwhite Hummer limousine parked beneath a palm tree on the other side of the bronze fountain that centered the circular drive.

"Yeah, that's her. Go around back to the pool. I'll be there in, like,one minute," Blake said, walking toward the limo.

Alexus emerged from the rear door and pounced on him as if she were a ravenous jungle beast, folding her legs around his waist, biting at hislower lip and kissing him at the same time. He smelled liquor on her breath.Tasted it. The twelve girls that climbed out of the limo behind her each heldbottles of Ace of Spades.

"You been drinkin'?" Blake asked between kisses.

"A little bit," Alexus admitted smilingly. "I'm also rolling off twopills." She snickered. "My panties are soaked."

Mercedes asked, "Where is Kenny?'"

"Out back by the pool," Blake said as he turned and headed that way, spreading and slapping the fleshy protuberances of his fiancée's rump.

"I'm not letting you get drunk and pass out on us tonight," she muttered, trailing a curve of kisses from his lips to the ten-carat white diamond in his left earlobe. "We're having a threesome with Tee-Tee beforewe go to bed. She hasn't had a dick in her in over two and a half years."

"I already got us somebody for that," he told her.She pulled back, eyeing him. "Who is it?"

"A stripper from K.O.D.""Is she cute?"

"'Cute' ain't even the word. She's bad, baby."

"Really?" Alexus became thoughtful. She inserted an index

fingernail between her teeth and lightly bit down on it. "I supposed wecould have a foursome."

"I suppose we could," Blake beamed.

She slapped him gently across the cheek, biting the corner of her bottom lip. They were passing a row of bright lawn lights on the side of the massive Spanish-style mansion, the lights to their right, an outdoor restaurant beneath a black retractable awning to their left. Three chefs were scrambling around in the stainless steel kitchen, preparing barbecue chickenwings and drumsticks, cheesy nacho platters, fried shrimp, crab cakes, and fruit and salad bowls for the impromptu pool party.

Thirty feet ahead lay the swimming pool. The Travelers and two of the Mafias—Kenny-Lord and Pat—were hunched over a crap game on the elevated patio behind the mansion, and the other three guys were already inthe pool with the girls.

There were five lounge chairs set up beside the pool. Blake thoughtlessly chose the middle one to recline in and found himself sandwiched between Tasia and Mercedes. Sitting on top of him, Alexustook off his shades and dropped them in her shoulder bag with her ownshades.

"So," she asked, flicking her eyes toward the pool, "which on areyou talking about?"

Blake followed her gaze and spotted Chyna sitting on the edge of the pool with her feet in the water, typing something on her smartphone. Hestarted to point her out to Alexus, but then Tasia began yapping.

"Starting tomorrow Cereniti and I are going to be busy shooting ourreality show in Chicago," Tasia said to Mercedes. "I need you to keep an eye on these two for me. Especially Blake's' black ass. Call me if you suspect anything out of the ordinary."

"Girl, you ain't even gotta trip on that," Mercedes quipped, "causeI'm on his ass anyway."

Alexus lowered her lips to Blake's and molded them together, silencing the critics with a passionate kiss; mumbling something about a bathing suit, Tasia stood and sauntered into the mansion via the rear patiodoors, and Mercedes—along with the rest of their entourage—followed behind her.

"Tee-Tee," Alexus shouted before Cereniti could make it into

117

themansion. "Come here for a minute." Then she looked down at Blake andagain asked him which girl was the K.O.D. stripper.

He waved Chyna over and was just about to introduce her to Alexuswhen suddenly Alexus leapt to her feet and grabbed a hold of his hand.

"Let's hurry up and go before the haters return," Alexus said, laughing ecstatically.

As the four of them were lancing back around to the front of the bigwhite mansion, Cereniti asked, "Yo, where the hell we going?"

"To the Hummer," Alexus answered.

Blake didn't really give a damn where they were going; they couldhave been en route to Mars for all he cared. He was about to be alone withthree bad bitches. Nothing else mattered.

The party started as soon as they climbed into the stretch Hummer. There were two twelve-count cases of Armand de Brignac—one open and empty, the other unopened—stacked on the hardwood floor inside the 220"limousine. While Blake cracked open two bottles, Cereniti turned on the CD player and the DVD player. Seconds later, Gucci Mane's latest mix- tape, "Trap Back," was blaring throughout the limo, and a Nyomi Banxxx porn was playing on the five flat screen televisions.

"Driver," Alexus said after pressing a button that lowered the blackprivacy glass. "Do you mind driving us to the Versace mansion?"

"Wait a minute," Chyna protested, turning to Blake. "My money's inthe trunk of your car."

Alexus spoke before Blake could. "The cars will be loaded onto a747 first thing in the morning and flown straight to Chicago," she said. "And you don't have to worry about anything being stolen out of them.

Whatever's in them now will be in them when they're unloaded inChicago."

"Chicago?" Chyna looked worried. "I can't go to Chicago. I have towork tomorrow."

"I'll talk to your boss about it," Alexus said. She was peeling off herjumpsuit, revealing the white-lace Victoria's Secret bra and thong set she wore beneath it. "Now, will y'all please get naked?"

Snickering, Cereniti and Chyna shed their dresses and

underwear. Then the trio of dime pieces hastily undressed Blake, kissing all over his bulging black muscles and gulping down mouthfuls of Ace of Spades.

Blake drank heavily, too, enjoying the moment, for he realized how fortunate he truly was. He was a black man living in a country where whites were twenty-two times wealthier than blacks, and thanks to Alexus he was one of the wealthiest African-Americans in the nation. He had to smile about that.

He stretched out on the long, milk-white leather seat, watching Alexus take off her bra and thong. She descended her glistening-wet pussy onto his mouth, and he started sucking and licking her clitoris. Looking down between her parted thighs, he saw Chyna slide her mouth halfway down his dick, while Cereniti's tongue slathered his scrotum.

The privacy glass rolled down again. "Your friend Tasia's standing in front of our vehicle," Enrique said. "Want me to have one of our men move her?"

"No, it's okay. We'll just stay here." Alexus was gazing down at Blake, biting the corner of her bottom lip and pinching her nipples.

The black window closed quickly, and Alexus climaxed a moment later. She was a "squirter;" her tasty juices arced out of her and spilled into Blake's mouth. He continued to suck her quivering pussy until she stumbled over to the other side of the limo.

His attention immediately moved to Cereniti as she tore open a Magnum condom packet. She rolled the condom onto his wet black pole, French-kissing Chyna in a very passionate manner. Chyna squatted over his rigid pipe with her back to him, and Cereniti guided it into Chyna's slippery juice box.

True to her word, Chyna rode him just as wildly as she'd danced for him at the strip club. Her pussy was warm and snug, her juices viscid and sweet-smelling. She bounced up and down so rapidly that he had to lift her off of him four times within the first few minutes just to keep from ejaculating prematurely.

Cereniti rode him next, and her pussy was way tighter than Chyna's.

At first he was surprised at how skilled she was at riding his dick, mainly because he'd never seen her with a man. But then he remembered that she had been a professional stripper a couple of years ago, which explained whyshe was so talented at working her hips.

Tasia's hating ass started banging on their window, but no one paidher any attention; Chyna was sucking Alexus's pussy, and Cereniti was reverse-cowgirling Blake with reckless abandon.

When he felt the ample load of semen bubbling up in his scrotum, Blake sat up and yanked off the condom. Alexus mounted him hurriedly and slipped his dick into her dripping-wet pussy. He sucked her nipples anddug his fingers into her massive derriere as his cum filled her womb.

The Cocaine Princess 3

Chapter 22
Costilla Resort Hotel Cancun, Mexico

Jennifer Costilla rolled off of her twenty-three-year-old lover and slumped onto the bed beside him, running her fingers through her unkempthair.

His name was Miguel Godinez, formerly an assassin for the Zetacartel, now a loyal member of the Costilla cartel.

He turned onto his side, curled his arm beneath his head, and stared at Jenny's beautiful face until their breathing returned to somewhat of a normal pace. Then, fingering a lock of hair from Jenny's forehead, he said, in Spanish, "I'm sorry I got here so late. I, uh... ran into a bit of trouble leaving my sister's villa. Gamuza's men ambushed me. They Swiss-cheesedthe Ferrari, killed a few innocent bystanders. I held them off with an AK-47while Sissy and the nephews climbed in her van; then I got us the hell out of there."

Jenny rolled her head to the left and gazed into the young man's eyes. He was a fearless cartel soldier, but she knew that he was afraid of Gamuza; virtually every human in Mexico was afraid of the perilous Zeta cartel leader. Gamuza was vicariously responsible for over fifteen thousandmurders, which included a president-elect, four mayors, and dozens of politicians, news reporters, musicians, federal agents, journalists, police officers, and private investigators. He ruled most of eastern Mexico with aniron fist, while the Sinaloa cartel controlled most of the other half of Mexico.

The Costilla cartel bosses—Papi, Flako, Jennifer and Alexus—detested Gamuza for a more personal reason: he had murdered Segovia Costilla, Jenny's father. He'd cut Segovia to pieces with a chainsaw, right infront of Segovia's wife and children, and though he was now in his early eighties, the Costillas still wanted the octogenarian drug lord dead.

"Well," Jenny said, "all you have to do is find out where he lays hishead. He won't live to see sunrise."

"Nobody knows where Gamuza lives," Miguel pulled on his briefs keeping his golden-brown eyes locked on Jenny. "I would have killed him long ago had I known where to find him. I pledged my life to the Zetas, and they turned against me for a mistake I had nothing to do with."

121

The "mistake" was last year's failed assassination on Alexus Costilla. A sniper had sent a hail of bullets through the windows of Rita Mae Bishop's high-rise office at the MTN Tower in downtown Chicago. Several rounds had come close to striking down the Costilla cartel leader,but she had escaped unscathed.

There were four one-gram lines of tan-colored powder stretched across the cover of a hardback Stephen King novel on the bedside table nextto Jenny. A short straw lay beside the book. Jenny picked up the book and the straw, and sat up in the bed. She used the straw to snort half a line up one nostril and the second half up her other nostril. Then she leaned her head back and squeezed her eyes shut as the cocaine and gun powder raced throughout her veins.

"You should really stop snorting that gun powder," Miguel advised."I've been doing pow since the eighties, and Papi's been doing it

since the sixties." She opened her eyes.

"Which explains why he's so prone to chopping off people's headswith that golden machete."

Sitting the book back on the table, Jenny laughed briefly. She stoodup, stark naked, cum oozing down her inner thighs. The pow— a sobriquet Papi had given the cocaine and gun powder mixture— had her feeling supercharged. She sashayed over to the floor to ceiling windows and separated the big white curtains. They were in a penthouse suite on top floor of the 43-story Costilla Resort Hotel, which, altogether, was a

220,000-square-foot paradise of water slides, hiking trails, swimming pools,jet skis, yachts, and exotic eateries. *Caliente*, the Mexican-style sports bar on the hotel's first floor, was never void of inebriated crowds of men and women from all over the world.

"What time is it?" Jenny asked, staring out the window. She adjusted her eyes to study Miguel's model-esque reflection as he checkedthe rose gold Rolex watch she'd bought him a few weeks ago.

"Two hours past midnight. Bedtime for normal people." His blacksteel Tec-9 submachine gun was on the nightstand, a fifty-round clip extended from beneath it. He picked it up and crossed the room to Jenny.He coiled his arms around her waist. "What are you thinking about?"

122

She took in a deep breath, leaned her back against his smooth chest, and exhaled. She was thinking about the nuclear war head, wondering how much longer she'd have to wait before its construction was completed. Her son Santiago had kidnapped a Russian physicist—Vasily Kramnik—from a vacation resort in Panama, and now Kramnik was being forced to build the bomb at an abandoned factory in the remote jungles of Cabimas, Venezuela.

But Jenny knew that, no matter how much she trusted Miguel, she could not risk revealing her plans to him—or anyone else, for that matter. she wasn't trying to get hauled back off to that military prison.

So, instead of telling him what she was pondering, she said, "I'm thinking about the new Ferrari I'm going to buy you."

"Really?" He showed her his wonderful little smile, sliding his free hand up to cup her breast. "Actually, I've had my eye on a Dodge Viper I saw at a dealership in Mazatlán."

"Then that's what you'll get." She turned and looked up at him. "But first I need you to get a message to the Mexican Mafia."

"To their boss?"

"Yes. Tell Sergio I sent you." "And what's the message?"

"Crash the Mercedes," Jenny said coldly.

Chapter 23
Chicago, Illinois

Alexus sauntered into the lobby of the 86-story MTN Tower at 9:30 the following morning, flanked by Enrique, her attorney Britney Bostic, and a phalanx of bodyguards. Her bloodshot eyes were stashed behind a pair of Dolce & Gabbana shades. She donned a white Prada skirt-suit and white, five-inch Louboutins.

She stopped and shook hands with several MTN employees before stepping onto the private executive elevator. Then she was on her iPhone, getting in some FaceTime with Blake, who unsurprisingly was still in bed with Chyna and Cereniti; they all had flown back to Chicago late last night on Alexus's one-hundred-million-dollar Boeing 757 private jet, which had two bedrooms, three full bathrooms, a kitchen, and a living room.

"Good morning, Bulletface," she softly intoned, watching Blake's mouth stretch open and tremble as he yawned away his tiredness. She liked the way he looked in the morning: black and ugly, yet handsome at the same time. "Ugh, get up and brush your teeth. I can smell your breath through the phone," she japed.

He chuckled sleepily. "Don't get beat up." He sat up, fingering the crust from his eyes. "Where you at?"

"I'm downtown at the MTN Tower. My mom wants to talk to me about something. Probably about us sending the kids to stay with Carolynn and Dale again."

Carolynn and Dale were Blake's parents. They resided in the affluent Brentwood area of California, in a hilltop mansion not far from Heidi Klum's. Savaria and King Neal were staying there until the end of Blake's concert tour.

"Tell Rita I said hi," Blake said.

"I will. Get yourself a few more hours of rest. Douglass would never let me hear the end of it if you passed out from exhaustion at one of those shows. I'll call you back at noon."

Britney said, "Tell that gangster I said hello and good morning." Blake heard her; he chuckled again. "Mornin', Britney."

"Bye, boy," Alexus said. She pressed END and turned to Britney, who was smiling as widely as she was. "What are you beaming about?"

125

"You two are so cute together. I love your love." Britney's eyes wereon the screen of her BlackBerry smartphone, perusing the e-mail Alexus had forwarded to her this morning, the e-mail from T-Walk. She had on a gray pinstriped Chanel pantsuit, and her hair was whipped up into a bun that complemented her chocolate face. "This proposal of T-Walk's doesn't sound like a bad idea. I mean, you have to admit, he knows what he's doingwhen it comes to these reality shows. Brick House of Jupiter Island is still the most-watched show on television, and Brick House of North Palm Beach is tied with American Idol. And don't forget that ever since he took the lead as executive producer of Mariah's Salon and 'Hood Affairs, their ratings have literally skyrocketed. I'd really take this proposal into consideration if I were you. Especially the Miss Black America beauty pageant."

Alexus was thoughtful for a moment, pondering T-Walk's two-showproposal, which she had read three times before forwarding it to her attorney, her mother, and the Costilla Corporation's board of Executives.

The first of Walkson's innovative ideas was the Miss Black Americabeauty pageant. He planned to select a hundred and fifty big-bootied models from magazines such as Straight Stuntin, As-sets, Dime Piece, Sweets, Craze, BlackMen, Stunnaz, Cheddar, and Smooth Girl.

The girls would then compete for the crown in a nationally tel-evisedbeauty pageant that would be aired live on MTN and hosted by T-Walk and —"Preferably," he wrote—Alexus Costilla, with three black celebrityjudges. He suggested the event be sponsored by McDonald's, Ciroc, Trukfit, AT&T, MTN, and Walkson Promo-tions, his own promotion company.

The second show was essentially a black version of E!'s *The Girls Next Door*, only instead of Hugh Hefner, the star male would be rap legend Too Short, and taking the place of blonde-haired, big-breasted white womenwould be black women with weaves and big butts.

"Both of them seem like shows a lot of people would watch," Alexus said as the elevator finally made it to her mother's fifty-sixth flooroffice. "I'll talk to my mom about it."

Alexus and Britney sailed through the expensively furnished

waitingarea, past Rita's assistant's desk, and into Rita's office, leaving the bodyguards outside.

Rita Mae Bishop was sitting behind her big mahogany desk, readinga paperback copy of Alex Haley's Roots and sipping from a Styrofoam cup of Starbucks coffee. She looked up at Alexus, her expression indecipherable. She bookmarked the poignant tome and set it on her desk asher two visitors greeted her with warm hugs. While they muttered their good mornings and how are you todays, Alexus discerned a thinly veiled coldness in her mother's voice; Rita let her know what it was about as soon as they were seated.

"Three days ago," Rita Mae said, "a columnist for the Houston Chronicle wrote about a secret drug cartel operating out of Matamoros, Mexico. He claimed to have had proof that the Mexican military was protecting the cartel, and the CIA was assisting the cartel in successfullysmuggling their drugs into the States."

"Sounds a little far-fetched to me," Alexus said timidly.

Rita Mae continued. "The columnist was found dead in his home thefollowing day. He'd been shot twice through the mouth, his throat was slit, and his tongue was hanging out of his neck." She paused for effect. "Now, that article has been deleted from the Houston Chronicle website. I called FBI Agent Josh Sneed and asked him about it. Want to know what he said?"She didn't leave room for an answer. "He told me to leave it alone. He said that the article was a lie, that I was wasting my time investigating a fictionaltale. But then, when I made it here to work this morning, this envelope was in my mailbox."

A wave of apprehension washed over Alexus as she watched Rita pick up a plain white envelope from the desktop and hand it to her. She accepted it with a tremulous hand, fearing that her secret role as the leaderof the Matamoros' cartel-the Costilla cartel had somehow been revealed.

Alexus said, "Who cares about some secret drug cartel in Mexico?""I do," Rita replied.

"Why?"

"Because your father was arrested two years ago for allegedly running a Matamoros-based drug cartel. And because, the day before Blake's album was released, that CIA director showed up at your mansionand demanded to speak with you. You claimed it was just to warn you thatyour psychotic aunt Jenny was coming home, but I know there has to be more to it than that." She sipped some more of her coffee. "Just read the papers."

Reluctantly, Alexus opened the envelope and took out two folded pieces ofpaper The FBI agent had typed in a small yet very readable Roman font:

'Ms. Bishop,

When your ex-husband and his brother Flako were released from the federal prison in Florence, Colorado, on the very same day that bin Laden was murdered in Pakistan, I immediately went searchingfor answers. This is what I have found.

#1 The names of Juan and Flako Costilla were deleted from all state and federal criminal databases on May 1st, 2011, roughly an hour after Jennifer Costilla was captured inside bin Laden's compound in Abbottabad, Pakistan, Juan and Flako Costilla-and Tasia Olsen, your daughter's friend-were released from federal custody a few hours later. Since then, the entire Costilla family has been granted diplomatic immunity, which exempts them from taxation, searches, arrests, etc. They, including Alexus and her son, are literally untouchable. Their files are Top Secret, accessible by only a handful of CIA agents.

#2 According to a friend of mind at the ONI (Office of Naval Intelligence), Alexus Costilla is next in line to be the chairman of the Council on Foreign Relations (CFR). I have in my possession several documents proving that the Council on Foreign Relations isthe absolute highest level of the Illuminati. Other branches include the Brotherhood of the Snake, the Brotherhood of the Dragon, the Open Friendly Secret Society (the Vatican), the JASON Society, the Mysteries, the Builders, the Illuminated Ones, the Order of the Quest, the Knights Templar, the Freemasons, the DeMolay Society,the Royal Institute for International Affairs, the Knights of Malta, the Bilderberg Group, the U.S. Central Intelligence Agency, the Trilateral Commission, the Skull & Bones, the Scroll & Key, the Thule Society, and there may be many more. The CFR controls ourgovernment, from the Justice Department, to the State Department,to the military, the press, the New York Stock Exchange, and the President of the United States...'

Alexus stopped reading and handed the papers to her attorney.

Shesaid, "Momma, if you believe this nonsense, you may as well believe in aliens. I'm not about to waste my time reading this crap." "No, I want you to finish reading it. Tell me if there is any truth towhat he's saying." "There isn't. I've never in my life heard of the Council on Foreign Relations. It probably doesn't even exist." Alexus was struggling to suppress the panic that was brimming inside of her. She shifted around uncomfortably in the black leather chair. Globules of perspiration burgeoned on her forehead. "Momma, I swear, I am not and never will be amember of the Illuminati. Now can we get on to business? Tell me what you think about T-Walk's email."

"Fine." Rita brought up the e-mail on her computer. "What's withthis six million dollars he's trying to invest?'

'Damnit,' Alexus thought. She'd forgotten about that part of the e-

mail.

"I don't know, Mom. I didn't really get a chance to discuss it with

him. We were at a club in Miami when he mentioned it."

Rita's umber-colored eyes moved from the computer to Alexus. Shespoke in a low, questioning tone of voice.

"You have a thirteen-man team of stock investors, and every one ofthem are ex-CIA agents and former Goldman Sachs executives."

"So what?" Alexus said, playing dumb. "I have the same accountants and investors that Granny Costilla had before she passed."

"Hmm." Rita went back to scanning the computer screen. Then shepicked up her desk phone, dialed a number, and put it on speakerphone.

"Who are you calling?" Alexus asked with a sigh. "The guy you should have stayed with," Rita retorted.Trintino Walkson answered on the fourth ring.

"Hey, Ms. Bishop." He sounded cheerful. "Hope you're having agreat morning."

"I am." Rita was already smiling; she loved her ex-son-in-law. "DidI catch you at a bad time?"

"No, not at all. I'm actually at the Redbone's strip club, on the set ofDown the Pole. We're shooting the first episode tonight. Me and the other producers are here making sure all the equipment is in working order, introducing ourselves to the film crew."

Alexus was excited about *Down the Pole*. It was going to be aired live on iBlack, a Cinemax-like television network of hers that had debutedin January. Cereniti and Tasia were among the five strippers that were selected to star in the highly-anticipated reality show.

Rita said, "T-Walk, what is it with you and all these booty models?Every show you've created is chock-full of black women with big butts."

T-Walk laughed briefly. "I'm just trying to correct the image of whata black supermodel truly is. Black women in the modeling industry nowadays don't stand a chance unless they're shaped like white women— tall and malnourished. Those are not the kinds of women black and Hispanic men are generally attracted to. Kiya Renae, Mesha Seville, Heather Bianchi, Buffie the Body... Alexus— those are the kinds of black women that we look at as supermodels. We want to see more women like them on television, and in movies. I feel like God has blessed me with the opportunity to reveal the unparalleled beauty of black women to the world, so that's what I'm going do. "

Alexus rolled her eyes, smiling. "You are so full of it, T-Walk."

"No, I'm serious." He protested. "Before I created the Brick House reality shows, there had never in the history of television been a show witha cast full of curvaceous black women. They couldn't even get on TV in a bikini without being blurred or edited out. The industry has for so long degraded and disregarded black women with thick figures, and now, thanksto your television networks, they are finally getting the national attention they deserve."

Rita was nodding her head in agreement. "So what kind of budgetare we talking?" She asked, twirling an ink pen in one hand.

"Around forty million for the beauty pageant, and—"

"You can forget about the other show," Rita said. "I'm on board withthe pageant. I have a meeting with the other executives in ten minutes.

We'll draw up a contract and work on getting all the details figured out.Talk to you later."

"Yes!" T-Walk exclaimed triumphantly, and then Rita terminated the call.

"Why couldn't I have thought of that?" Alexus said to no one in

particular.

Tapping the Bic pen on her desk, Rita Mae Bishop became contemplative; she sucked in her bottom lip and gazed at the pen for a longmoment, "We need to hurry up and contract T-Walk to Costilla Corporationbefore another network gets him," she mused. "I say we sign him to a five-year, two-hundred-million-dollar contract. That amounts to a fourth of the money he's made us so far."

"Two hundred and fifty million sounds better," Alexus said, gettingup from her chair. "He deserves it."

"Sit back down. I'm not through with you yet." Rita's expression changed as she raised her eyes to her daughter's. She put on a mask of scrutiny, and waited till Alexus was again seated to resume the conversation. "I've been looking into your investments, trying to ascertainthe source of this perpetual influx of cash you've been receiving. Like all the other inquiring minds, I can't find a thing."

Alexus sighed. "Derivatives are an eighty-trillion-dollar market, it'scompletely unregulated, and it's all confidential. Of course you can't find anything. No one can. Carlos Slim made twenty-five billion the year beforelast, and every investor in the world wanted to know how he did it. But it'snot for them to know. Some investments are made public, and some are kept private. Mine happens to be the latter." The blatant lie felt like vomit as it escaped Alexus's mouth.

Truthfully, the fourteen billion dollars she'd recently acquired came from dealing kilos of cocaine and heroin to the United Kingdom, Japan, Spain, France, Iceland, the Netherlands, and the United States of America, but Alexus couldn't tell that to her mother. Rita Mae Bishop was a religious zealot, a devout Christian who followed the laws of the New Testament to a

T. Criminal activity was one of her many pet peeves, and in her book drug-dealing was right up there with murder.

Rita placed her elbows on the desk and leaned forward. Her browsfurrowed, and her eyelids moved closely together. "Alexus Costilla," she said tightly. "You are the wealthiest person on this entire planet. I personally believe God blessed you with those riches for a reason. Do notlet me find out otherwise."

Chapter 24

Kush smoke curled up into the air from the end of Blake's blunt as he toked on it. He was standing in his vast walk-in closet, beads of shower water dripping from his muscular frame, a custom-made Louis Vuitton bathtowel wrapped around his waist, Chyna and Cereniti were drying him off with another towel, while he eyed his wardrobe and tried to decide on whatto wear.

"You must be taking steroids," Chyna said, sliding the towel alonghis powerful left arm. "You're about as big as Busta Rhymes."

Blake looked over at the sexy redbone stripper. She and Tee-Tee were both naked, and they, too, were laden in globules of water from the shower the three of them had just taken together. When he was re-awakenedat 10:45a.m., Chyna's mouth had been noisily slurping up and down his dick, and Cereniti had been fucking Chyna from behind with a strap-on dildo. He had ejaculated in Chyna's mouth for the second time in less than twenty-four hours. Then he'd sat up in bed and devoured a breakfast of steak, hash browns, and cheese eggs while the two dime pieces licked and sucked each other to trembling climaxes. In the shower, he'd fucked both ofthem.

Now it was eleven-thirty, and Blake was ready to hit the streets. "I need to go out and buy me something to wear," Chyna said.

"I go you," Tee-Tee promised. "We gottta hurry up, though. Me andTasia gotta be at Redbone's by four."

"Y'all go 'head," Blake said, putting on a pair of Calvin Klein boxer-briefs. "Chyna, I'll send somebody to pick you up before my Garyshow. I want you to come onstage and dance when I perform "Money InThe Air." So wear somethin' sexy."

"I'm always sexy," Chyna proclaimed arrogantly. "I need my moneyout of your car, too,"

"I told Enrique last night to have somebody put it all through the money machines and put it in some duffle bags. They should be sittin' by the front door." Blake grabbed a pair of Black denim Trukfit shorts—baggyenough to fit his usual thirty-grand bundles of Franklins in each pocket— and stepped into them. Then came a matching cap and tee shirt with TRUKFIT stretched across the chest in gold letters; a pair of Air Yeezy 2 sneakers; a Louis Vuitton belt with a blinging, white diamond-encrusted LVbuckle; and a Louis Vuitton bandana, which he left hanging out of his rear left pocket.

He then bejeweled himself with a Cartier watch that had a hundred carats of white diamonds spread around its frame; a bracelet with twice as many white diamonds; four platinum necklaces that were replete with five-carat white VVS diamonds; a pair of platinum and white diamonds skewered through his earlobes.

Chyna and Cereniti studied him with intrigued eyes as he put on thejewelry and sprayed on a dash of Versace cologne. The two of them went back into the bedroom and got dressed while Blake visually scanned the section of the east wall where his collection of designer sunglasses was stored. He grabbed a pair of gold-framed Louis Vuitton shades and headed into the bedroom.

"Time for the walk of shame," Chyna said sheepishly. She pulled her hair into a ponytail, smiling at Blake as he picked up four large bundles of hundred-dollar bills and his iPhone from his nightstand.

"Welcome to the good life," Blake chuckled. "Good sex, good Kush,good money." He stuffed the cash in his pockets.

Cereniti said, "There isn't enough room in my Lamborghini for herand I to go shopping. Mind if we take your Phantom—well, *one* of your Phantoms? Yo, I promise not to crash it."

"If you crash my Rolls, I'm crashin' you," Blake threatened.

"You already did that." Cereniti giggled, and then preceded Chynaout of the bedroom.

Blake sat on the bed and made a call to his mother to check on thekids. Carolynn sounded frustrated.

"Hello?"

"Hey, Momma. How you doin'?"

"This little devil of yours is getting on my last nerve.""Who, King?"

"I'm talking about Savaria. She's driving me insane. And your father isn't making it any better, wrestling around with her in my bed after I just made it."

Blake grinned. He heard Dale and Vari's laughter through the phone."What's up wit' King Neal?" He asked, attaching a Bluetooth earpiece to his left ear, puffing on his blunt.

"He's all smiles as usual. Trying his best to walk and talk like you.

Thinking he's tough already. He gibbers the way you did when you were hisage."

A wider grin burgeoned on Blake's dark brown visage. "That's myli'l nigga," he boasted with pride. Getting back up from the bed, he headedout of the bedroom to the hallway safe and punched in the combination.

Pulling open the heavy steel door, he said, "I'll be out there in California allthis weekend.'

"Good. Maybe I'll get a little peace with these kids out of my hair."

Blake clipped the Smartphone to his hip and stepped into the safe, astainless steel vault with a gold and crystal chandelier suspended from the ceiling and an eighty-inch Sony camera monitor on its left wall that displayed images from the estate's thirty-nine cameras. The rear and right walls were three long shelves of hundred-dollar bills. The bank-new notes were papered together in ten-thousand-dollar bundles.

Flanking the door on both sides were three long rows of 24-karat gold-plated guns: Kalashnikovs AK-47s, equipped with 125-round drums;

.50-caliber Desert Eagle handguns with 13-shot clips; Uzis and Tec-9s, Ruger P90s and Glock 18s, all gold-plated and fitted with red laser sightingand extended magazines. On the floor beneath them were forty brand-new Louis Vuitton duffle bags; Blake picked one up, unzipped it, and placed it on the 24-karat gold rectangular table that sat in the middle of the vault's steel floor.

"What are you doing?" Carolynn asked.

Blake stared for a brief moment at the piles of cash—all $537 million of it. Then he began filling the brown leather duffle bag with cash. "Getting' ready to start my day, Momma. I got two shows today. One at thestadium where the Pacers play in Indianapolis. Eighteen thousand people."

"Thank the Lord. Mmm," Momma intoned. "I don't know how youdo it. I'd probably faint if I had to perform in front of that many people."

"It ain't nothin'. I was born to be a star. Pops would have been a startoo, if he hadn't been a dope-fiend. It's cool, though. At least

he ain't doin' it no more. And it's my time to shine now anyway."
He looked at the touch-screen camera monitor and saw that Chyna and Cereniti were just entering the eighteen-car garage. Another image showed Alexus and what seemed tobe the entire Costilla family-Jenny excluded-conversing in the basement's soundproof shooting range.

"You'd better be careful in Indianapolis. I've been reading the blogs.A lot of them still think you had a hand in that big shooting that took place two years back. Make sure you put on that vest, and don't let anyone prepare your drinks or roll up your weed."

"I know the game, Ma," he chuckled.

"Well, I'm just making sure. I know how much you love those streets." She sighed a motherly sigh of love and worry. "Here, talk to yourdaughter."

Savaria quickly broke into her standard line of questioning. She wanted to know how he and Alexus were doing; if she should be expecting any new gifts; when she would be seeing him again. Blake finished stuffing
$500,000 into the regular-sized duffle and zipped it shut while he spoke with his little angel. Then he ended the call, tucked a Desert Eagle behind the waistline of his baggy Trukfit shorts, grabbed an AK-47, and went downto the shooting range—after shutting and checking the safe's door.

The elevator ride lasted less than thirty seconds. When the doors opened and Blake stepped out, the Costillas all turned to look at him. A deafening silence fell over the massive room. Blake walked over to Alexusand kissed her on the cheek, then hugged Mercedes and Isabella, and shookhands with Papi, Flako, Pedro, Antoney, and Santiago. Instinctively, Blake wondered why the cartel bosses were all here in Chicago. They usually stayed in Mexico.

Eyeing Blake's gaudy attire, Papi grumbled, "Seems like your diamonds multiply every time we meet. Who do you think you are, BigMeech?"

"I think I'm Bulletface," Blake replied tightly. He dropped the duffle, but kept the AK-47 in hand. "What's goin' on?"

Mercedes was dressed in a multicolored Marchesa sundress and black Gucci ankle boots. She grabbed her hips and said, "Papi thinks I'm insome kind of danger. They think my aunt Jenny—who I've never even met

—wants to kill me."

"That could very well be the case," Alexus said, turning to Blake."We have Jenny's suite at the Cancun resort wired with listening

devices. Enrique and Papi listened to the recordings this morning andoverheard Jenny say something about Mercedes."

"What did she say?" Blake blew out a stream of weed smoke.

Alexus said, "We can't really tell. She was standing about ten feetaway from the nearest bug, and she was whispering. But we're absolutelysure that the last word she said was 'Mercedes,' and she said it venomously."

"So what?" Santiago interjected. "My mother could have been talking about buying another fucking Mercedes, for all we know. Stop assuming that she's always planning on killing somebody. All she's beendoing is relaxing and enjoying her freedom."

This sparked a fiery debate among the Spanish-tongued Costillas.

Unable to understand the conversation, Blake picked up his duffle and strolled over to one of several white marble-topped tables. He took a seatand laid the AK-47 on the table. Mercedes joined him.

"I'm really starting to believe that the drug cartel Papi used to run isstill around," she said, casting a timorous glance at the cartel bosses. She was completely out of the loop as far as the cartel was concerned. No one had told her a thing about her paternal family's international drug- smuggling operation.

Blake shrugged indifferently as he snubbed out his blunt in an ashtray. His mind was on his money. Upcoming concerts for him and hisMBM team, Mocha's new R&B album, Lil Meach and Young-D's new mix-tape, the album his new R&B group was working on in Atlanta, andthe kilos of heroin and cocaine and pounds of Kush he had stashed at a River Forest mansion.

Mercedes said, "Do you think I should be worried about my own auntie trying to kill me?" When Blake didn't reply, she added, "I mean, it'snot like I'm scared. Kenny won't let anything happen to me. You know him and his niggas stay strapped up." She stepped in front of him and touchedan index fingertip to his white diamond-flooded bracelet. "How much didyou pay for this?" She asked.

"Eight hundred and sixty-one thousand," Blake said, letting his eyescrawl slowly up Mercedes' thick pair of caramel-hued legs. He pulled his smartphone from his hip and looked up at her. "Kenny'll be wit' me all daytoday. I want you to stay close, too. I'll make sure you're safe."

He sat back and dialed his music manager's number, gazing from behind the dark shades at the nineteen-year-old's perfectly sculpted face. The more he looked at her, the more he realized how closely she resembledurban modeling legend Mesha Seville.

"Just got off the line with Freddie Gibbs and Young Jeezy," Douglass said as soon as he answered the phone. "They're ready to makeappearances at the Genesis Center. King Louie and Chief Keef will be there, too."

"That's what's up," Blake said. "You on the way over here?"

"We just finished gassing up the tour buses. I'll be there with the rest of the MBM team in about forty-five minutes""A'ight. See you then."

Blake ended the call and returned his attention to Mercedes. The other Costillas were still chattering in Spanish.

"I can't believe this shit," Mercedes said, still eyeing the bracelet."Can't believe what?" Blake asked.

"All this money," she replied. "Just last year, I was broke as hell, sellin' pussy to some old-ass man to keep food on the table for me, Porsche,and the kids. Now I'm able to walk into the Gucci boutique and buy all the designer bags and shoes I can carry. Now I have a Maybach and an eight- million-dollar condo at the Trump. Now I have thirty-two million dollars inmy bank account, and the government isn't even making me pay taxes. I feel like I'm dreaming."

"Crazy what a forty-million-dollar check can do, ain't it?"

Mercedes smiled dimly. "Speaking of checks have you seen that dissvideo T-Walk put on WorldStarHipHop.com?"

"A diss?" Blake frowned. "What kinda diss?"

"Oh, you haven't seen it?"

"Evidently not if I'm askin' you about it… genius." He had his phone in hand, typing his way toward the website.

"It really ain't nothin'," Mercedes said. "You know how niggas be hatin'. He said you ain't really no hustler, and that you'd still be a broke-assdope boy if Alexus hadn't given you that five-hundred-million-dollar check.Oh, and he said thanks for takin' care of his son."

Blake was already livid by the time the video started.

It began with T-Walk leaning back against the driver's door of a baby-blue Bentley convertible on big blue DUB rims. He had on an expensive blue suit and Mauri shoes, and he was drinking from a bottle of Ace of Spades like the other eight black men that were crowded around him, clad in similar blue suits. An equal number of black and Hispanic women in tight dresses and tall heels were mixed in with the men. One of them was Ashley "Thunder" Hunter, a dark-skinned big-bootied former video and urban magazine model who was now the main star of MTN's Brick House of Jupiter Island reality show. She was standing beside T-Walkwith a glass of champagne in hand. Sunlight was escaping the sky above.

The cameraman said, "So, Trintino, um, how are you liking Miami?

Pretty nice down here, huh?" It was a black man's voice.

T-walk adjusted his Gucci shades and displayed a cocky grin. "Realnice weather," he said. "It's a perfect location for a real boss like myself.

I'm out here eating good wit' my folks, you feel me? My gangstas. Shoutout to Larry Hoover and all the other stomp-down bosses, all the Board Members, all the real shot-callers. Shout out to all the real niggas worldwide." He turned and motioned toward the three-story gray-stone mansion that stood about twenty feet ahead of his Bentley. "You see thatcrib?"

The cameraman laughed. "How could I miss it?'

"I just dropped nine mill' on this mansion," T-Walk bragged. "I'm flying all my family and friends down here this weekend to break it in, andtonight"—he planted one hand on Thunder's huge derriere and squeezed it

—"I'm planning to break it in a little myself."

"Isn't Bulletface one of your friends? I know y'all are from the samecity, right? He's probably the hottest rapper to come out of the Midwest since Kanye. I know you've got to be excited to finally see a real niggafrom your hometown gettin' it."

T-Walk sipped from the golden bottle. "Nah... not really. I'm glad tosee him succeed, but I don't fuck wit' dude like that. He's really not the king of the Midwest on any level; if anything, I'm the king. That li'l nigga was coming to cop work from me when we were out there hustling in the streets. He couldn't even afford a whole thang! I was chargin' that li'l niggafifty-five hundred for nine-pieces, you feel me? Now all of a sudden he's a boss, moving hundreds of bricks?" He scoffed dubiously. "Yeah right! Just because he handcuffed a billionaire dime piece, he thinks he's a boss. If shehadn't blessed him with that five hundred million, he would still be broke, and he definitely wouldn't be lying to the world about all the dope he supposedly moved."

"Wow. I, uh… thought you two were close friends."

"Once upon a time we were. But then he started creepin' with Alexus behind my back, so I broke up with her and sent my li'l niggas toteach Blake a lesson, you feel me?"

"Is that when he got shot ten times?"

T-Walk regarded the camera with a conspiratorial grin. "Is this goingup on YouTube?" He asked.

"I'm actually putting it on my blog, but it'll probably end up on YouTube. Bulletface will end up seeing it."

"In that case," T-Walk said, stepping closer to the camera, "I mightas well give him a shout-out, huh?" His grin widened. "Right on for takingcare of my son. I highly appreciate it. But I need you to do me one more favor. Keep that "king of the Midwest" bullshit out of your mouth, li'l nigga."

The video ended abruptly. Clenching his teeth tightly together, Blake looked up at Mercedes and said, "I can't believe this hoe-ass nigga."He turned and shouted for Alexus.

"She already watched it," Mercedes said as Alexus walked to-wardthem. "She was waitin' on you to wake up to talk to you about it. The fullvideo's on YouTube. It already has, like, seven hundred thousand views, and it's only been on there two days."

Just as Alexus made it to Blake's side, his smartphone started ringing with a call from Fly.

"Man," Fly said, "you gotta check out TMZ. They got a video onthere of T-Walk talkin' shit about—"

"I just watched it," Blake interrupted.

"Nah, bruh. You gotta watch it again. Look at the two niggas standin' off to his right. They're the same niggas we got in that shootoutwit', when Lil Mike and Terry got killed."

Blake closed his eyes and took a deep breath. He had been right allalong, he realized. Lil Mike was dead because of T-Walk.

"I'll talk to you when y'all get here," Blake said. He ended the calland took off his shades. An unprecedented fire filled his brawny chest. He considered stomping over to one of the firing lanes and emptying his AK- 47 at a paper target, but Alexus sat down on his lap before he could get up.Holding his face between her hands, she sighed and gazed into his eyes.

"Please don't go crazy over that stupid video," she said, tapping her soft lips against his. "He's making us a lot of money. I can't afford for anything bad to happen to him. Just give me a day or two and I'll get him tomake a public apology."

"It's cool," Blake said calmly. "We need to get that DNA test for King Neal. I want it now."

"I've asked you to take that test a hundred times." She let go of hisface. "I'll make sure we get it done this weekend, okay? I'll have a doctorwaiting at your parents' house after Sunday night's awards show. But firstyou have to promise not to go after T-Walk."

"I promise."

"You promise what?"

"I promise not to go after T-Walk," Blake mumbled.

'And promises were meant to be broken,' he thought.

King Rio

Chapter 25

Alexus went up to her and Blake's bedroom with Mercedes while everyone else headed out to the massive eighteen-car garage. She exchanged her white skirt-suit for a white, one-shouldered Louis Vuittondress and a matching pair of heels.

"We should wear pants today," Mercedes suggested as she roved hereyes over her sister's extensive shoe collection

They were moving around inside Alexus' walk-in closet, which wasessentially a high-fashion clothing store. Lining the walls were hundreds ofpairs of designer shoes; furs, dresses and other clothes; as well as, purses, sunglasses, watches, bracelets, necklaces, rings, and earrings. Altogether, itwas a seventy-million-dollar collection, Alexus' second-most expensive wardrobe next to the one she had at her mega-mansion in Matamoros, Mexico.

"I'm not wearing pants," Alexus said, putting on a pair of Louis Vuitton shades. "I'm not even wearing panties. All I want to do to-day is watch Blake perform and give him all the pussy he can han-dle, because I know that if I leave him alone for one minute, he'll send a team of killers atmy best executive producer."

"So what? T-Walk shouldn't have been talkin' shit. I think the nigga's just jealous 'cause he ain't as rich as Blake."

"That's not it." Alexus put on a white diamond-encrusted Le Viantennis bracelet ($125,000), a matching necklace ($410,000), a platinum Rolex watch with a hundred carats of white diamonds em-bedded throughout its frame ($190,000), and a pair of tear-shaped ten-carat whitediamond earrings ($350,000).

"Well, what is it, then?" Mercedes asked.

"T-Walk wants me back," Alexus said "and to be honest, I kind of want him back, too. He's the type of gentleman my mom would love to seeme marry. He's handsome, business-minded, loving— everything about himis just so perfect. When I was with him, he wanted me and only me. Blake wants to fuck every bad bitch he lays his eyes on."

"You *let* Blake fuck Tee-Tee and that other girl last night, and he probably did it again this morning. That's your fault."

Alexus sighed. "I was testing him," she somberly admitted. "I

143

half expected him to say something like, 'Baby, I don't want any-body but you.' Ididn't think he would actually fuck Tee-Tee. The only reason I went along with it was because I had just popped those X pills and I was feeling all horny."

"It's still your fault," Mercedes said with a shrug.

They stepped out of the closet and left the bedroom. As they were passing the hallway safe, Alexus pointed at it and said, "Do you know I putfive hundred and sixty million dollars in brand-new hundred-dollar bills in there about two months ago, and Blake has already blown through over twenty million of it. He tossed over three million at that stripper last night."

"Trina said she hasn't seen anybody blow money the way Blake does since Big Meech left the streets" Mercedes turned to squint at Alexus."How does Papi know who Big Meech is?"

"What?"

"When Blake got off the elevator, Papi said something about Blake'sjewelry. Then he said, 'Who do you think you are, Big Meech?' How does he know Big Meech?"

"I don't know," Alexus lied. "He probably saw the BMF episode onGangland."

She grabbed her smartphone from her white leather Louis Vuit-tonshoulder-bag and hopped on Twitter before Mercedes could question herany further.

Alexus' twenty-eight million Twitter followers were already buzzing about the diss video. A lot of them wanted to know who King Neal's father was. Some of her followers were taking sides, as if Blake andT-Walk were Edward and Jacob from the Twilight Saga. Shaking her headin disbelief, she decided against sending out a tweet and phoned her attorney instead.

"Why is it that every time I pick up my phone to call you, you call me?" Britney answered laughingly. "I hope you're still dressed I've set up ameeting with Mr. Walkson to discuss that video he made about Blake. He'swaiting on us at Reesie's gentleman's club on Sixteenth and Trumbull, on the set of *Down the Pole*."

A brief silence followed. Alexus put her thumbnail between her teeth, thinking "I guess we can do that. Blake and all his MBM art-ists are about to give away five thousand pairs of shoes in that same neighborhood,but they'll be blocks away at that park on Albany

Street."

"I'm pulling in behind Kenny now. Get your butt out here." Alexus smiled as she returned the smartphone to her shoulder bag.

She and Mercedes exited the east end of the mansion through large Frenchdoors that led them into the garage/basketball court.

There were fifteen cars and SUVs lined up across the garage's polished hardwood floor. The five white-painted vehicles—a Bugatti Veyron Grand Sport convertible, a Mercedes Maybach 62 convertible, a Lamborghini Urus SUV, a Rolls-Royce Phantom Drophead Coupe convertible, and the Rolls-Royce Phantom limousine—belonged to Alexus.Blake's ten black-painted whips consisted of his three Bugattis, two Phantoms, a Mercedes-Benz SLS AMG coupe, a Ferrari 458 Italia, a Maybach 62 convertible, a Lamborghini Aventador, and a 1973 Chevy Caprice convertible on 24-karat gold-plated 28-inch DUB rims. All nine ofthe garage doors were open, and Mercedes' snow-white Maybach 62 convertible was parked in the driveway between Cereniti's Lamborghini and the security team's eight Chevy Tahoes.

Blake was sitting on the trunk of the drop-top Bugatti with his shirtoff, rolling a blunt of Kush and talking into his Bluetooth earpiece. The Trukfit tee shirt lay next to him beneath a Louis Vuitton bulletproof vest and a Ziploc bag containing about four ounces of Purple Kush. The Ak-47was stretched across his lap.

Glancing toward her collection of gaudy vehicles, Alexus spotted her paternal family standing in front of her limo, conversing in whispers. She sashayed over to Blake, her arms extended for a hug. He embraced herlimply.

"Hold up a minute, bruh," Blake said into the earpiece. He smiled a little as her lips touched his. "Let me call you back in a few minutes. Matter of fact, I'll catch you at the park... yup, one hun'ed." He hung up

"Who was that?" Alexus asked, kissing the Old English-written DOPE BOY tattoo that ran across the top of his chest.

"That was Douglass," Blake said, "just callin' to let me know thatI'm getting' a quarter mill' to show up at a strip club in Indianapolis afterthe stadium show. I'm pullin' in one point eight off that show already. A hundred off every ticket."

Alexus flicked her eyes over to her attorney's sleek gray

Mercedes Benz GL320 SUV as it pulled into the driveway behind Kenny's Panamera. "I, uh, kinda have an important business meeting to attend, so I'm not goingto make it to your first show. I'll fly down to Nap-town for the second one. Mercedes said she's going with you, so I'm sending twelve bodyguards with—"

"I ain't ridin' wit' no bodyguards." Blake grumbled. "She'll be a'ight. I don't know why y'all worried 'bout Jenny anyway. She way down in Mexico some-muhfuckin-where." He slid on the bulletproof vest, then fired up his blunt. "And besides"—he patted the golden assault rifle—"ain'tno water drippin' out this Super Soaker."

Papi appeared beside Alexus. He kissed her and Mercedes on theircheeks and said. "If anyone is sent to harm either of you, I assure you thatJenny will pay dearly for it. Blake, you take good care of my angels. And be a gangster about it."

"I'm gangsta twenty-fo'-seven." Blake shook Papi's hand. Then theold drug lord turned and went back to Alexus' limousine. He climbed in ahead of the other cartel bosses, and the limo sailed out of the garage. Theywere on their way to O'Hare Airport to board a plane to Hong Kong, a plane that was carrying twenty-two thousand pounds of uncut cocaine.

Bostic honked her car horn once, and Alexus placed another kiss onBlake's lips before rushing off to join the attorney.

Chapter 26

Trintino Walkson, now a Senior Regent of the Gangster Disciples, entered Cup's office at Redbone's clad in a navy blue Armani suit and carrying a Gucci duffle bag. Due to his imminent face-to-face meeting withAlexus, a Colgate smile was pasted on his face.

"Three hundred and seventy thousand?" Reesie Cup said; eyes fixedon the camera monitor, he was studying the trio of SUV's T-Walk and his crew had arrived in.

"Exactly." T-Walk sat the bag on Cup's brand-new desk—a gold- plated five-pointed star centered between two golden canes with a thick slabof glass laid over it. "Nice desk," he complimented.

"Yeah... just got it last week, joe. Paid damn near a half a mill'." Cup turned to T-Walk and pointed at the three-foot-tall card-board box that stood beside his desk. "There you go right there. Forty bricks, and you oweme the other three seventy."

"This better be that raw shit." "Ain't it always?" Cup grinned.

T-Walk opened the box and took a look at the kilos of cocaine. Theywere individually wrapped in greenish-blue cellphone, just as they always were. He pulled out the key to his brand-new baby blue Lamborghini truck and used it to skewer one of the blocks of co-caine. He dabbed a bit of the powder on his tongue, and his mouth went numb.

"Is that the new Lambo truck?" Reesie Cup asked, gazing again atthe wall-mounted camera monitor.

"Yup," T-Walk said. "It's the Lamborghini Urus. Got it squattin' onchrome thirty-inch Asantis. That's my folks Squirms' Hummer on thirty- twos sittin' behind the Lambo, and my nigga Lil Ant just bought that blackCadillac truck on thirty-twos."

Cup nodded his head and unzipped the duffle, pressing a button on the cash-counting machine that sat next to his computer. "I watched that li'lvideo you put on YouTube. That was a dumb move. You know how triggerhappy Bulletface is." He fed a stack of hun-dreds into the machine, then leaned back in his hair and trained his eyes on T-Walk. His expression became quizzical. "I hope you're ready for what's comin'."

"Nigga, we strapped up. Fuck Blake and every nigga ridin' with

147

thathoe-ass nigga. And you can tell him I said it, too. You think I'm going to just forget about that li'l nigga shooting' up my Rolls? He shot me twice, fam. One bullet went through my shoulder and missed the jugular by an inch. Me not gettin' at him would be like Obama not gettin' at Osama."

"I'm not sayin' you don't have the right to be upset. But timing is everything. Right now he's responsible for most of the dope coming into theMidwest. You're buying his product; I'm buying his product—think about all the money you'd fuck up if you took Blake out of the game. Like I told you before, find me a cartel connect who can flood the streets wit' snow like Blake can. Then *I'll* have him taken care of."

T-Walk grabbed a roll of duct tape from the corner of the desk andstarted ripping long strips from it, taping the cardboard box shut. His mindwas jumbled with thoughts of how to do away with Blake. He looked up and followed Cups' gaze to the camera monitor… and smiled.

A Mercedes SUV and two white Tahoes were parked in front of hisUrus. He showed a beamed lightly as he observed Attorney Bostic step down from the driver's door holding a phone to her ear.

Just then, T-Walk's smartphone rang.

"Would you mind tailing us to another location?" Bostic asked. "It'sonly a block away. We can drive right up this alley behind Redbone's."

"That's cool. I'll be down there in a minute." T-Walk picked up thebox and gave Cup a nod. "Holla at you later, fam."

"You're leaving? I thought you said Alexus was meetin' you here.""Change of plans," T-Walk said tersely.

"Well," Cup said, getting up and walking his guest to the door, "if I were you, I'd be trying to get Alexus to plug me wit' that cartel she pluggedBlake in wit'. I know she did it, 'cause I used to get my dope from her."

"I'm already on it," T-Walk replied, and stepped out of the office.Chapter 28

Money Bagz Management's three tour buses--Blake's lime-green one, Mocha's hot pink Newell, and Young-D's jet-black Newell—lanced down Roosevelt Road ahead of seven lime-green 1973 Caprices on chrometwenty-eights.

The Cocaine Princess 3

There were five others on the tour bus with Blake: Mercedes, Kenny, Fred Douglass, a studio engineer, and Blake's older brother Terrence "Streets" King.

Standing before the microphone in his soundproof recording booth, smoking a blunt of Kush and sipping from a Styrofoam cup of cold orange juice, Blake put on his white diamond-encrusted Beats by Dre headphones and nodded for his studio engineer to start the track. It was the second track on the "Certified Boss" mix-tape he was working on, a track that would soon feature verses from Rick Ross, Yo Gotti, and Birdman.

The beat started, and Blake began lacing the hook:

'Three Bugattis, couple Phantoms, I'm a kingpinA hun'ed carats in my Hublot, I'm a kingpin

I'll show you niggas how to floss, like a kingpinBulletface, Baby, Gotti, Ross-we some kingpins

Last night I hit King of Diamonds, threw three mill in a bitch faceMy money tall, like six-eight, and I keep the yay like Kim K.

Keep the K for you fuck-niggas who be actin' hard on the Internet That forty-seven'll Swiss cheese you, cook ya squad up for dinner nextHun'ed twenty racks in my denim, yeah nigga that's Trukfit

Hun'ed twenty-five rounds in this choppa, dare you try to get that fuck shitI go to places you cain't go, be in hoods where you cain't be

You on YouTube 'cause you hate to see that I'm ballin harda than Jay-ZAll in thanks to my queen bee, and that's Queen A, we on fire, trust me Her body looks just like Maliah's, doesn't it?

Cannon wit' me, I ain't talkin' 'bout Mariah's husband…'

The fiery lyrics spilled out as if Blake had written them. He was free-styling, so deep in his own zone that he hardly even noticed the five faces that were staring in at him from behind the glass window. By the timehe completed his verse, the tour bus had stopped moving. Taking in a mouthful of potent weed smoke, he stepped out of the booth and told his manager to send the track to Ross, Birdman, and Yo Gotti. Then he put on ablack-and-gold leather Pelle Pelle jacket to conceal the .50-caliber in his shoulder-holster, passed the half-smoked blunt to his brother, and looked out the Newell's tinted side windows at the huge crowd of black men, women, and children that was packed into the Albany Street park. Thanks to the $150,000

King Rio

Blake had spent on food, drinks and prizes, the Chicagoanswere enjoying themselves in the 79-degree weather.

"Was that freestyle?" Streets asked, slapping a coal-black hand ontoBlake's shoulder.

"Man, bruh, you murdered that shit," Mercedes commented. "I wanta copy of that as soon as it's done."

"I'm freestylin' through the whole mix-tape," Blake said. "I might freestyle from now on. Fuck writin'; I can go hard without a rhyme book." He watched as a large gathering of ghetto girls converged alongside his tourbus. "On my kids, y'all just don't know how bad I wanna get at that nigga."

Everyone knew who "that nigga" was.

"Calm down, li'l bruh," Streets advised. "Remember what Ross saidon that Rich Forever mix-tape? 'When you get a li'l paper, get ready for haters.' Niggas hate to see real niggas gettin' money. You gettin' paid off words on paper, li'l bruh. Talkin' in rhymes on a beat. So what Alexus gaveyou all that bread. The money you gettin' now ain't comin' from her. She ain't dropped no albums. She ain't sellin' out no stadiums. All she did was give you the money to start this MBM Empire. So fuck what T-Walk got tosay about it. Reply to the diss and leave it alone."

"Oh I'm gon' reply to it a'ight. Straight gunshots," Blake retorted sharply as he strolled toward the door.

He ended up signing over a hundred autographs. Then the loadingdoors on two U-Haul trucks were opened, and he and his MBM artists passed out boxes of brand-new Jordans to the men and children, and Louboutins, Pradas, Zanottis, and Louis Vuittons to the women. The ecstatic smiles Blake saw on their faces left an indelible warmth in his heart. He wished he could help out every poor black neighborhood in America.

He was handing a box of $3,400 Christian Louboutins to a pretty- faced redbone when he suddenly spotted Nona Malden standing behind her.Nona was dressed in a white Gucci halter and skirt, and she was gazing intently at Blake, smiling and aiming her smartphone at him like so many others were doing. He immediately noticed that she wasn't wearing a bra; her nipples were poking at the thin fabric of her halter top. He pulled her tothe side of the truck, where twenty members of his original crew—the Dub Life Good

Squad—were standing.

"Have you seen the latest issue of Straight Stuntin Magazine?" She quickly asked. "I'm on the cover with Mesha Seville and Meek Mill." She reached out and pinched his cheek. "Kayslay told me you asked him to put me on the cover. Thanks. As soon as that issue was released, I started getting calls from photographers all across the country. Next month I have acover shoot for Dime Piece Magazine."

"Yeah? That's why you stopped callin' me, huh? You done got allfamous and forgot about me."

"Negro, please. I called you every day for a week straight after wetalked that night. You never even let me know if you liked the video."

"I didn't watch it. Had to erase it the next mornin' before Alexus had a chance to see it."

Nona flicked her eyes around the bustling street, which was lined onboth sides with cars, pickups, and SUVs. Most of them had big chrome rims, because their owners were either drug-dealers or business-owners working beneath Reesie Cup.

"Let me ask you a question," Nona said. "Where are your bodyguards? I mean, you can't just be walking around out here in Chicago wearing all this jewelry. These niggas are crazy. More people get killed inthis city than soldiers in Afghanistan."

"I don't give a fuck how many niggas get murked out here, I'm notwalkin' around wit' no bodyguards. I'm a TVL like all the rest of these niggas. I was comin' out here when I was broke, fuckin' wit' Cup and Lil Cholly n'em. My nigga Lil Lord came up under Cup and other guys off Fifteenth and Trumbull. I'm doin' this shit for him."

"Didn't you shoot up T-Walk's Rolls-Royce on this same street?" "Who told you that?" Blake asked, staring through his shades at

Nona's huge breasts.

"My friend was out here when it happened. She said you pulled out two guns and started chasing his car down the street, shooting through the back of it. Then I saw on the news that he'd been shot twice, in his left handand shoulder."

"Hmm. So, uh…what's up? What made you come over here?"

"I live a few blocks down from here, on Fifteenth and

Spaulding.""You walked?"

"Hell no," she laughed. She pointed up the crowded street. My girlgave me a ride. I dropped my car off at a detail shop this morning to get itpainted lime-green like those Bugattis you had in that video. I already hadsome twenty-sixes put on it, and I had the MBM logo stitched into the headrests."

Blake's grin flourished as he scanned Nona's perfectly formed bodyfrom head to toe. She was definitely a dime piece; her yellow-ish-brown visage was flawless, her breasts were large and round, her stomach was flat,and she had an ass like Diana Escotto.

"What are you grinning about?" She asked, grabbing her hips.

"What, are you surprised that I'm so down with MBM? I told you I wasyour biggest fan, didn't I?"

"I think I do remember you sayin' that," Blake laughed. "Listen, I want you to stay right here. I'm about to pass out some signed copies of myalbum, then we're headin' straight to G.I. for a show at the Genesis Center."

"You're taking me with you?"

"Just to the Gary show. Alexus'll be at the one in Indianapolis."

"She'd go crazy if she caught you with me, huh?""Prob'ly," Blake said.

He turned his attention back to his fans and started taking pictures with them, handing out copies of his now triple-platinum album, hugging the women and shaking hands with the men. He discerned an undiluted money-lust in the eyes of the women, and an equal abundance of hatred in the eyes of some of the young hustlers. The latter of which was understandable; last year, on the eve of Blake's very first stadium concert, he had opened fire on a group of teenaged Traveling Vice Lords on the corner of 15th and Trumbull, killing several of them. He had done it shortlyafter he'd learned that Reesie Cup had been responsible for the kidnapping of his daughter and murder of his daughter's mother.

His manager approached him timidly as he was taking a picture witha pack of seven 'hood chicks. Once the picture was taken, Frederick nudgedBlake's elbow and canted his head toward a beat-up, rust-laden Buick sedanthat was parked behind Fly's drop-top Caprice. Three Hispanic men with bald, tattooed heads and faces were seated inside the car. Their frigid eyes were trained on Blake.

"That car followed us here from the mansion," Frederick mutteredtensely.

"They've been staring at you since you stepped off the coach."

'*Aww shit,*' Blake thought as he studied the glowering trio. He knewthat they must have been sent by Jennifer Costilla, to do whatever it was shewanted done to Mercedes, who was still on the tour bus with Kenny.

Blake turned and headed onto the Newell, waving for Fly and Nonato follow him. His crew of Dub Life Goonz—all clad in black Trukfit outfits with Louis Vuitton accessories, Air Yeezy 2 sneakers, and blinging white diamond-encrusted jewelry—split up and hopped into their Chevys, and the MBM artists boarded the other two coaches.

Upon entering the tour bus, Blake found Kenny sitting on the black leather sofa across from the recording booth with his black Trukfit sweatpants pulled down to his knees. Mercedes was kneeled between his parted legs, sucking his dick in and out of her throat; she twisted her head tolook at Blake, Fly, Frederick, and Nona, then continued her highly skilled blowjob.

"Damn…," Fly commented. "She's damn near better thanSuperhead."

"She done popped two of them Blue Dolphins," Kenny chuckled. "Itold her not to take 'em both at the same time."

"Oh, my God, she looks just like Alexus," Nona murmured. "Isn'tshe Alexus' long-lost sister or something?"

Blake kept quiet. His adrenaline was already pumping. He went tohis bedroom door, unlocked it, and stepped inside.

There were four guns lying next to the Louis Vuitton duffle bag at the foot of his bed: two 9-millimeter Uzi submachine guns with 32-round clips, a Smith & Wesson AR-15 assault rifle, and the gold-plated AK-47. Blake was tucking the Uzis inside his duffle when Fly and Nona walked into the bedroom. Fly plopped down on the bed and pulled a rubber-bandedbundle of fresh Benjamin's out of his hoody pocket. Nona stayed near the doorway, flicking her eyes around the lavishly furnished room.

"This bus is literally a mansion on wheels," Nona said, her cottonvoice replete with awe. She looked at the cash-filled duffle and gasped. "Oh, my… how much money is that?"

"A whole lot," Blake said. He turned to Fly. "Let me see your car keys, bruh. I'm about to, uh…. Drive down to that corner store on Sixteenthand Drake. I ran out of cigars. You can hop in Spyda's Chevy."

Frederick Douglass barged into the room with a grim frown on hisface. "Did I just hear you correctly?" He asked Blake. "We can send someone to get your blunts. You have a show in less than an hour, Blake.Time is money, and you'd be foolish to waste it."

"It'll only take thirty minutes to get to the G from here," Blake argued, zipping the duffle shut. "I'll be back in 'bout ten minutes." He picked up a long cylindrical gym bag from the black fur carpet on the other side of his bed and laid the assault rifles inside it. "Come on, Nona. You canride wit' me,"

"She can stay wit' me," Fly said, counting through the bundle of hundreds and casting a suggestive stare at Nona. "How much I gotta dropfor some wet-wet? I'll blow a rack on you."

"I am not a groupie, Mr. Whatever-Your-Name-Is." Nona rolled hereyes, crossed her arms, and sucked her teeth. "There are over a thousand girls packed into that park outside. I'm sure one of them will gladly let you"blow a rack" for some pussy, but it won't be blown on me."

Blake laughed aloud as he closed the gym bag, showing Nona a veridical smile of appreciation. "Damn, you can't give my nigga no pussy?I'll give you ten racks on top of what he wanna give you, got it in my pocket right now."

"And you still got it," Nona retorted snidely.

Her belligerent remark elicited laughs from everyone, including Kenny, who had just appeared in the doorway behind her, buckling his YSLbelt and smoking a Newport cigarette. Mercedes wrapped her arms around his waist and peered over his shoulder.

Frederick released a sigh of frustration as Blake walked past himand handed the gym bag to Kenny.

"You and Mercedes come wit' me," Blake said.

Chapter 27

"How did I get myself into this predicament?" Alexus murmured thoughtfully, gazing across the room at Trintino Walkson as he folded a lineof Kush into a Swisher Sweets cigarillo.

They were seated on separate white Italian leather sofas in the spacious living room of Alexus's five-story Trumbull Avenue home, whichhad been a foreclosed apartment building when she'd purchased it early lastyear.

Now, after $3 million in renovations and upgrades, the former eyesore boasted heated white marble floors, seven bedrooms, seven full bathrooms, an exercise gym, a seven-seat theater, twenty-one indoor andoutdoor cameras, and a four-car garage.

"I didn't even know you had a house out here," T-Walk said.

"There are probably a lot of things you don't know about me,"

Alexus fired back. "Now, do you mind telling me why you felt the need to put that video on the Internet? And hurry up before I call my mom and haveher shred the new contract we just put together for you."

"New contract? What new contract?"

"Two hundred and fifty million for five more years with the Minority Television Network. But you can forget about the contract if you're not planning on apologizing to Blake."

T-Walk's face became locked in an expression of sheer disbelief. "Fifty million every year till twenty seventeen?" His voice was an octave above a whisper, and his eyes were flicking rapidly from Alexus to the TikaSumpter-looking attorney sitting beside her.

The attorney said. "Yes, Mr. Walkson. You'll get fifty million everyyear, a little over four million every month. And due to the epic success ofyour reality shows, the cast of both Brick House shows will now be paid four hundred thousand per episode. MTN will also be financing the budgetfor your pageant. It's all included in your contract."

Drying his blunt with a Zippo lighter, T-Walk took a moment to ponder his situation. He quickly decided that his beef with Blake was not worth losing $250 million. He wanted that money just as bad as he wantedAlexus.

"I'll apologize," he said. "It ain't no big deal. I didn't mean for thatto hit the Internet in the first place."

Just as the lawyer's smartphone started ringing, Alexus uncrossedher legs and then re-crossed them, and T-Walk got a brief glimpse of herclean-shaven pussy; its plump lips were glistening with moisture.

Phone to her ear, Attorney Bostic suddenly shrieked, "Ooh, Jesus. My sister's in labor?! Girl, I am on my way. Be there in less than an hour."She hopped up from the sofa, snatching up her Prada bag and briefcase in the process. "Alexus, I'm sorry, but I have to get on the highway immediately. Kia's having the baby."

"Go ahead," Alexus said, her emerald eyes trained on T-Walk. "I'll drive myself to the airport. My Ferrari's in the garage. Call and let me knowhow she's doing."

T-Walk put fire to the end of his blunt and drew in a cheek-bulgingmouthful of smoke. Sucking it into his lungs, he watched the lawyer rush out the front door. Then he glanced at the camera that was mounted abovethe door and said, "Where's your security team? Usually they're everywhere."

"They're watching from the camera room." Alexus leaned forward and grabbed a remote control from the glass-topped coffee table. She aimedit at the camera, pressed a button, then pointed it at the 150-inch flat-screen television and turned it on. Three rows of seven different camera feeds appeared on the screen. Only one of the rectangular boxes was black. "Well,they were watching from the camera room; now it's just me and you."

Smoke curled up into the air from the glowing end of T-Walk's bluntas he filled his chest with another potent cloud of Kush. "Last year, you toldme Blake had taken a paternity test for King Neal. You said the results proved that Blake was the father. Were you telling me the truth?"

A dramatic pause ensued. T-Walk's smartphone was lighting up andvibrating on his hip, but he wasn't about to answer it. He was anxious to know if King Neal Costilla was his or not; the phone call could wait.

Alexus sighed and readjusted her modest ponytail. "I… I don't know," she stuttered. "Not having it done was Blake's idea. He didn't wantto take the test. We're getting it done this weekend for sure."

'Damn,' T-Walk thought, 'I might have kidnapped my own son.' Gazing at his ex through a haze of thick smoke, he reflected on the day he and three other men—Squirm-G, Lil Ant and Lil Regg— had kidnapped the baby from Earls' Jewelry in downtown Chicago. Tasia had set it all up for him. She'd talked Alexus into letting her babysit King Neal, then she'd allowed him to be taken from her after Trintino and his goons had gunned down four Costilla family bodyguards.

Alexus shattered T-Walk's reverie by uncrossing and re-crossing her legs again. This time he was certain she'd done it on purpose.

She dug in her purse and pulled out a box of Magnum condoms. "I picked these up on the way here," she said, getting up. She walked slowly toward T-Walk. "Let's get some frustration out before we do any more talking. I haven't had my daily dose of dick today."

King Rio

Chapter 28

"Drive faster!" Blake shouted at Nona.

He and Kenny were sitting in the backseat of Fly's drop-top Caprice. He was holding his gold-plated AK-47, and Kenny had the AR-15with a 120-round drum.

The suspicious Buick sedan remained five car-lengths behind themas Nona raced the old-school Chevy down 16th Street, veering the big- rimmed convertible around other vehicles and street-crossing pedestrians.

"What are they chasing us for?" Nona asked nervously.

"Just drive." Blake said. "Make a left on Drake and park across from the corner store. Mercedes, call Alexus and let her know she was rightabout Jenny."

Mercedes didn't listen to him; instead, she ducked down in the passenger seat and began whispering a prayer. She had no idea of what was going on, but she'd seen Blake whisper something to Kenny as they had gotten into the car, and now the two Vice Lords were holding assault rifles, constantly glancing at the dirty Buick that was speeding up the street behindthem.

"Sent some muhfuckas to murk my bitch?!" Kenny grumbled heatedly. "Don't even trip, I got 'em."

The candy-painted Chevy zipped swiftly along the two-way street, through a seedy ghetto that had recently undergone a two-hundred-million-dollar renovation, courtesy of Costilla Corp. Although the neighborhood was still replete with drug-dealing gang members, the houses, apartment buildings, and businesses—previously boarded up and dilapidated—were now thoroughly revamped and new-looking. With the top down, Blake noticed everything.

As Nona sped past Redbone's on the corner of 16th and Trumbull,Blake spied a white Hummer H2 on big chrome rims parked at the curb infront of the gentleman's club. Something occurred to him, but he quickly dismissed the thought; he was too focused on the rapidly approaching Buick.

Just as Nona was nearing the Drake Street convenience store, two ofthe Buick's passengers dipped their upper bodies out the rear windows.

Their faces were covered from the nose down by black-and-yellow bandanas, and their guns—a Tec-9 and a .45 caliber pistol—were pointed atthe lime-green Chevy. At the same time, Blake and Kenny rose up and squeezed the triggers of their fully-automatic assault rifles.

Blake's first three rounds spiraled through the Buick's windshield, hitting the driver twice in the chest. Out of the corner of his eye, Blake sawthat, like his own assault rifle, Kenny-Lords' AR-15 barrel was sneezing flames into the air before them. The sound of the gunfire was deafening.

Blake saw a quick flash from the Tec 9 one of the Hispanic men was holding. The dense crowd of black men and women standing on the cornerof 16th and Drake scattered quickly.

As Nona was veering onto Drake Street, Blake witnessed the Tec-wielder's brutal demise. Eight 7.62-millimeter rounds tore through the man's bare chest, and two more created macabre twin circles beneath his left eye; his brains exploded out the back of his head.

It took Blake a moment to realize that he had just killed the man. Bythat time, the Hispanic thug who'd held the.45 was slumped limply out of one rear window, bleeding profusely; the guy Blake had just wet up was tumbling alongside the Buick after having fell out of the rear passenger's side window; and the Buick itself was careening into a parked minivan.

When Nona finally stopped the Chevy, Blake got out and fired over fifty more shots into the wrecked Buick. Then he turned around… and sawthat Kenny had been shot.

160

Chapter 29

"Mmmm... I love you, Trintino... keep licking me right there," Alexus moaned. Her perfectly manicured fingernails were digging into theback of T-Walk's head. Lying naked on the U-shaped leather sofa, with hergenerous thighs spread apart and her throbbing clitoris stuck between T- Walk's lips, she let out another salacious moan.

Then a sudden barrage of distant gunfire startled them both. "What the...?" Alexus murmured.

Trintino lifted his head and frowned. "That sounds too close," hesaid, wiping her tasty juices from his mouth and chin.

"This is Chicago," Alexus said. "What do you expect to hear, birdssinging? And besides, it's not like we have anything to worry about. The exterior walls are bulletproof, all the windows are bulletproof, and that thick slab of glass on the wrought-iron fence is also bulletproof. This placeis as safe as the White House."

The gunfire continued for a couple of seconds. T-Walk set his eyeson the big Sony television and studied the camera feeds until the gunshotsceased a moment later. He automatically assumed that his clique of Gangster Disciples were involved in the shooting, but he wasn't about to call any of them. His name alone was a multimillion-dollar brand, and speaking on an open line about the shooting could put his entire career in jeopardy.

Clad in a fresh blue pair of Gucci boxers and an equally expensivepair of matching socks, he watched Alexus as she slipped two fingers intoher damp vagina. His concrete erection was like a flagpole in his boxers.

"What made you buy a big-ass house in the middle of ghetto?" He asked, pulling out his erection and stroking it gently. "If I had your kind ofmoney, I'd be living somewhere in the Hamptons."

"I spent two hundred million dollars of my own personal money rejuvenating this neighborhood. Don't you think I deserve a place here?"She replied, still fingering herself. "Now, will you please put on that condom so we can fuck? I don't have all day."

Trintino frowned at her. "Let me get some head first." "You know I can't do that, T-Walk. Blake would kill me."

"What?!" He exclaimed. "You got me fucked up. On Larry you

gotme fucked up." He leapt to his feet, snatching his Armani suit from the armof the sofa. "You got me like this last time; I'll be damned if it happens again."

Alexus sat up and grabbed ahold of his wrist. "Wait a minute," shewhiningly pleaded.

Turning to face the Maliah bodied billionaire, T-Walk gazed down ather angelic visage, admiring her salacious green eyes, and her succulent, heart-shaped lips as they parted to welcome his rigid manhood into the warm interior of her mouth. Just as she'd always done back when they werea couple she pursed her lips around his hard muscle and sucked it as if she'dbeen personally trained by Pinky.

T-Walk dropped his head back and stared at the overhead chandelier,enjoying the feeling of Alexus' rapidly fluctuating tongue. He tried to focuson her, but the $250 million contract had him geeked up. Trintino had been raised by his parents to be an ambitious man. He'd struggled through six years of college to achieve his dream of one day becoming a legendary television and film producer, and now he had finally made it. His reality shows were the most watched on prime time television; two weeks prior, he'd joined Tyler Perry for an Esquire magazine cover shoot; and his girlfriend Ashley "Thunder" Hunter, the most aggressive cast member of the Brick House franchise, was now four months pregnant with his first child—well maybe his second child, depending on the paternity test results of Alexus' son.

His thoughts shifted back to Alexus just as she pulled his dick out ofher mouth and kissed its glistening head. She grabbed the condom from the glass-top coffee table, tore open the wrapper with her teeth, and then rolled the rubber onto his saliva-dripping erection.

"You miss this pussy, don't you?" She said, turning to kneel on the sofa. Rubbing the fingertips of one hand over her clitoris, she arched her back, lowered the left side of her face onto a fluffy white leather pillow, andlifted her rotund ass into the air. "Beat it up the way you used to," she moaned.

T-Walk wasted no time. He got behind her, eased his thick eight inches into her juicy pussy. A lot of people said Alexus looked just like Nicki Minaj but Trintino thought she looked more like Cubana Lust than anything, and in his opinion, Cubana Lust was the world's second mostbeautiful woman.

Alexus was number one on that list.

Clamping his hands onto her narrow waistline, he slowly began to fuck her from behind, sliding all the way in and halfway out, watching her plentiful juices accumulate along the length of his tan serpent. Alexus's meaty buttocks jiggled wildly at his every thrust, and her euphonious moans grew louder and louder as Trintino picked up the pace.

He pounded in and out of her warm, gushy pussy with piston-like speed while she massaged her clitoris and couple of minutes later, her bodywent rigid, her vaginal walls tightened around his dick, and her orgasmic juices spilled down onto the sofa.Chapter 32

"Nigga, what the fuck was you thinking'?" snapped Terrence "Streets" King. Tall and dark, with a medium build and a low-cut fade, Streets was only a few years older than Blake, but he was still Blake's bigbrother, and now was the time for a big brother speech.

But Blake was far too overwhelmed with emotion—anger and fear,for the most part—to pay his brother any mind. After the shooting, Nona had sped back to the tour bus, while Blake tried again and again to call Alexus. Then Nona and Mercedes had rushed onto the tour bus behind Blake and Streets and watched from a darkly-tinted window as Fly hoppedin his Chevy and raced away with Kenny's blood-soaked body (he'd been shot once through the chest) stretched out across his back seat.

Now, sitting between Mercedes and Nona on the black leather sofa across from his recording booth, smoking a seven-gram blunt of Purple andsipping on a bottle of Ace of Spades, Blake studied his angry-faced brotheras Streets paced to and fro in front of him.

"Question," Blake said, glowering at the ribbon of smoke curling upfrom the crimson tip of his blunt. "What did you expect me to do, let them kill me? Let them kill Mercedes? Nigga, I ain't about to be playing' out here in these streets! Look at what happened to Pac and Biggie, and Jam Master Jay, and 50 Cent. Shit, look at what happened to me! You think I'malet myself get shot up again?"

"You could've had one of the goons take care of that, li'l bruh. The only thing you should be focused on is getting' money, ex-pandin' the MBMbrand in the same way Birdman and Tunechi are doin' with YMCMB."

"And that's exactly what I'm doin'." Blake filled his lungs with smoke, shifted his eyes to the smartphone that was lying on his lap amongsta hundred and twenty thousand dollars in hundred-dollar bills, and then turned to Nona. "You a'ight, li'l momma?" He asked, nudging her voluminous thigh with the golden champagne bottle.

"I'm fine," Nona mumbled. "Shit like this goes down in Detroit allthe time. I'm just glad I wasn't shot."

Blake turned up the bottle and gulped down another mouthful of Jay-Z's $475 bubbly. For a while, no one spoke, and Blake got a chance torelax and think as the tour bus rumbled up the mildly congested expressway. He wondered why Alexus wasn't answering his calls, and if Jenny Costilla had sent the crew of Latinos to murder him and Mercedes. That had to be the case. Why else would they come after Mercedes while hewas with her?

A third perturbing thought suddenly invaded his contemplation. TheH2 Hummer that had been parked in front of Reesie Cup's strip club—it was identical to the Hummer Fly had described as being present during Lil Mike's murder.

But—if it was in fact the same white H2—what was it doing in Chicago, parked at the curb of Cup's second-most lucrative establishment?

Abruptly, Blake snatched up his iPhone to call Reesie Cup, but anincoming call from Cereniti halted him.

"Chyna's on her way to the Genesis Center now," Tee-Tee said. "She's driving the Phantom. Took me an hour to teach her how to use the navigation system, but I think she got it, yo. And I gave her your number. She'll call you as soon as she makes it into Gary." Before Blake could reply,she sailed on. "Yo, if I tell you somethin', you gotta promise not to tell a soul."

"Tell me somethin' like what?"

Tee-Tee let out an audible sigh. "I, uh… just pulled into the parkinglot at Redbone's. Three of the guys who were in that video with T-Walk arestanding out here by the back door. I think he brought them out here to copsome… stuff from Cup. Tasia sent me a text a few minutes ago saying Alexus and T-Walk were somewhere having a meeting."

"What?!" Blake exclaimed, tearing off his shades.

But then it clicked. Of course, T-Walk should be in town for the firsttaping of *Down the Pole*, which was being filmed at Redbone's. "Yeah," Tee-Tee continued. "MTN's supposed to be signing T-Walkto a quarter-billion-dollar contract for five years, and I guess Alexus is meeting with him to discuss that."

"Right on." Blake was grinding his teeth-together. He glanced overat Mercedes and saw that she was still bawling uncontrollably. "Are the police out there?"

"How'd you know that?" Tee-Tee asked "They're *mad* deep out here, b. *Mad* deep. Three people just got killed outside that cornerstore onDrake. Somebody shot their car up with a machine gun, Swiss-cheesed thatmother-fucker, too. I'm hoping that shit won't affect the show."

A volcanic heat boiled up from Blake's midsection and tensed the herculean muscles in his chest. Think, he told himself, just calm down andthink. If Alexus was somewhere with T-Walk, there was nothing he coulddo about it. Not now, at least.

Still clinching his teeth tightly together, he said. "See if you can getin good with his li'l buddies. Give 'em some pussy if you have to. I got a hundred thousand for you."

He ended the call abruptly and stood up, causing the four thick bundles of hundreds to fall to the floor as he stormed off toward his mobilebedroom.

"Don't be stupid," Streets shouted after him, but Blake's ears werepractically closed as he entered the bedroom and slammed the door shut behind him.

He attempted calling Alexus three more times, and all he kept getting was her voicemail. The same thing happened when he called theirattorney. Frustrated, he threw the phone at one of the many silkencased pillows that were stacked across the head of his bed.

"I'm bodyin' that nigga on sight!" He shouted lividly. He scowled atthe large face that covered most of his heavy black blanket. It was his own face, split in half in black and white to resemble the infamous Scarface poster, and beneath it, the name Bulletface was written in big white letters.

He sat on the bed and ran his hands up and down his face, wondering where Alexus was and what she was doing with his archenemy.An image of her lying naked under T-Walk flitted through Blake's mind, and he gritted his teeth again.

'She's fucking him right now,' Blake thought, knowing he was rightbut hoping he was wrong. He couldn't remember the last time he'd called Alexus without having gotten an answer. She always answered her phone, even when she was busy.

A soft knock at the door made him lift his head.

"It's me," Nona said.

Blake hesitated. "Come in," he finally said, as he picked up the TVremote and started flipping through channels.

Nona walked in holding Blake's rubber-banded bundles of hundredsagainst her bountiful bosom, and the wonderful scent of her perfume, combined with her pretty smile, beautiful face, and pleasant disposition, somehow managed to brighten Blake's mood a bit. She sat the cash down on the middle of the bed, then shut and locked the door and sat down besidehim.

Blake tried to ignore her. He wanted to focus on ESPN, to not think about the triple-murder, Kenny's potentially fatal gunshot wound, and Alexus' questionable fidelity. But there was something about a woman witha sexy face and a fat ass that never failed to snag his attention, and Nona Malden was not lacking in either of those departments.

"I hope Fly got your friend to the hospital in time," Nona said. Hersugary voice was as soft as her knock had been. She placed a hand on his knee and rubbed it gently. "Your brother's giving you some good advice. You shouldn't have to jeopardize your freedom for anything. Defending yourself is one thing, but going out looking for trouble is a whole nother subject."

"They came at me," Blake said, turning to look at the perfectly-builtdime piece seated next to him. For a brief moment, he studied her juicy, pink-glossed lips, already considering fucking her as revenge for whatever Alexus was out doing with T-Walk.

And then it hit him.

He leapt to his feet and grabbed his smartphone off the pillow.

"I know they came at you, but you could've easily paid somebody todo what needed to be done. Don't end up like T.I., bouncing in and out of prison. Some bad situations are avoidable, Bulletface. Your fans need you out here in the free world. Not behind bars and definitely not in an early grave."

Blake was only half-listening to Nona. He was tapping into Safe

Home, a smartphone app that granted him full access to all of the surveillance cameras at every one of his and Alexus' many homes. He immediately scrolled down to the 15th and Trumbull listing and touched it.

And what he saw made his blood boil.

T-Walk was sitting on their living room sofa, and Alexus was on herknees in front of him, bouncing her head between his parted thighs.

Suddenly, Blake became very calm. Clicking out of the mobile app,he sat back down and smoked the rest of his blunt, gazing vacantly at the TV. He tried vehemently to delete from his memory the image of Alexus sucking T-Walk's dick, but it was to no avail; he doubted if he'd ever forgetthat painful reality.

He finished off the Ace of Spades in three gulps, then flung the bottle as hard as he could at the wall and watched it shatter to pieces.

King Rio

Chapter 30

Alexus stroked and sucked T-Walk's thick phallus until he doused her face with semen. Out of the corner of her eye, she saw that her iPhonewas ringing incessantly, and she was glad that she'd remembered to put iton silent mode as she, Britney, and Trintino had walked into the living room.

"Damn you, T-Walk," Alexus complained as she got to her feet.

Trintino looked at her and smiled. Ribbons of cum were streaked across her sexy face. She stepped into her snow-white Louis Vuitton heels, grabbed her hip with one hand, and used the other to wipe two dangling ropes of goo off her chin. Standing before him wearing nothing but her five-inch heels and a bunch of white diamond jewelry, she looked just as beautiful as she was rich.

"I'm glad I muted this stupid phone," she said, picking it up. There were seven missed calls from Blake, five from Mercedes, and one each from Tasia and Cereniti. With an agitated sigh, she sat the smartphone backon the table and turned to T-Walk, grabbing her hips with both hands this time. "I hope you don't think I'm going to let you get away with skeeting on my face every time we hook up. Do I look like a porn star to you?"

T-Walk's smile widened. "You really want me to answer that?"

"Fuck you, T-Walk," Alexus said with a smile.

Being around T-Walk always made her smile. She knew that his love for her was genuine, and that, if she let him back into her heart, she would never have to worry about him cheating. He was the most honest, loving boyfriend she'd ever had, and she was considering dumping Blakeand taking T-Walk back.

She raked the side of an index finger down her seraphic face, collecting his cum and pushing it into her mouth. T-Walk chuckled.

"That's the Alexus I remember," he said.

"Shut up and get dressed, boy. We don't have all day. I want to be inIndianapolis before Blake and his guys get there. He has a concert at the stadium where the Pacers play."

"I really don't give a damn what he has going on. You could've keptthat to yourself." T-Walk pulled on his boxers and slacks, then tucked his 9-millimeter Ruger behind his waistline before putting on the rest of his suit.

Alexus picked up her smartphone and went to the bathroom in her master suite to get cleaned up. She dialed her sister's number, put it on speakerphone, and sat the iPhone on her white marble sink, gazing into themirror at her cum-striped face and listening to Mercedes' Chief Keef call tone. Her idiosyncratic smile—more of a half-smile than anything—was still pasted on her face.

"Bitch," Mercedes answered, sounding upset, "I've been calling youfor the past hour and a half. You were right about Aunt Jenny. That crazy bitch really did send some people after me. They shot Kenny in the chest."

"Oh, my God, are you serious?!" Alexus gasped.

"Does it sound like I'm playin' around?" The pain in Mercedes' voice was palpable. "Blake and Kenny shot them motherfuckas up. ThreeSpanish-lookin' dudes in a rusty-ass Buick."

"Is Kenny okay?"

"I don't know yet. Fly took him to the hospital, and I stayed on thetour bus with Blake. We just pulled up outside the Genesis Center in Gary.I'm hoping this concert'll calm my nerves a little, 'cause Lord knows I'm scared as hell right now. I've seen my fair share of shoot-outs, but never have I been the damn target! What the hell is wrong with Aunt Jenny?"

Alexus turned on the faucet and rinsed the viscid curds of semen offher face. "Have you talked to Papi?" She asked.

"Not since we left the mansion this mornin'."

"Call and tell him what happened. I'll send a few men to the shooting scene to clear Blake and Kenny's names. Where'd it go down?"

"On Sixteenth and... Drake, I think. Right in front of that corner-

store."

"Yeah, that's Drake," Alexus said, suddenly realizing that the rapid

gunfire she'd heard had come from that same shooting. "Listen to me,Mercedes. I want you to stay on that tour bus until—"

"Bitch, you must be crazy," Mercedes cut in. "That stripper y'all brought from Miami last night just got here in Blake's Phantom. I'm aboutto take it and speed home to my kids right after I watch Jeezy perform with Blake. I really want to go up to the hospital and stay with Kenny, but I don'twant my name tied to that shooting."

Alexus sighed, shaking her head and closing her eyes. Mercedes hadabsolutely no idea how dangerous their aunt was. Over the past couple of years, Jenny—along with several other members of the Costilla family— had attempted to kill Alexus on numerous occasions.

Following a brief moment of silence, Mercedes continued "You know what, big sis? I'm really starting to think that... somehow... Papi'sfamily had something to do with my mother's murder."

"What do you mean 'Papi's family'? He's our father. His family is our family." Alexus was saying whatever she could to shift the topic away from where her sister had just taken it. "Let's talk about this later. Where'sBlake?" She quickly added, "Never mind, I'll call him. You be safe out there. And make sure you call and let Papi know every detail of what wentdown."

"Over the phone?"

"Yeah. Our lines are secure. Call me when you're on the way home.

I'll have some guys stay over there with you for the next few days.""All right. Love you, girl."

"Love you, too." Alexus hung up and was getting ready to dial Blake's number when her phone started vibrating in her hand.

New text message:

'Just to let you know, I watched you suck that nigga's dick. Forgotabout the Safe Home app, huh? I ain't trippin' though. Fuck you and that nigga. I'm done fuckin' witchoo. Bitch!'

The message was from Blake.

Alexus felt her heart sink down into her intestines for the second time in less than a minute.

PartTwo:

Bein' Single, Seein' Double, Makin'TripleChapter 34

October 1, 2012

Blake went a full fifty-six days without speaking to Alexus after witnessing her sexual tryst with T-Walk. He'd only called her to check on King Neal, who was now back in her custody. She and T-Walk were again acouple, living in the $125 million South Beach mega-mansion she had purchased from Versace.

The call had lasted a mere one minute and fifteen seconds.

"Wow… I never expected to hear from you again," Alexus had said."I'm sure you didn't," Blake had replied. "I'm just callin' to see

what's up wit' my li'l nigga. My momma told me you said he was sick."

"He has a cold, that's all. It's nothing to worry about. Our doctor'staking good care of him. He's probably just missing his daddy."

Just then, an awkward silence occurred. Blake had been sitting on the trunk of his brand-new triple-black 2013 Maybach Landaulet 62S convertible on the corner of 15th and Homan watching a group of teenageVice Lords as they talked shit, rolled dice, and smoked blunts on the sidewalk next to him.

"Check your email when you get a chance," Alexus had finally said,breaking the uncomfortable silence. "I received King's paternity test resultsvia e-mail this morning. You should have it by now. I forwarded it straight to you."

"What did it say?" "Read it and find out.'"Just tell me."

"I want you to read it, Blake."

He hung up on her without even a good-bye, and now, two months after that heart-wrenching phone call, he was lying in bed with Nona on histour bus, reading King Neal Costilla's paternity test results for the umpteenth time on his new iPhone5 and wondering how he'd allowed himself to lose the woman of his dreams. Although he was enjoying the single, no-strings-attached life he missed Alexus more than anything in the world. He had seen her on the red carpet at the MTN Music Awards, and ithad taken every ounce of his energy not to walk over and speak to her.

Otherwise, though, the past few months had been grand for Bulletface. His North American tour had grossed $43 million in ticket sales,his newest mix-tape had gone platinum before it was even released, and the MBM compilation album featuring himself and nine of his recording artists had added $2.35 million onto his growing fortune. Mocha's album had also gone platinum. And in early September, Blake had signed a seven-year contract with Reebok for $100 million, sixty-two million of which was given to him immediately after he'd signed the contract.

Now that his tour was over, he spent most of his days in the studio, and most of his nights inside strip clubs all across the country, throwing thousands of dollars at some of the most gorgeous big-bootied women God has ever created. On September twenty-first, his twentieth birthday, he had thrown $2 million in drug money at the sexy ladies who had danced for him at Kamal's 21 in Atlanta, Georgia.

"What are you looking at?" Nona asked as she sat up and glanced at his smartphone. She had on a red-lace Victoria's Secret bra and panties set, and the red Derrick Rose jersey dress she'd worn today was folded up at the foot of the bed beneath her red Bulls cap. "What is that, an e-mail?" She persisted.

"Stop bein' so muhfuckin nosy," Blake said, exiting his Yahoo e-mail account. He turned to Nona and kissed her on the cheek as he sat up beside her.

"Don't kiss me, nigga." She crossed her arms over her big breasts and pouted, staring straight ahead at the TV. They were watching Rick Ross' "Hold Me Back" video on BET's 106th and Park.

"So," Blake asked, "I can't kiss you now?" "Nope."

"Why not?"

"'Cause I said so, nigga, that's why," Nona snidely retorted. But she was smiling happily, and when Blake pressed his lips against the side of her neck and slipped a hand into her panties, she did not resist. A moment later she was on top of him in the reverse cowgirl position, her panties pulled to the side, her slippery pussy coasting up and down the length of his dick with the celerity of a jackhammer. Blake took ahold of her waist and endured the ride.

Looking up at the mirrored ceiling, he opened his mouth and studied the blinging reflection of his new grille: $75,000 worth of platinum and white diamonds installed permanently into his gums. The dental procedure had taken nine hours to complete, and to Blake, it had been worth every minute and dollar spent. It went well with the white diamond-encrusted MBM pendant attached to his white diamond necklace, the white diamond-flooded Cartier watch on his left wrist, the 300-carat white diamond Jacob bracelet on his other wrist, the pair of round-cut 10-carat white diamond earrings that were gleaming in his lobes, and the jumbo pinkie rings that were sparkling on his hands. Altogether, the jewelry he was wearing had cost him close to two million dollars, about the same price as his new four- door Bugatti Galibier.

Through the Newell's bedroom door, Blake could hear the thrumming bass of Chief Keef's "Don't Like," along with the boisterous voices and laughs of his MBM team and the many women who were partying with them. Among the scantily clad women were four of Blake's favorite adult film stars—Roxy, Pinky, Cherokee, and Nyomi Banxxx—andseveral urban video/magazine models, including Jazzie Belle, Maliah, Ms. Damn, Dream Girl, Cubana Lust, Leoncia, and Mesha Seville. They'd all just left Bulletface's "Dime Pieces Everywhere" video shoot, which had been shot inside a forty-million-dollar Highland Park mansion and had featured Lil Wayne, Birdman, and French Montanan. Now the tour bus washeaded to the Highland Park mansion that Blake had shared with Alexus.

He had been staying there since their split.

The melodic tune of Nona's moans and the creamy tightness of her pussy became too intense for Blake to handle. He let go inside of her and his cum oozed down his twitching pole. She rode him a few seconds longer,then dropped her full weight down onto him and gyrated around a bit beforeturning around and collapsing onto his chest.

For a moment she was silent. She was breathing just as heavily asBlake was, and tiny globules of seat were glistening all over the both of them. Caressing and kneading Nona's ample mounds of derriere, Blake inhaled the sweet scent of her Beyoncé Heat perfume and waited for hisbreathing to settle.

"Can I ask you a personal question?" Nona asked."You just did, genius."

She rolled her pretty eyes, smiling up at him with her chin resting onhis chest. "How'd you feel when Alexus gave you that five hundred milliondollars? I mean, what was going through your head?" She didn't give him achance to answer. "I'm only asking because I was watching CNN the other day and saw that Warren Buffett had just given his three grandkids six hundred million apiece for his eighty-second birthday. I can't even imagine having that much money. I'd probably buy a mansion for every one of my family members, cars for every one of my friends, food and clothes for

174

thousands of homeless people." She giggled softly, toying with his massive quarter-million-dollar MBM pendant. "I'd be broke in a week."

"That's that genius in you," Blake said, combing his fingers throughher curly blonde-dyed hair. "When I got that money, the first thing I did washit my momma and my pops wit' a couple million. Then I looked out for my Dub Life niggas in Michigan City and the Travelers I fuck wit' out herein Chicago. I didn't really spend nothin' after that. Alexus was spoilin' me. She bought my clothes, my jewelry, my cars—basically everything I ever wanted. Money, hoes, cars, and clothes, a dope boys' dream, and she gave me all of that. She moved Momma and Pops into a big-ass mansion in California, right down the road from Heidi Klum's mansion. She bought methat Bugatti Veyron Super Sport. She bought me a four-million-dollar necklace full of big-ass yellow diamonds, with a diamond-flooded pendant of my face like the one Rick Ross had. On some real shit, I felt like I was dreamin'. That bitch bought a hundred-million-dollar Boeing 757 jet earlierthis year and had it *customized*! Ain't that some wild shit? Niggas in my hood ain't never even had a *half* a million till I got on. Now I got all my niggas eatin'. The whole clique iced out. I can't even lie, I'm kinda upset about how shit ended, but I'm still good. At least I'm alive. Not many niggas who done been shot twelve times can say that."

"You're gonna get shot twelve more times if you keep hanging outin this fucked up city," Nona warned. "Word on the street is that you killedsome niggas on Fifteenth and Trumbull last year, and I hear Reesie Cup isn't too happy about it."

"So muhfuckin what? I'm a boss. Ain't no nigga finna run me out of Chicago. Cup can get murked just like I can get murked."

"Yeah, but he's a gang chief, a five star universal elite of the TVLs.

You know how ruthless the Vice Lords can be. My girl Jessica said her boyfriend told her that the Travelers were only fucking with you becauseyou had kilos of cocaine and heroin for the low, and now they're gettingtheir dope from some GDs in Gary. Jessica said they're the same niggas who were in that YouTube video with T-Walk."

"Was one of 'em in a white Hummer?" Blake asked.

"Yup. A white H2 on some big chrome rims. I think his name's Worm or… no, it's Squirm. I met him at The Visionary Lounge a few weeksago. Twista and Chief Keef were there performing that night. He came in with a big black nigga named Gusto, another dark-skinned dude name Ant, and a third nigga who I didn't get to meet. They were popping bottles of Ace of Spades and smoking Kush all night. Squirm was with Cereniti, the stripper chick from *Down the Pole*."

Blake stowed the information in the back of his mind. He would ruminate over it later. Ever since Alexus' unforgettable betrayal, Blake hadbeen focused solely on his music career. Though most of his guys were stillknee-deep in the dope game, he'd decided to leave the game alone, to distance himself from the Dub Life Goons and the Traveling Vice Lords sothat he could enjoy his riches without having to look over his shoulder every second of every day. It made more sense for him to fall back and let his goons do all the trapping; with a net worth of $715 million, he was far too wealthy to be directly involving himself in any criminal activity.

He and Nona got up and stepped into the full marble shower for a while. Unable to keep his eyes off of her enormous ass, he took his time showering and dressing. He put on a white Trukfit hoody with matching sweatpants, a white Louis Vuitton skullcap, a white pair of Reebok Classics, a white leather Pelle Pelle jacket, and a gold-framed pair of LouisVuitton sunglasses.

"Am I Doug E. Fresh?" He asked once they'd made it back into thebedroom.

"More like Gucci Mane," Nona said as she put on her Chicago Bullsmini-dress and black, red-bottomed Louboutin heels. She paused in front of the TV, glanced at the fifty-thousand-dollar pile of hundreds that was stacked up next to Blake's gold-plated .50-caliber on the bedside table, andsaid, "Blake, I need, like, seventeen grand to buy this new Birkin bag I sawonline this morning. It's gray leather with diamond hardware, and I've justgot to have it."

"Shiiiit," Blake said, stuffing the cash and pistol in his hoody pocket. "Seventeen racks for another purse? I done already bought youabout twenty of 'em."

"I know, but this one's different.""I bet it is."

"I'm serious, Bulletface."

176

"I am, too." He slipped his hands around her waist and squeezed hermammoth rear cheeks, smiling his signature half-smile. "I think it's about time you gave me a threesome. What's up wit' that bad bitch from Nap yoube hangin' wit'?"

"Who, Crysta or Jonae?""Both of 'em."

"Fine. Give me the money for the purse, and I'll get them to buss down with us." She checked her red diamond-encrusted Audemar watch forthe time. Blake had bought it for her on his birthday, along with a three- hundred-thousand-dollar cherry-red Aston Martin DBS and a rented oceanfront mansion in Malibu, California. "They're still in Indianapolis right now. I think they're throwing a birthday party for one of the other Cream Team girls, the one Yo Gotti used to fuck with."

"Cream Team? What's that, the name of their clique?"

"Yeah. They're a bunch of bad bitches from all over Nap-town. Their asses and tits are fake, but they're all pretty much dime pieces. Everystreet nigga who's ever kicked it in Nap knows them: especially the ballers.Crysta and Jonae won't even fuck you without receiving some kind of payment. I'll give them five hundred apiece and tell them it's from you."

Someone knocked on the bedroom door, halting their conversation.

Blake stared at her ass—it looked like two big watermelons in that tight-fitting dress of hers—as she sauntered over to the door and opened it.

Slim and brown-complected and clad in a gray Akoo sweatsuit, Young-D barged into the room holding a bottle of Ciroc in each hand. "Bruh," he said, talking to Blake but staring at Nona, "Cubana and Leoncia wanna take some pictures with you." He kept his squinted eyes glued to Nona's fat ass until she crossed her arms and scowled at him. Then he turned to Blake, who was at the bedside table putting on four more white diamond necklaces. "Get out here and join this muhfuckin party, nigga. Yougot a tour bus full of big-booty bitches, and you in here cakin'. How much bread have you blown on this rat today? Ten racks? Twenty?"

"I gotcho rat, nigga," Nona retorted. She sat on the bed and put on her Bulls cap, leaning it slightly to the left the way Blake always wore his."Whatever Blake gives me is none of your business."

Blake said, "Watch how you talk to my nigga."

"Yeah, what he said," Young-D added with a vague grin.

Nona turned to the television, cantankerously rolling her eyes andsucking her teeth.

"Stop disrespectin' my bitch, too, nigga," Blake muttered, snatchinga bottle of Ciroc out of Young-D's grasp. "What's up wit' Fly?"

"I just talked to him. He's flyin' in from Turks and Caicos wit' some'hood bitches and a couple niggas he been trappin' wit'. They should be at the mansion in about an hour. He got Tootie and that bad li'l bitch from St. Louis wit' 'im."

"He took some hood rats to the Bahamas?"

Shrugging his shoulders dismissively, Young-D curled an arm around the nape of Blake's neck and ushered him out of the bedroom.

'Oh, my God,' Blake thought to himself as he and Young-D traversed the ambulant crowd of women. He'd always been most attractedto black women with cute faces, small waists, and massive asses. Now he found himself surrounded by them. All the girls—there were two dozen ofthem—had on strapless white Dolce & Gabbana dresses ($12,500 apiece) and five-inch Giuseppe Zanotti ankle booties. "Dime Pieces Everywhere" was blaring loudly from the coach's state-of-the-art sound system, and a few of the girls were bouncing to the beat.

'Birds just landed, I got nine pieces everywhere

In the club throwin' racks, dime pieces everywhereNew Bugatti Galibier, this four-door is very rare

Engine loud, can barely hear, it's supa fast, can barely steerSo buss it open, come pop that pussy over here

Say I'm the king, king of the Mid just so we clearBulletface, Money Bagz, I'm the king of shinin'

All these chains on, just call me the king of diamonds...'

Blake was taking a picture with a few of DJ Kayslay's Straight Stuntin Magazine models—Mesha Seville, Jazzie Belle, and Ms. Damn—when Young-D walked up and whispered in his ear.

"Baby-momma just texted me saying T-Walk is s'posed to be in Michigan City tonight just for some kinda event at The Swagger. We cancatch that nigga on the Boulevard when he leavin' and…shit, you alreadyknow."

Blake pulled Young-D to the side and gazed silently out his tour bus' side window. He'd been patiently waiting on the perfect opportunity toavenge Lil Mike's death, and now was his chance. Tonight he had a sold- out show at the United Center, with special guest appearances from Rozay, French Montana, Gucci Mane, Yo Gotti, and Twista. The concert would give Blake the perfect alibi if the cops ever were to come around asking questions.

'Fuck it,' he thought.

"Yeah, get the goons ready," he said. "Tell 'em to load up the choppas and mask up. And make sure they empty *every*thing into that nigga."

King Rio

Chapter 31

Financially, things were going all wrong for Alexus Costilla.

Six weeks ago, she had invested over twenty-two billion dollars intovarious European and Chinese corporations, including multiple television networks, casinos, oil refineries, theme parks, and Internet websites. She'd put another billion into renovating decrepit African-American and Hispaniccommunities all across the U.S., and an additional seven hundred million had gone to Feed The Nation, the Costilla family's non-profit organization that was dedicated to feeding thousands of starving families in America's most poverty-stricken regions.

But just a week after Alexus's $22.1 billion oversees investment, Beijing Holdings' stock had plummeted, and since it had been the recipientof $18.7 billion of Alexus's investments, she's suffered a devastating fourteen billion dollar loss.

Then things had gotten worse.A lot worse.

She'd been lying out on the upper-deck of her father's 470-foot mega-yacht on the coast of Mazatlán, Mexico, reading Leo Sullivan's captivating *Innocent's Revenge* on her Kindle Fire tablet and occasionallyglancing up at Papi, Uncle Flako, and T-Walk as they hammered golf ballsinto the Pacific Ocean, when suddenly her iPhone5 had jingled to life.

"Ms. Costilla?" CIA Director Bowden had said."This is I," Alexus had answered.

"I, uhh…hate to be the bearer of bad news, but per the director ofHomeland Security and the President himself, Operation Matamoros is being shut down until further notice."

"What? You cannot be serious."

"I'm sorry, Ms. Costilla, but with the recent disappearance of Jennifer Costilla and our lack of knowledge as to the whereabouts of so much highly-enriched uranium, we simply cannot risk allowing your familyto continue to import goods into this country. Or any other country, for thatmatter. Thirty-four hundred U.S. troops have already been deployed to the Mexican border, and we'll have drones monitoring your family indefinitely.I'd advise you to, uhh, maybe get out of the business for a while. Focus on Costilla Corporation.

Raise your kid and enjoy your wealth. And as for Jennifer Costilla…we're almost certain she's up to no good, so be careful.If you hear from her, contact us immediately."

Ever since that daunting phone call, the Costilla cartel hadn't been able to move a single kilogram of cocaine or heroin into the states, and the kilos they had stored at their Feed The Nation Facility in southern Texas were selling out more rapidly than an A-list celebrity's sex tape. Alexus wasnow down to eleven thousand kilos of coke, thirty-eight hundred kilos of heroin, and eight thousand pounds of marijuana.

Recumbent on an Italian-made lounge chair beside the outdoor swimming pool at her massive South Beach mansion, Alexus sat her Kindleaside (this time she was reading Leo Sullivan's *Innocent's Revenge 2*) and took a moment to reflect on her situation. She looked at T-Walk, who was busy teaching King Neal how to swim. Mercedes and Cereniti were sunbathing in their bikinis on two of the other twelve lounge chairs.

Alexus sighed and said, "You know what? Screw this. I'm done stressing myself out over money. I have a child to take care of, and a fine-ass man to cater to, and—"

"A big-ass mouth," Cereniti said. "We don't have to talk all the time, yo."

Mercedes burst out laughing.

Sucking her teeth indignantly, Alexus glowered at Cereniti, brieflyconsidering cracking her friend upside the head with the Kindle.

"Back in Harlem," Cereniti continued, "we used to hit bitches in thethroat for talkin' too much. Just *whop*! Fuck a bitch whole voice box up."

"Well, hit me in my throat and see what happens," Alexus retorted."Keep talking like that. Go ahead. Let's see if you make it to the second season of *Down the Pole*. I'll send your ass back to Harlem in a beat-up Honda."

Mercedes laughed again. "Ooooo, she got you on that one." She reached across Cereniti and gave Alexus a quick high-five.

"Fuck both of you half-Mexican-ass, Nicki Minaj-lookin' hoes," Cereniti said, offering two middle fingers to the Costilla sisters. She tuned them out with her iPod ear buds, and seconds later she was shouting out thelyrics to Ciara's latest jam.

Shaking her head and smiling, Alexus went back to reading the novel, feeling like the queen of the world inside her castle-like mega- mansion.

Formerly known as the Casa Casuarina, the three-story white-painted Versace mansion—with ten bedrooms, eleven bathrooms, and overtwenty-three thousand square feet of living space—had been the most expensive mansion in the U.S. when Alexus purchased it for $125 million.An avid swimmer, she'd checked out the estate online and had instantly fallen in love with its swimming pool, which was 54-feet-long, lined with twenty-four karat gold, and adorned with tile mosaics and fresco paintings.

About twenty minutes later, just as Alexus was nearing the end of her favorite author's latest novel, and as T-Walk was climbing out of the pool with King Neal mounted on his back, Mercedes sat up and said, "Do you think Papi...made Aunt Jenny disappear? I can't stop thinking that somehow our daddy's family might have had something to do with my mom getting killed. Maybe the same thing happened to Aunt Jenny. I don'tbelieve it's a coincidence that my mom was killed in the same city where your mom was almost killed."

"Some doped up crack head killed your mom and a bunch of other woman named Whitney that night," Alexus said. "On the other hand, I know who planted that bomb on my mom's front porch. It was Aunt Jenny.She chased me down I-94 in an eighteen wheeler, shooting my Bentley up with a fucking machine gun. Then she went to my mom's house and bombed it. There is no connection between what happened to your mom and what happened to mine."

"You don't know that. Not for certain."

"Yes, I do. Aunt Jenny was in that military prison when your momwas killed." Alexus fixed her eyes on T-Walk's dripping muscles as he toweled himself dry with a fluffy white Versace towel. "She shot up my Bentley the morning after T-Walk sent his friends to shoot Blake."

"I wonder why T-Walk never brings his friends around. Doesn't itseem like he's been antisocial ever since you two got back together?"

Alexus struggled. "He's a family man, the type of man King

needsin his life. A real man will always put his family first. That's why I'm withhim and not with Blake. All Blake ever cared about was his niggas and hismoney. T-Walk actually cares about *me*. I might have been blinded by loveat first, but now I see why everybody wanted me to get back with T-Walk.He's the kind of man I need. I don't like to share. I want a man I can call my own."

"Yeah, yeah, yeah," said Cereniti. She had just yanked out an ear plug. "You know you got mad love for Blake. Word is bond, yo, I got madlove for dat nigga, too. He reminds me of—I don't know—like a Midwestversion of Gucci Mane, you know what I mean? Or a younger version of Birdman. Every real street nigga in America looks up to him, 'cause he's just like them. The only difference is he made it out of the hood and they haven't."

The girls fell silent as T-Walk strolled toward them, with King Nealambling beside him. Alexus sat up, scooped her little man into her arms, and pulled him in for a kiss. He laughed jubilantly.

"Where's my kiss?" T-Walk asked with a smile. He leaned downand gave her a quick kiss on the lips. "What the hell were y'all over heretalking about?"

"Oh, just girl stuff. And this new Leo Sullivan book," Alexus said."Papi and my uncle Flako should be here in a few minutes. I believe Bellaand Santiago are coming with them."

"Those Rosetta Stone lessons aren't working fast enough. Bella'salways speaking Spanish when she comes around me. Sometimes I thinkshe's talking about me, cussing me out on the low," T-Walk said.

Alexus sucked her teeth and rolled her eyes as she stood up, settlingher son on her hip. "Do you think I'd let her talk about you behind your back?"

He shrugged. "Mexicans are inclined to stick together," he japed,curling an arm around Alexus's narrow waist.

A brief giggle escaped her throat. There was something about T- Walk that never failed to warm her up on the inside. She didn't know if itwas his confident swagger, his model-esque physique, his romantic disposition, or his Drake-ish yellow complexion, but whatever it was had her head over hills in love, a love so profound and complete that shecouldn't even put it into words.

They gathered their things and headed inside to change out of their swimming attire. In the master bedroom suite that Alexus shared with T- Walk, she traded her Mint Swim bikini for a snow-white Emilio Pucci dressand a matching pair of Christian Louboutin heels. She sat down at her twenty-four karat gold dressing table, applying her makeup and watching T-Walk's reflection in the mirror as he dressed himself in a dark blue Ermenegildo Zegna suit.

"Look at you." Adjusting his tie, he approached her from behind andplanted a gentle kiss on her cheek. "I don't know why you bother wearing all that makeup. You're just as perfect without it."

"Whatever. Do you see these bags under my eyes? I look like an oldwitch, and I'm not even twenty-one yet."

"Sexiest witch I've ever seen." He drew back abruptly, checking hisrose gold Rolex for the time. "About how long do you think it'll be before you make it to Chicago?"

"I'll definitely be there by midnight. The family and I have to attendthat Democratic Fundraiser dinner at the White House, but we won't be there for long, so tell Tasia she doesn't have to send me a thousand messages asking where I'm at. I'll make it to her little book release party intime for the celebrations."

Tasia had recently penned a tell-all memoir detailing her exploits asone of New York City's most well-known strippers, and tonight her book release party—the twelfth one in two weeks—was being held at The Swagger, T-Walk's nightclub in Michigan City, Indiana.

"Are you bringing any of your friends?" Alexus asked as she penciled on her eyeliner. "The girls want to, wh...you know."

"I know what?"

"They're interested in seeing those guys you brought to Club Livthat one night. I forgot their names."

"Oh, you're talking about Squirm and his guys." T-Walk chuck-ledonce. "I can't have them hanging around me anymore. I'm television's highest-paid producer now. Squirm's pushing all of that dope your family been giving me, and he's a fucking lunatic, too. Keeping a safe distancebetween them and myself is only logical. And besides…"

Alexus got up and followed Trintino's unwavering gaze to King Neal, who was on his hands and knees, rolling his toy Escalade across the floor. She crossed the room to T-Walk, slipped an arm around his waist, andmurmured, "Finish what you were saying."

What T-Walk had wanted to say was, "And besides, Squirm's right-hand man, Lil Regg, is still pissed off about his girlfriend and son being killed when your cartel people rescued King Neal from Regg's apartment."But of course he could not say that. So instead, draping an arm around the nape of her neck and planting a warm kiss on her temple, he said, "King needs a safe environment to grow up in, and it's my responsibility to provide that for him. Bringing a bunch of killers and drug-dealers around our kid is a recipe for disaster. He's already been kidnapped once. We can'ttake any more chances. The kidnappers might not be so dumb next time."

"There won't be a next time," Alexus said.

"I know there won't. I wouldn't have let it happen the first time, totell you the truth."

Just then, the ever-cantankerous Cereniti walked into the bedroom with Mercedes and Porsche; all three of them had on tight black leggings with BULLETFACE stitched across the rear, black tee shirts with Blake's face on the front and MBM TEAM on the back, and MBM visors that madethem look like dealers in Vegas.

T-Walk grinded his teeth together in disdain.

"I'm not goin' to no stupid-ass book release party," Porsche said,plopping down on the white leather Versace sofa. "Shit, I'm fuckin' withmy nigga Bulletface today." She flicked her eyes at T-Walk and regardedhim with a sneaky little smirk.

"Shut the hell up, Porsche," Mercedes snapped.

"Straight up, yo," Cereniti said. "We're going to Michigan City forTasia's party right after we leave Blake's concert. I mean, for Christ's sake,if we don't support each other…"

The welcoming sound of T-Walk's smartphone ringing took himaway from the girls' boisterous conversation, and he was grateful for the interruption. He hated Blake, plain and simple, and seeing how much theworld was beginning to love "Bulletface" made T-Walk hate him even more.

He strolled over to King Neal's side, squatted down, and ruffled thelittle guy's hair as he answered the phone.

"T-Walk?" Reesie cup said, sounding distressed."Yeah, what it is, fam?"

"Man, Joe…the DEA just raided three of my spots, got me for

twohundred and ninety bricks and damn near twenty-seven million."

There was a 72-inch flat-screen television secreted in the bedroomceiling. T-Walk grabbed the TV remote, pressed a button that made the television descend from its hiding place, turned it on, and flipped throughthe channels until he landed on CNN.

And sure enough, there it was.

DEA agents arrest 47 in Chicago drug sting; seize millions in drugs,cash, and luxury vehicles.

"Goddamn," T-Walk muttered, and the room suddenly became quietas everyone zeroed in on the newscast.

Then they heard a single gunshot from somewhere outside the mansion.

The girls gasped in unison, and T-Walk rushed to his spacious walk-in closet to retrieve his Ruger pistol.

King Rio

Chapter 32

"Rest in peace, you son of a bitch," Papi said. He was standing on the front steps of the Casa Casuarina with his gold-plated Desert Eagle inhand, glowering down at what was left of his nephew Santiago Costilla'shead.

The two obese figures flanking Papi were Flako and his daughter Isabella, both of whom had long ago grown used to Papi's savage behavior.Their indecipherable expressions betrayed the coldness in their hearts.

"Jenny's really gonna flip out now," Bella commented, throwing aglance back at the Ocean Drive traffic; the vehicles were already speedingaway from the sound of gunfire, and the dark-suited Costilla cartel henchmen who'd occupied the black Range Rovers that had trailed Papi'ssleek black Maybach Landaulet to the mansion were hustling toward Santiago's dead body.

"You didn't have to kill him, Papi," Flako said.

Waving off his younger brother's comment, Papi handed the smoking .50-caliber to one of his men, then watched as they picked upSantiago's limp corpse, tossed it in the back seat of a Rover, and disappeared down Ocean Drive.

"Think of it like this," Papi said. "I just made him famous, shot himdead in the exact same spot where Gianni Versace was killed. This'll go down in history, no? Jenny should be proud." He looked at Bella, and saw that her eyes were brimming with tears.

"Why'd you kill him?" She murmured emotionlessly.

"He was working with the Zetas," Papi said, "and I'm pretty damn sure Jenny's working with them, too. His phone records show numerous calls to a Zeta underboss, one of Gamuza's closest friends. There were alsodaily calls to an unlisted number in Venezuela, and that same phone was tracked to Belize two days ago, Mexico City, yesterday morning, and"—helooked at his Bulova watch—"an hour and forty minutes ago in Laredo, Texas. It's Jenny. I'd bet my soul on it. She probably sweet-talked Gamuza's underboss, got him to let her use one of their tunnels to enter the U.S. undetected."

He turned toward the large front door as it swung open. His two beautiful daughters were in the foyer, nearly hidden behind a wall of vigilant bodyguards.

Alexus timidly stepped forward, pushing a lock of hair behind herear. Her usually exuberant green eyes widened in shock as she took in thegrotesque sight of her brain-splattered marble steps.

"He was working with the Zeta-cartel," Papi explained, assum-ingAlexus had watched the murder on her camera monitors.

She put a hand over her eyes and squeezed. "Who was it?" She asked with a hopeless sigh. "Please don't say it was Santiago."

"Fine, I won't, then," Papi said. "I need you and Mercedes to gatheryour things right this minute and come with us. Send someone out here to clean off these steps."

"What about the White House dinner?"

"Forget about the dinner. I believe Jenny's found her way back intothe States, and there's a very really possibility that she may have a nuclearweapon with her."

Chapter 33

There were more than thirty pretty young Black women mingling around the indoor swimming pool at Bulletface's Highland Park estate.

Some of them were lying in white chaises, sipping glasses of Ciroc vodka,while others were bouncing to the beat of one of Bulletface's club bangersand talking with the other MBM artists. Blake was sitting at the wet bar on a white leather stool between Nona and Lakita, a big-bootied stripper he'd dated last year. He had talked her into becoming a dancer at Reesie Cup's strip club in hopes of learning the identities of the men who'd kidnapped his daughter and murdered his daughter's mother a few years ago. Now he knew that it had been none other than Reesie Cup himself, but since Cup's crew accounted for over half of Blake's kilo sales, Blake had set aside his ill feelings and focused on accumulating more cash.

But now things had changed.

"Yeah, it was crazy," Lakita was saying. "Feds just swooped in andsnatched up damn near every nigga Cup fucked with. I'm really surprised they didn't get his ass, too. I thought for sure he was goin' down. He's thebiggest drug-dealer in Chicago."

Out of the corner of his eye, Blake regarded Kita with a look of suspicion, wondering if she was somehow responsible for the demise of Reesie Cup's crew; with the way she was talking, she definitely could havegotten some people busted.

"Loose lips sink ships," Blake said, watching Cherokee D'Ass' phatbooty shake as she and Pinky sashayed away from the bar with their drinks in hand.

"Boy, please," Kita retorted. "Everybody and they momma knowabout Reesie Cup."

"Doesn't mean you can just broadcast it to the whole world." Nona was rolling up a blunt of Kush for Blake, and her eyes, replete with disdain,were fixed on Kita. "Big-mouthed bitches are the main reason why so manyreal niggas are locked up now."

Kita waved off Nona's comment, and Blake chuckled at their obvious dislike for each other. He liked Nona a lot, but he certainly did not love either of them. Alexus had taken his heart in her hand and mutilated itwith an icepick of betrayal, and the experience had extinguished his need for love. Now all he wanted to do was eat pussy, get his dick sucked, and fuck.

He smoked the blunt without speaking, feeling like he was on the setof French Montana's "Pop That" video shoot. An Indian-looking dime piecewho'd introduced herself as Shanel Nelson was standing maybe ten feet away from the bar, chatting with another urban model, and Blake couldn't stop looking at her. Her eyes happened to meet his just as Fly walked into the room, and Blake almost motioned for her to join him.

But then he spotted Tameka, the girl he'd met at his Michigan Cityhome on the night of Lil Mike's murder.

She was strolling in behind Fly and three other guys. Tootie was right next to her. Awestruck, the two girls ogled the retractable glass ceilingas they followed Fly to the bar. Both of them had on tight fitting multicolored leggings, spiked heels, and Gucci accessories.

"What it is, bruh?" Fly shook hands with Blake, the Dub Life handshake. He was wearing a fresh white Trukfit outfit that was similar toBlake's. "Man, I know you heard about that sweep."

"Talking 'bout Cup n'em?" Blake asked.

Fly nodded somberly. "I hope that shit don't fall back on none of ourniggas. You know how them indictments go. First it's one clique, then it's another." He turned and introduced the three guys he'd brought with him.

Blake had already met two of them—Smoke and Lil Lew—and the third nigga was Nutso, a dark-complected cat who looked like a shorter versionof Rick Ross. All of them had on heavy fur coats and a bunch of diamondjewelry.

"I'ma have to get my ice game up," Blake joked as he shook theirhands and smoked the last few inches of his blunt.

Suddenly Nutso closed his eyes, leaned forward, and inhaled thepungent aroma of Blake's weed. "What's that, some Purp?"

Smoke laughed. "My nigga Nutso is a weed connoisseur. He can name every kind of Kush that's out there."

"Crazy part about it," Blake said, "this is some Purp."

"That shit ain't on nothin'." Nutso took off his chinchilla coat, laid iton a barstool, and pulled out a Ziploc full of loud-scented weed that was covered in a whitish sheen. "This shit right here is the champagne of strains.They call it White Russian. It's the most potent Kush in the world, my nigga. Blowin' one blunt of this White Russian Kush is like smokin' eight blunts of Purple Kush." He opened the bag, and the powerful stench made Blake's head spin.

Blake ended up buying two ounces of White Russian Kush for sevenhundred dollars apiece, and in the process, he gained a new weed man.

Nutso, claimed to have numerous "grow houses" all over the Midwestwhere he routinely grew and packaged all kinds of Kush. He agreed todump thirty pounds of White Russian on Fly for $5,000 a pound.

Needless to say, Blake was elated.

He hung out with everyone for nearly an hour, smoking blunts, talking to his artists, and taking pictures with the models. Then he sneakedoff to his master bedroom with Nona, Tootie, and Tameka.

He had no idea how crazy his night was about to get.

King Rio

Chapter 34

"You do know that we can't land at O'Hare or Midway right?

Security's been stepped up at every major airport in the country, and it'sbecause of you," said the Mexican pilot.

Seated behind him, Jenny Costilla was gazing out her window as thepilot steered the small Cessna plane through a pall of clouds. She was wondering why Santiago had not yet called her, especially since he knew that today was the big day.

'He must be with Papi,' she thought to herself.

"Hay, are you listening to me?" The pilot said, looking over his shoulder at Jenny. "You're gonna have to parachute, Jenny. There's reallyno other way. And I need that payment before you jump."

"Will you please stop talking? I'm trying to think back here."

"I'm...just saying. Favor for a favor. My daughter's college loans are through the roof. That eighty grand'll set us straight."

There was a stainless steel briefcase on the seat next to Jenny. She put it on her lap, opened it, and examined its contents: $500,000 in hundreddollar bills; an MP-5 submachine gun with an additional silencer and shoulder strap; and two smartphones—an iPhone5 and a Samsung Galaxy SIII.

She used the iPhone to send her son another empty text message. Itwas the seventh one she'd sent since they had stopped to re-fuel at a small landing strip in Poplar Bluff, Missouri.

"Where are we now?" Jenny asked.

"We'll be crossing over into Chicago in fifteen minutes.""Turn east and head to Michigan City."

"Indiana?" He glanced over his shoulder again. "What's in Indiana?

Is it where you're hiding all that weapon-grade uranium the FBI says youstole?"

"First off," Jenny snapped, slamming the briefcase shut, "I'd never even heard of uranium until the FBI accused me of stealing it. Now shut thehell up and mind your business. My boyfriend is waiting for me in Michigan City. Get me there."

The pilot shrugged. "You're still gonna have to jump.""I said shut up," Jenny hissed.

She sat back in her seat, took the Samsung smartphone out of thebriefcase, and turned it on. Only one number was programmed into its contacts list.

And dialing that number would start the one hour timer on the nuclear weapon that Jenny Costilla was so proud of.

Twenty minutes later they were in Michigan City, soaring over the beach at Lake Michigan. When Jenny spotted the small boat Miguel had rented, she put on a parachute, pulled a Glock from inside the blazer of herblack Prada pantsuit, and shot the pilot twice in the back of the head.

Then she opened the plane's side door and jumped.

Chapter 35

"How did she even get into the country?" Alexus said as she paced back and forth through the cabin of Papi's sixteen-passenger Gulfstream 5. "Isn't she barred from entering the US?"

The daunting notion of Jenny Costilla being in the United States— possibly with a nuclear warhead—kept everyone quiet for a moment. Papi and Flako were smoking Cuban cigars, drinking Ace of Spades champagne,and staring thoughtfully at the ceiling, and the others were eating the lobsterand crab cakes that the two flight attendants had just served.

But Alexus had lost her appetite the second she'd learned that Papihad blown Santiago's brains out. The macabre image of her blood- splattered front steps was still fresh in her mind. She wanted to call Blakeand let him know what was going on, because Aunt Jenny was known for attacking the loved ones of her enemies.

Alexus didn't know what she would do if something bad happenedto Blake.

"Has anyone reached out to Bowden?" She asked.

Papi looked at her and shook his head. "Screw Bowden. Screw the whole fucking Central Intelligence Agency. I'm no snitch, you know? Thisis family business, and we will handle it as such."

"Are you serious?" Alexus was incredulous. "This is a matter of national security. Hundreds of thousands of American lives could be lost inan instant if Aunt Jenny has what the CIA thinks she has. We have to alert them."

Bella scoffed, shaking her head and swallowing her last bite of lobster. "See what I mean, Uncle Papi? Your daughter's weak. There's noway she'll be able to run the family business."

Alexus scowled at Bella, then flicked her eyes at Mercedes and Porsche; they were on the edge of their seats, taking in every word. Cerenitiwas sitting in a window seat beside T-Walk, and they too were silently watching Alexus, perhaps remembering the terror the nation had experienced back when Jenny Costilla and her al Qaeda affiliates had hijacked a Boeing jet and crashed it into Alexus's Miami Beach house.

"How about you focus on losing some weight, fat ass," Alexus snapped at Bella. "Just because I'm not as ruthless as our grand-mother was doesn't mean I'm not smart enough to run this cartel. And I am not going tocontinue to be disrespected by you or anybody else in this family."

"Take it how you wanna take it," Bella said, "but snitching is a trait that is only possessed by the weak. Granny Costilla never went to the policeon anyone."

"Yeah, but she never had to deal with a raving lunatic who could wipe out an entire city with the push of a button," Alexus reasoned.

Flako raised his hands to stop the bickering. "Nobody's snitch-ing,okay? We're going to find my sister and...do away with her."

"And how exactly do you plan on finding her?" Alexus asked. "We won't have to find Jenny," said Flako. "She'll find us."

*****

The Gulfstream descended into O'Hare at 8:40 p.m. central time.

The Phantom limo was waiting, and thirty minutes later, they pulled into thefront entrance of Blake's Highland Park mansion. Alexus immediately noticed the emptiness of the vast circular drive-way, which was usually congested with foreign sports cars and tour buses. Now there was only one car, a red Aston Martin, parked near the front door.

"I don't think it's a good idea for us to come here," Alexus said asshe gazed out at the looming mansion. "T-Walk and Blake are bitter enemies. Things could quickly go bad if they bump into each other."

"I'm going to Tasia's book release party," T-Walk said, wrap-ping anarm around her lower back and kissing her on the temple. "I'll get a room atthe Trump tonight. Just make sure you stay the fuck away from him. I want you on the phone with me until you go to sleep."

As they were all getting out of the limo, Papi said, "No place is saferthan here. Half the world knows that you and Trintino are a couple. Jenny would never expect you to be anywhere near Blake. Plus, it's going to be pretty difficult for her to make it all the way up here to Illinois without being spotted by a cop, and I'm sure every state and federal police agency in the country's looking for her."

"I'll have our guys fan out around the neighborhood," Flako said.

Alexus didn't argue. She lifted her sleeping son out of the limo andcradled his head against here shoulder.

"Hurry up and get my nephew out of this cold air," Mercedes said."Right after the concert, I'm picking up my kids and driving straight backhere."

"I'm coming back too," Cereniti added, flicking a nervous glancearound the dark estate.

An ominous feeling of fear washed over Alexus as she envisioned anuclear explosion like the one that had decimated Hiroshima decades ago. Holding her son tightly against her bosom, she hurried into the mansion, and for the first time in a long time, she prayed.

Chapter 36

'I'm just another rich gang memba, like Tunechi and Game, nigga
Vice Lord in my veins, nigga, no mercy on lame niggas
I'm fuckin' niggas' bitches, go run and tell CheatasI got alotta
cheese, call me Mr. Velveeta
Hit her from the back, make her spine tingle Married to the da
game, but tonight a nigga singleStacked chips, got a pocket full of
Pringles
Make it rain, hun'ed thousand worth of singles…'

Of the twenty thousand Bulletface fans packed inside the United
Center, more than half knew the lyrics to every one of his songs,
and they were rapping along with him as he moved from one side
of the stage to the other, flailing his Louis Vuitton bandana in the air
and gripping his diamondencrusted microphone.

The flashing cameras, the screaming fans, the money-hungry
groupies who were shouting "I love you Bulletface!" at the top of
their lungs—it was all the motivation Blake needed to keep his
gangster rap career in motion. He loved his fans just as much as they
loved him. The factthat millions of people loved him after all the
dirt he'd done in the past made these long days and nights he and
his MBM recording artists spent in the studio all the more worth it.

When Gucci Mane, Yo Gotti, and French Montana joined him
onstage to perform "Real Niggas Don't Snitch," the crowd went
wild, andthey became even more frenzied when Ross came out and
hit them with "Hold me Back."

Blake wasn't wearing his white Trukfit hoody; he was shirtless
wearing the Louis Vuitton bulletproof vest and five white diamond
necklaces, and his baggy Trukfit sweatpants were sagging down
around hisLouis boxer-briefs.

It was a few minutes past 10:00 p.m., and Blake was performing
aslow song for the ladies with Mocha, his R&B superstar, when he
lookedback and saw Mercedes, Cereniti, and Porsche. The three
girls were standing with MBM's production manager, a few other
MBM staff members, and Kenny-Lord. Blake sent a blinging smile
their way, then turned back to the crowd and finished the song.

The concert ended with a bevy of local artists—Twista, Chief

Keef, Shawnna, Freddie Gibbs, Kaos, and Will Scrill—joining Bulletface onstagefor a song off his album titled "Gangland." And as always, Bulletface spoketo his fans before leaving the stage.

"I just want y'all to know how much I love my fans," he said. "A couple of years ago, I was sittin' in crack houses wit' my niggas, sellin' dope and dodgin' indictments. I remember writin' raps and sayin' to myself, 'Man, ain't nobody gon' buy this shit. The industry don't even fuckwit' the Midwest like that.' But now look at me. Like my nigga Lil Wayne said, 'I'm sittin' on these motherfuckin' millions like a bean bag,' sellin' more albums than any other rap nigga in the country, and it's all because ofmy fans. Y'all don't know how much I appreciate that shit. I hit the studio every day to put on for each and every last one of y'all. Have a safe drive home, everybody. Dub Life or no life, Money Bagz Management. One hun'ed."

He turned and walked straight over to Mercedes, who was wrapped up in Kenny's mammoth arms. She pulled away from Kenny and gave Blake a hug, and Blake could clearly see the fear in her eyes. He noticed thesame fear in Porsche and Cereniti's eyes.

"Yo, we need to talk," Cereniti said as they headed backstage.

"About what?" Blake was wiping sweat from his brow with the towel his assistant had just handed him.

Before Cereniti had a chance to reply, a fist slammed into Blake's jaw, followed by several more vicious punches that sent him sprawling against the wall. Too dazed to defend himself, Blake shielded his head withhis arms until the raining blows stopped.

He regained his equilibrium a moment later. Spitting out a mouthfulof blood, he looked up the brightly lit corridor and found that the culprit, whoever it was, was balled up on the linoleum floor beside the men's restroom door, taking punches and kicks from a phalanx of Blake's friends,including Kenny, Fly, and Young-D.

Blake pushed through the circle and bloodied his white Reeboks against his attacker's face. It took him a minute to realize who it was he wasstomping on, and when he did, he turned to Mercedes and glowered at her.

"He must've stolen my backstage pass," Mercedes shakily admitted.

Rubbing his throbbing jaw, Blake delivered another kick to

Duke's battered face, then went to his dressing room and grabbed his golden DesertEagle. "Nigga wanna fight?" He muttered as he spun around to return to thehallway.

But a slew of CPD officers and security guards were already spillinginto the hall to break up the fight.

"Are you trying to get arrested?" Cereniti asked, nudging him backinside the dressing room.

Blake was furious. Examining himself in the mirror that was attached to the back of his dressing room door, he saw that his right eye wasa bit swollen, and there was blood all over his diamond teeth. Cereniti stoodbeside him with her hands on her hips, looking like Draya Michele from theBasketball Wives of LA show.

"Listen," she said, "I know you're upset right now, but there's something very important I have to tell you before we leave this stadium." She raised her hands and cupped them against the sides of her neck. "Remember when you asked me to get in good with one of T-Walk's guys?It was the day you caught Alexus...you know. Well, anyways, I've been talking to Squirm for a few months now, and he slipped up and told me something the other night, something about collecting a million dollars afterthis show tonight. I, uh...I think he's planning on killing you."

Blake only nodded.

'Good,' he thought. 'I'm in the mood for some gun play.'

King Rio

Chapter 37

"...I'm live here in Michigan City, Indiana, where just hours ago a small plane crashed into this secluded beach area behind me. The plane's pilot, thirty-eight year old Jorge Godinez, has been confirmed dead of an apparent gunshot wound to the head. Eyewitnesses report seeing someone jump from the plane shortly before the crash..."

Papi muted the television, lit his Cuban cigar, and blew a ring of smoke toward the gold-and-crystal chandelier that hung from the ceiling ofBlake's marble-floored living room. Alexus was pacing a tight circle in front of the gold-framed fireplace, smoking a joint of Blue Dream Kush to calm her rattled nerves. Flako was leaning forward beside Papi, using a razor to split open the kilo of cocaine that was sitting on the white marble coffee table in front of him.

"Blake sure does have good taste when it comes to choosing furniture," Papi said, shifting himself deeper into the white leather sofa.

Actually, it had been Alexus who'd purchased the Italian leather sofa from a furniture store in Dubai, but the sofa was the furthest thing fromher mind. She looked at the television and sighed. "It's Aunt Jenny," she said in a despondent tone of voice.

"We don't know that," said Papi.

Alexus rolled her eyes. "Come on now, Papi. Name another personyou know who's brave enough to kill the pilot of a plane they're flying in.Go ahead. Name one."

"Even if it is her, there's no way she'll find us here.""Where's the guy who was tracking her phone?"

"Matamoros," Papi said, ashing his cigar. "Doesn't matter now. Welost track of her in Texas. She must have switched phones."

Alexus tossed the joint in the fireplace, shaking her head worriedly.Her nerves were crumbling more and more by the minute. It was days like this that she wished her grandmother Vida Costilla was still alive. Vida hadkept the Costilla Family together. She'd ruled over all the other Mexican drug cartels with an iron fist, and not once had she been forced to deal witha disloyal family member.

"So, why do I have to deal with this shit?" Alexus thought.

She watched her Uncle Flako scoop a small pile of coke out of the kilo and dump it on the table. He separated the uncut powder into four long lines, then snorted two of them through a rolled up hundred dollar bill. "Back to the money," he mumbled, slouching back on the sofa and pinchingthe bridge of his nose.

"What was that?" Alexus asked.

"We need to get back to the money," Flako repeated. "Our supplies are running low, and the Colombian cartels are wondering why we haven't been buying from them. Same with the Bolivian and Peruvian cartels. Theyall think that we are buying from everyone, but them. Tensions are brewing.There may be a war if we don't do something soon."

"No thanks to the fucking CIA," retorted Papi.

"I think I have a solution." Flako snorted up another line. "We can drop around forty million to the North Valley cartel, have them build us twosubmarines. The Medellin cartel has been doing it for years. We'll be able to move six to eight thousand kilos in each sub."

Alexus sat down in an easy chair, crossed her thick legs, and slowlyran her thumb beneath the heavy platinum and white diamond necklace encompassing her neck. The submarine plan didn't sound like a bad idea, she had to admit.

"So," she asked, "What's the catch?"

Flako shrugged. "Eight out of nine cartel submarines make it to thecoast of California without incident. Pretty good odds, if you ask me."

"Well…get us eight of them. We'll do two shipments per week. Hopefully that will be enough to keep us ahead of the Zetas. From here onout, we're charging everyone eighteen grand per kilo. They can take it or leave it."

"They can take it *or else*," Papi threatened.

The approaching sound of high-heeled footsteps paused their conversation. Seconds later, Isabella Costilla entered the living room with adiabolic grin stretched across her chubby face. A bodyguard followed her into the room, and he was holding an RN-P90 to the ribcage of a strikingly attractive redbone in a red Bulls minidress. The girl looked frightened— just as frightened as Bella was happy.

"Look at what I found on Blake's bed," Bella said, winding a bunch of the girl's hair around her fist. "Looks like he's found himself a slut with abigger ass than yours." She was grinning at Alexus, perhaps hoping to discern a tinge of jealousy in her cousin's face.

And sure enough a hurricane of intense jealousy spun a path of destruction through Alexus's already torn emotions. But she wasn't going toallow Bella the satisfaction of seeing her pain, so she put on an indecipherable expression and ordered the bodyguard to lower his weapon.

"I told you Alexus was soft," Bella said. She opened her mouth to speak again and caught a mouthful of knuckles as the girl in the red jersey dress hit her with an ugly right hook that sent her stumbling backward. Shefell on her ass, clutching her aching mouth with both hands.

Alexus cracked up laughing…until Flako stood up, drew a pistolfrom his hip, aimed it at the girl's face, and pulled the trigger.

Chapter 38

"What are you reading?"

Startled, Rita Mae Bishop looked up from her Kindle reading tabletand locked eyes with her lover. He was leaning against the frame of her open office door, clad in a gray cashmere sweater and slacks, holding a plastic-wrapped dozen of red roses in one hand and a bottle of Ace of Spades in the other.

"How'd you get in here?" Rita asked smiling affectionately as Fredrick rounded her desk and kissed her softly on the lips. She gratefullyaccepted the roses from him.

"Janitor let me in," he said, taking a seat on the edge of her desk. "Itold him it was a special occasion."

"Special occasion?"

"Absolutely. Every second I spend with you is special, isn't it?"

"Hmm. I suppose it is." Her smile burgeoned.

"I know it is." He treated her to another kiss then turned to study theKindle. "What is this, a love story?"

"Yeah...kind of. My daughter's been reading these Leo Sullivan novels for a while now. This one's titled *Life*. Our film company's about tobegin shooting the movie tomorrow and I'm just going over the screenplay."

Frederick walked over to the water machine and pulled off two paper cups. "Is he a black author?"

"Yeah, he's an urban writer. We're in the process of shooting severalfilms by other urban novelists as well. I'm hoping to get Cash Money to work with us on K'wan's *Animal* and Wahida Clark's *Justify My Thug*.

These two short novels would make great movies."

Frederick nodded his head thoughtfully. They were at Rita's officeon the top floor of the 86-story MTN Tower on North Wabash Avenue, across the street from the Trump International Hotel and Tower where Fred's lavish apartment was located. He took a moment to admire the darkChicago skyline through the tinted floor to ceiling window, and Rita creptup behind him, curled her arms around his waist, and pressed her cheek against his shoulder. She was wearing a form-fitting Valentino dress that accentuated her

King Rio

generous curves, an ensemble that was certain to leaveFred's tongue dangling over his fuzzy beard.

"How's everything going over at the record label?" She asked, lightly scraping her fingernails across the soft fabric that covered his chest.

"Business couldn't be better," he said, "but Blake's becoming a horrible CEO. He isn't even Blake anymore; he's Bulletface, a full-time gangster. All he does is smoke Kush, throw cash at strippers, and spend hismillions on exorbitantly priced cars and jewelry. His older brother Terrancehas been handling most of the company's business. I have to commend Blake for his work ethic, because he's always in the studio. He just blows through way too much money, and he's digging himself deeper and deeperinto the Chicago gang life. Some guy just jumped on him at the United Center concert. Mercedes' boyfriend and a few more of Blake's friends gotarrested for beating up the guy who jumped on Blake. Now, instead of making the scheduled appearance at The Visionary Lounge, Blake's probably driving around with a bunch of guns, seeking revenge. It's a perpetual cycle of violence with him, and I'm hoping it'll stop before he lands himself in prison. Or worse, an early grave."

"That boy needs counseling," Rita said.

Shaking his head, Frederick pushed a cup into Rita's hand, popped open the gold bottle of Ace of Spades, and filled both cups with thesmooth intoxicant. "What he needs is your daughter. Alexus is the only person he'll listen to."

"Well, I'm sorry, but that's not going to happen. I won't let it." Rita took a step back and crossed her arms defensively. "T-Walk and Alexuswere meant for each other. She's happier than she's ever been. T-Walk's with her and the baby every day and night, like a real man's supposed to be,and he's the most talked about black man in Hollywood. In fact, he's the one who's directing and producing the movie I was just telling you about.

There's no way I'd allow my daughter to take Blake back into her home. Iabsolutely refuse to let that man influence my grandson with his gangster ideologies."

Frederick turned around and leaned back against the window, smiling at Rita's resolute frown. The soft glow of her desk lamp illuminated her curvaceous figure, exacerbating her fiercely

210

determined expression.

Stop smiling at me," she said, and swallowed her drink in two gulps.

"You look so sexy in that dress." "Don't try to change the subject.""I'm serious. You look amazing."

Rita glanced down at her fuchsia-colored dress. "For thirty thousand dollars, I'd better look like something," she muttered.

Her iPhone started rattling around on her desk. She walked over and put it on speakerphone, smiling coyly as she noticed that Fred's eyes were stapled to her voluminous backside.

But the panic-stricken tone of her daughter's voice wiped the smirk away and replaced it with a straight-lipped worry.

"Hello? Momma?" Alexus sounded like she was crying. "What's wrong with you? Are you okay? Is it the baby?" "No, King's fine. I just--I need you to be careful, Momma We think Aunt Jenny may be back in the country, and she might have brought anuclear weapon with her."

"A nuclear weapon?" Rita's heart sank faster than her body as she dropped down into her leather Fendi swivel chair. "I thought the FBI had permanently banned her from the United States?"

"They did. But she's been missing since the day those men tried to assassinate Mercedes."

"Somebody tried to kill Mercedes?"

"It's a long story," Alexus said with a sigh. "I'll send someone over to pick you up in a few minutes. I'm at Blake's house."

"What?!" Rita regarded Fred with an accusatory scowl. "Don't worry, Momma. It's not what you think. I'm here with Papi and Uncle Flako. Blake probably won't even make it home tonight. Ifhe does, I'll make him sleep in the guest house."

It was Rita's turn to sigh, and hers was a sigh of relief. She wanted to ask Alexus why they had chosen to stay at Blake's place, but thegrim possibility of a nuclear weapon in Jenny Costilla's possession took precedence over that frivolous question.

"I'm still at the office," Rita said. "Just sit tight, okay? Fred and I will be there in--" She paused for a long moment, and an icy chill raced down her spine. Alexus got quiet too.

Rita's last two lovers—Neal Miller and Nat Turner—had both been killed by the Costillas; bringing Frederick around them was too muchof a risk.

"I'll be there shortly," she finally said.

"Good idea," Alexus caught on quick. A couple of seconds later, she said, "I, uh, watched your show earlier today. That was a goodinterview you did with Kerry Washington."

Suddenly, Frederick walked up behind Rita and started kissing on the side of her neck. He sat his bottle and cup on the desk, then kissed her neck again, filling his palms with her heavy breasts.

"I… have to go, Alexus," Rita said as Frederick spun her chair around and kneeled in front of her. He pushed up her dress, saw that she wasn't wearing any panties, and immediately went to work sucking and licking her clit, shifting his incredibly flexible tongue in different shapes and sizes.

"I love you, Momma," Alexus said. "Please be safe, okay? If you see anyone following you, call that FBI agent right away and tell himwhat's going on."

"Oh… okay. Love you, too." Rita ended the call abruptly.

Leaning back in her swivel, she dug her fingers into Fred's thick crop of hair—a Dr. Cornel West-like afro—and let out a tremulous moan.

*****

Down in the lobby, a fifty-something black male janitor was busy buffing the floor and listening to Al Green's "Love And Happiness"via a pair of Beats by Dre headphones when he looked up and saw the pretty Hispanic woman. She was knocking frantically on the steel-framedglass door, her shoulders bunched against the gelid winds.

The janitor pushed the headphones down around his neck. "Doors don't open till six a.m.," he shouted, turning off the buffer. He walked to the door. "You hear me? I said the doors don't open till six. Comeback then."

"Restroom?" The lady asked."Can't."

"Not even for a hundred bucks?" She reached in her coat pocket and pulled out a bankroll.

"Two hundred and we got a deal."

Jenny Costilla showed a wicked smile as she peeled off two hundreds. *'Greedy fucking Americans,'* she thought, handing him the cashas he opened the door.

She stepped inside and looked around. There were cameras in every corner, and another janitor was cleaning windows on the other side ofthe lobby. He was younger, with cornrows and a goatee.

"Restrooms right down there by the elevator," said the olderjanitor. "Try to make it quick."

Jenny glanced at the black Maybach that was parked at the curb in front of the skyscraper. "Is that Rita Bishop's car?"

"Yes ma'am, it is. Hard to believe she's turned into the new Oprah practically overnight, isn't it? My wife records every episode of theRita Bishop show on that damn TiVo thing I got her last Christmas."

"Where's her office?"

The janitor frowned at Jenny. "I thought you had to use the restroom?"

Jenny didn't reply. Instead, she turned and looked out the door again, this time focusing on the black Audi that was idling across the street.Miguel was lying back in the driver seat, wearing a black cotton ski-mask and holding an AR-15 assault rifle in his leather-gloved hands. Knowing that he was watching her gave Jenny a tad bit more confidence as she drew her Glock and put the barrel of its silencer to the janitor's temple.

"Don't you fucking move," she hissed, waving for Miguel to join her and keeping an eye on the other janitor, who was too busy squeegeeing the window to notice what was happening twenty feet behindhim.

Seconds later, she and Miguel had the two janitors face down on the floor with their fingers interlaced behind their heads.

"Two questions," Jenny said. "Number one: how many people are there in this building? And number two: where is Rita Bishop?"

"I don't know, man, I don't—" the younger janitor said, but his words were cut short by the suppressed *phoof* of Jenny's pistol; blood, brainand bone splashed across the marble floor.

"Wrong answer," Jenny said, moving the Glock to the otherjanitor's head. "Let's hope you can do better."

King Rio

Chapter 39

A stunning fleet of Ferraris, Lamborghinis, and Range Rovers was zipping down Chicago Avenue ahead of Bulletface's matte black, four-door Bugatti. Recumbent in the tan leather passenger seat, he was eyeing the side of Mocha's chocolate-hued face as she drove his multi-million- dollar toy through the darkness of Chicago's west side.

Leaving the United Center, Blake had been livid. So livid, in fact, that he hadn't even remembered to run the cash he'd made off the concert's ticket sales through his money-counting machines. The only thing on his mind was revenge.

But then, just as he'd been getting ready to ride down on Duke's clique of Four Corner Hustlers, he received a phone call from Jay Z, the one real nigga in the rap game who he respected and honored most.

The call had lasted a mere ten minutes, and it was life-changing.

Afterwards, Blake had forced himself to calm down. Then he'd given his assistant the money to bond his guys out of jail, rolled up a blunt, popped a Molly pill, and left the stadium.

Now, he was sweating like a Hebrew slave. His eyes were in-credibly red, and the tantalizing sight of Mocha's succulent lips had the crotch of his black Akoo jeans bulging out.

"Stop looking at me like that," Mocha said, flicking her eyes at him. She was wearing a brown Louis Vuitton romper with matching shades and heels, and her full-length fur coat was draped over her seat. She looked a lot like Kisha from the movie Belly. "Don't even start giving me that look, Face. Keep your freaky little eyes over there."

Blake laughed as he snatched off his black Akoo sweatshirt and dabbed a line of sweat from his brow with his Louis Vuitton ban-dana. He had changed out of the Trukfit sweatsuit before leaving the concert.

"Ain't nobody lookin' at you," he said, and went right back to ogling her juicy lips. "What kinda perfume is that you got on? That shit smell so good."

Nakisha "Mocha" Newsome sucked her teeth, rolled her eyes,

twisted her neck, and smiled all at the same time. She turned the volume upon the radio. Lil Wayne's "No Worries" was playing on 92.3.

"You are so full of it," she said. "I hope you don't think I'm about to let you sweet-talk me out of my panties. Especially not after you did whatever it was you did to Nona and those other two bitches."

"What?" Blake grinned. "When?"

"Before we left for the concert. I saw you creep off with them, and I know y'all did the nasty 'cause I walked by your bedroom and heard it through the door."

Another laugh escaped Blake's throat. He had fucked Nona and Tootie; but Tameka hadn't joined them; she had sat aside and watched.

Blake's smartphone started ringing, and he was surprised to see that it was Alexus calling. His brows furrowed together in wonder. *'Fuck is she callin' me for,'* he thought, adjusting the straps on his bulletproof vest. For a brief moment he considered ignoring the call. He didn't want to talk to Alexus. Not after all the heartache she'd forced upon him. Not after she'd left him for his number one enemy. But the truth was, he still loved and missed Alexus, and just the idea of hearing her cotton voice was all the motivation he needed to answer the phone call.

"What up." He curled an index finder around the trigger of the golden Desert Eagle that was lying on his lap; Cereniti's warning was still fresh in his mind.

"My aunt Jenny's back," Alexus said. "I… just wanted to let you know that. Just in case…"

"I ain't worried about that bitch."

Alexus sighed. "There's something else." She paused. "My family and I are at your place, and… umm…. Your girlfriends' been shot."

"What?!" His eyes went wide.

"It's only a graze. The bullet cut across the side of her head. I stopped Uncle Flako before he got a chance to shoot her again. My medical team is tending to her now. I'll have her call you when—"

"I'm fuckin' yo' uncle up," Blake said, emphasizing every word. "On my momma I'm beatin' his ass."

216

He was staring straight ahead as they approached the crowded intersection at Laramie and Chicago Avenue. On one corner was The Visionary Lounge, a tall yellow brick edifice that stood over the other buildings like Shaq in a room full of midgets. A long line of club-goers— mostly thuggishly-comported black men and scantily-dressed black women, a few non-blacks sprinkled in here and there—were wrapped around the opulent nightclub, all of them eager to get inside and be a part of the MBM team's official after party. Power 92 radio DJs had been announcing it for weeks.

"I miss you so much, Blake," Alexus said, "I'm not trying to win you over, but... you... I'm sorry for what I did. God knows I am. I loveyou more than I love myself."

The statement of love made Blake's blood boil. He hung up on her without saying another word, then rested the back of his black Louis Vuitton skullcap against his seat's headrest and let out his own sigh, angrilygritting his diamond-laden teeth as he remembered seeing Alexus sucking T-Walk's dick. There was no way he could forgive her for such a betrayal.

"So, are we going to this party or not?" Mocha asked, glancing at her icy Chanel watch. "Let me know before this light turns green."

He didn't have a chance to decide.

In his side view mirror, Blake watched the dark blue Dodge Magnum on thirty-inch rims as it pulled up alongside his Bugatti. The Magnum's tinted windows rolled down, and from them pistols emerged.

Gunfire ensued.

King Rio

Chapter 40

Gentle moans blew from Rita Mae Bishop's parted lips asFrederick thrust his rigid pole into her slick love tunnel.

Her bountiful butt cheeks were cradled in his strong black hands, her thick legs locked firmly around his waist to pull him deeper inside her. He had her back pressed against the cool window pane, and hewas licking her nipples and kissing all over her neck and face while he pounded in and out of her pulsating wetness, driving her to a fourth breathtaking orgasm. When it happened, she dropped her head back, dug her fingernails into his powerful shoulders, and held on until she felt himempty his warm seed inside her.

Then, breathless and covered in perspiration, they fell to the floor. Rita propped her chin on his heaving chest. Stared up into his deep-set smoldering eyes. Grabbed his veiny hands and slapped them onto her ass.

"Good God, Rita," he said in his throbbing baritone. "You're as hot and wet as a Jacuzzi down there."

"It's the champagne. Gets me every time.""You hardly took a sip."

"That's not true. I drank two whole cups.""Two whole baby cups."

Rita shrugged. "I might have had more if you weren't such an alcoholic. We should get you into some kind of AA meetings. Maybe that'll—"

The chilling sound of distant gunshots silenced Rita. She and Frederick became frozen in place.

"You hear that?" Fred asked.

"Of course I heard it," Rita whispered.

And then it came again: rapid gunfire from a fully-automatic weapon.

They got up and dressed hurriedly. Rita ran to her desk and brought up the building's camera system on her computer. What she sawmade her gasp in horror.

There were two stiff bodies stretched on floor of the lobby, four more near the third floor's elevator doors; a woman who'd clearly been shotin the head lay motionless in front of a snack machine inside Britney Bostic's law firm on the fifteenth floor.

"Jesus Christ," Fred murmured from behind Rita, "What the…"

Rita's hands clamped down over her open mouth, and she groaned into her palms as she spotted Jennifer Costilla standing beside anassault rifle-toting masked man on the floor directly beneath her office.

Sprawled out in the hallway behind Jenny and the masked man were seven dead men. They were Rita's bodyguards.

"Oh, my God." Rita was shaking like a wet dog. "We've got to get out of here, Fred. She'll kill us."

Rita kept a loaded .38 revolver in her bottom drawer. She took itout and turned to Fred; he had stripped back down to his underwear, and was busy tying an arm of his sweatshirt to the leg of his slacks.

"What in God's name are you doing, Fred?"

"Getting us out of here," he replied, hastily tying the arm of his long-sleeved thermal shirt to the other arm of his sweater. "You're gonna have to swing down to the floor under us as soon as they make it onto this floor. Take the elevator down to the lobby, get away from this building, andcall the police."

Rita crossed the room to her office door and locked it."They have guns, Rita. Locking the door won't—" Another barrage of gunfire echoed into the office.

Frederick snatched the revolver out of Rita's hand as shestepped back around to her computer.

"They're in the elevator!" She said.

"Turn off that desk lamp. The computer too," Fred replied. He pointed the gun at the window he and Rita had just desecrated and sent a bullet through the center of it.

Rita yelped at the sound of the gunshot. The window shattered, and most of it got sucked out into the frigid night sky.

"Come on, Rita. I need you to hold on to this shirt sleeve and letme lower you to the window underneath us. Here's your gun. Shoot out the window, swing yourself into the room, and run to that elevator, you hear me?"

Outside of Rita's office, the elevator emitted an audible *ding* as it reached her floor. Without thinking, she mashed her lips against Frederick'sand gave him a passionate two-second kiss.

"Go now," Frederick urged.

Rita coiled one end of the makeshift rope around her fist, holdingthe pistol in her other hand, and reluctantly walked over to the window. With the other end of the makeshift rope secured in Frederick's mighty hands, he held on tight and quickly lowered her out the window.

Which is when the grim reality of the situation set in.

Dangling from an outfit eighty-six stories in the sky was not Rita's idea of a good time. Ice-cold winds battered her against the building. Flung her from left to right. She had a hard time aiming the gun, but somehow shemanaged to shoot a hole in the glass a millisecond before a powerful gust ofwind slammed her through the window. She landed on her back, and her head smacked the floor hard enough to leave her thoroughly dazed.

But she wasn't too dazed to hear the machine gun blazing upstairs.

Turning to look out the window, she caught a brief glimpse of Frederick Douglass' bullet-riddled body as it plummeted to the ground farbelow.

"NOOOO!" she screamed hysterically. "God, please!"

"God cannot hear you from here," said a voice that sounded like an evil Sofia Vergara. "Come with me. I'll take you to Him."

Rita looked up, and through teary eyes, saw Jenny Costilla standing in the doorway.

King Rio

Chapter 41

Every once in a while, Trintino Walkson abandoned his ridiculously expensive suits for the gangster attire he'd worn back when hewas riding around the Midwest in his canary yellow Chevelle, selling ounces of coke and crack to the corner-hustlers.

The parking lot in front of his Michigan City nightclub was packed full of vehicles when he pulled up in his dark blue Range Rover Evoque. He eased into his parking space between Squirm-G's white Hummer and The Swagger's front entrance, then stepped out clad in a brand-new Pelle Pelle ensemble that matched the color of his Rover, its 30-inch rims, and the sparkling blue diamonds in his Cartier watch and six- pointed star earrings.

"GD Folks!" Squirm shouted as he got out of his H2 and walked around to T-Walk's side. "We got that nigga, G. Folks n'em just caught himin traffic on the west side of Chicago. Say they tore that Bugatti up."

Demonstrating the Gangster Disciple handshake with Squirm, and checking out the incredibly fat ass of a brown-skinned girl who was standing in line to get in the club, T-Walk smiled and said, "That's the kindof shit I like to hear. About time that nigga got taken care of."

He turned to Squirm. "Is he dead?"

"He *gotta* be dead. Regg and Ant emptied two thirties at dude. Close-range too. Ain't no way he could've lived through that."

"Call and make sure. And have somebody get on Facebook and Twitter; they have to be talking about that shooting. If he's dead, it won't bea secret for more than two minutes."

Suddenly, a fight broke out between two of the girls who were standing in front of the line. T-Walk watched in amusement as the brawl quickly turned into a three-on-one handicap match. The three attackers— Tiffany, Jessica, and Makayla, a troublesome trio of brown-skinned dime pieces from 10th and Lafayette, T-Walk's old neighborhood—were landingbrutal punches and knees to their victim's rapidly swelling face.

Squirm's twenty-man crew of GDs swarmed around him and T-Walk to get a better view of the fight. All of them wore Gucci and

Pelle Pelle outfits; blue diamond necklaces with blinging six-pointed star pendants; Gucci sneakers, shades, and bandanas. One particularly large GDnamed Gusto stepped in front of T-Walk and Squirm, essentially shielding them from any potential threats.

Shaking his head incredulously, T-Walk turned and strolled into the club, smiling his brilliant Colgate smile at what looked like at least two thousand men and women. After stopping to take pictures and network witha few people he made his way to the glass-enclosed VIP section at the rear of the club. Tasia was sitting at one of the tables behind a stack of her books. She had an unpleasant look on her face.

"Where are Alexus and Mercedes?" Tasia asked in a chilly voice.

"They, uh—it's a long story," T-Walk replied as he slipped into the seat beside her. "Cereniti's not coming either. They're all in Chicago atthat old Michael Jordan mansion."

"Blake's mansion?"

"Yeah." He gave a head nod to a clique of his guys that were seated and standing around another table. "Blake won't be there with them.Somebody told me he just got shot up again."

Momentarily, Tasia's expression brightened.

"Did they kill him?" She asked, sounding half-excited. "I think so. I'm not sure yet, though. We'll find out soon enough. Until then..." T-Walk waved over a waiter and ordered a hundredbottles of Ciroc.

Tasia seemed to relax a bit as the drinks started flowing, but her scowl returned when a hippopotamus-shaped white girl walked up and asked Tasia to sign her book.

"Isn't Alexus supposed to be here?" The hungry hippo asked. "This is my book release party." Tasia was furious. "The only person who's supposed to be here is me."

Hippo scoffed. "Most of us in here follow Alexus on Twitter. Weonly came because she tweeted about this party and we thought she was gonna be here. My friends and I canceled our plans to hit up the *Bulletface*concert, for Christ's sake."

T-Walk cracked up laughing as he watched Hippo storm away from their table, and he laughed even harder when Tasia angrily grabbed her smartphone from inside her Gucci bag and dialed

Cereniti's number.

"Stop fucking laughing," Tasia snapped at him.

"Aww man, that was too funny. If you could've seen the look on your face…" T-Walk sipped from his bottle and kept right on laughing, vibing to the stentorian bass of Chief Keef's "Love Sosa" as it boomed throughout the club.

Cereniti didn't answer the phone. Neither did Alexus. By the time Tasia scrolled down her list of contacts to Mercedes, she was fuming.

"What's up, Tay?" Mercedes answered.

"Don't fucking 'what's up' me, yo. I'm *mad* heated right now. Y'all got me sitting here all by myself while y'all partying out in big assmansions and shit. That's fucked up, b."

"Ain't nobody partyin', bitch. Me and Tee-Tee just got back from the Bulletface concert with my li'l sister. We ain't even walked in thedamn house yet."

"So, y'all ain't comin' to my book release party?"

"We can't. Some crazy shit's happenin' with my daddy's sister. Everybody's staying here with Alexus."

Grinding her teeth together, Tasia took a deep breath… and said something she'd been itching to say for months.

"How can you kick it with the same person who got your mother killed? I mean, sister or no sister, I'd be *pissed*, yo. Lexi would have to answer for that."

Mercedes ended the call abruptly.Tasia smiled.

King Rio

Chapter 42

Mercedes slowly lowered the iPhone to her side. Her hurt greeneyes landed on an aluminum gum wrapper that was stuck to the rear right tire of Porsche's pink Bentley, and they stayed there until Cereniti, grabbingher purse off the Bentley's hood, turned to Mercedes and spoke.

"Yo, I can't remember where I put my phone charger."Porsche said, "You left it on Papi's jet." She picked up

Meyoncé, Mercedes' two-year-old daughter, and put the little girl on herhip. Then she noticed the troubled expression on her sister's face. "Girl,what the hell is wrong with you? Who was you just talkin' to?"

They were all standing in the circular driveway at the Highland Park mansion. Strategically placed lawn lights revealed a bevy of dark- suited bodyguards positioned all across the estate, from the still open wrought-iron gates at the end of the driveway, to the impeccably landscapedmulti-acre lawn, to the mansion's gray-stone porch.

"This bitch done went mute on us," Cereniti joked, walkingtoward the porch stairs.

But her words collapsed and perished before they made it to Mercedes' ears; Mercedes was still hearing Tasia. *'How can you kick it withthe same person who got your mom killed?'* The daunting question bouncedaround in her head like a hyperactive child.

Was Alexus responsible for the Whitney murders?

After all Mercedes had heard during the flight to Chicago, the idea of Alexus orchestrating a killing spree did not seem far-fetched.

The front door of the mansion behind Mercedes opened, bathing her in a lake of foyer light just as her son, Baby Duke, who was not even five years old yet but sometimes wise enough to be twenty-five, tugged on her pant leg and murmured, "Is you okay, Momma? 'Cause you don't look okay."

"Momma's okay, baby." She turned around and watched Alexus and Papi step out onto the porch. There was blood all over the front of Alexus's white Pucci dress and Louboutin heels. "Everybody go in the house. I need to have a long talk with Papi and Alexus,"

Mercedes said.

But just then, Blake's matte black Bugatti Galibier came roaring up the driveway, followed by a smoke gray Ferrari and two Range Rovers. The passenger's side of the Bugatti was covered in bullet holes.

*****

An overwhelming sense of dread washed through Alexus as she took in the sight of Blake's car. Golden Eagle in hand, he got out of the car and slammed the door shut. Streets and Young-D hopped out of the Ferrari, and several more members of the MBM crew exited the Range Rovers holding pistols.

"Bitch ass niggas tried to do me in," Blake said, looking at Alexus and slapping the roof of his Bugatti. "They didn't know this muhfucka was bullet proof. Better hope theirs is, too."

"Do you know who it was?" Alexus asked.

"Of course I know who it was! I know who sent 'em too. It's all good. On Vice Lord, this shit gon' end tonight." Blake turned to his crew. "Come on, y'all. We finna load up and roll out."

He and his MBM team breezed past Alexus and disappeared into the mansion leaving behind Mocha and two pretty girls who were sitting in the back of one of the Range Rovers.

Dropping her head, Alexus pinched the bridge of her nose and sighed. Everything seemed to be going bad at once. *Everything.* And what was Mercedes looking so angry about? Was it because she'd found out on Papi's jet that the Costilla cartel was not just a myth?

When Alexus finally lifted her head, she found herself alone with Mercedes and Papi; Cereniti and Porsche had taken the kids into the mansion, and Mocha was driving away in the Range Rover with the other two girls.

"Let's go inside," Alexus said. "We'll talk after I calm Blake down. You know how crazy that boy can get."

Mercedes was shaking her head. "Have Enrique pull your car around. I have a lot on my mind, and I don't want anybody interrupting this conversation we're about to have."

With another sigh, Alexus sent a bodyguard to fetch her purse, and Enrique went and got her pearly white Phantom limo. She got in back with Papi and Mercedes, then Enrique headed down the driveway ahead oftwo white Tahoes full of Costilla cartel henchmen.

Mercedes crossed her arms over her chest and scowled at Alexus.

"What's this all about?" Papi asked.

"It's about my mother." Mercedes regarded Papi with the same cold scowl. "You remember her, don't you? The cosmetologist you hired foryour wife about twenty years ago? The woman you got pregnant behind your wife's back? The woman you sent here to Chicago without a dime to feed *your* child?"

"That is not true, I loved Whitney. I gave her more money than you can ever imagine. But the bottom line is, I was a married man. I was wrong for cheating on my wife with Whitney. To be honest with you, I hadplanned to spend some time with you and your mother after Rita and I divorced, but Whitney was already too..."

"Too what? Too strung out on crack? Is that your excuse forbeing a fucking dead-beat?!"

Papi's expression remained placid, but Alexus knew how much he hated being cursed. An outsider would have certainly been killed for such a transgression.

He lit his Cuban cigar and said, "What are you complaining about? Huh? Alexus gave you forty million dollars. That's a little over twomillion for every year I missed of you growing up. You should be happy."

Mercedes shifted her steaming emerald eyes to her sister's, and for a moment she didn't speak; then, "I want to know who killed her, and Iwant to know why." Her accusatory stare was frigid and replete with emotion.

"Why are you looking at me?" Alexus said."Who killed her?" Mercedes persisted.

"How the fuck should I know? You and I didn't meet until after your mother was killed. For all we know, it could have been a drug deal gone bad."

"Bullshit! Tasia told me *you* had it done!""I don't give a damn *what* Tasia told—"

"Quiet!" Papi said, raising a wrinkled brown hand to cease the burgeoning argument. "Now, Alexus I want you to tell her the truth. Get itover with. It's not like it was intentional."

Although Alexus had nothing to truly be angry about, she tried earnestly to match her sister's wrathful expression. They locked eyes, and the stare down began.

'Damn you, Papi,' Alexus thought. 'Why'd you have to tell her?'

She looked down at her blood-stained dress. "Okay, Mercedes. Here's what happened. I, uh… was doing something with Blake last year, atthe house on Trumbull Avenue, and, uh… I tasted another girl's stuff on him. I asked him who the bitch was, and he said Whitney."

"So you had somebody go to Michigan City and kill everyWhitney in the phone book?!" Mercedes was stunned.

"I told them to find the girl he was cheating with, and to make sure it didn't happen again. If I had known that they were going to kill allthose women, I would have stopped them." Alexus's head was weighed down with shame and guilt. She didn't want to look back up at her sister, but she did it anyway—just as her iPhone started ringing inside her purse.

To avoid her sister's intense gaze, she answered the call. "Hello, my dear niece." Aunt Jenny's voice was a cold whisper.

"If you ever want to see your mother alive again, come to the First Baptist Church on the corner of Eighth and Willard Avenue in Michigan City. Andlose the two SUVs behind you. I only wish to see you, Mercedes, Juan andEnrique. Anyone else and she dies."

In the background, Rita shouted, "No, Alexus! Don't come! It's a set—"

Then the call ended.

Chapter 43

"I can't believe that motherfucker shot me," said Nona. She was driving Blake's charcoal black Rolls-Royce Phantom coupe down Interstate-94, her head wrapped in gauze to cover the deep gash streaked across the left side of her head. Her hands were trembling on the steering wheel, and she kept swatting away the smoke that was drifting up from theend of Blake's blunt.

"Pull over at the next rest stop so I can drive," he said.

"I told you, I'm good," she replied. "It's just a graze wound. Don't worry, I won't pass out on you. At least not while we're on this highway." She tossed him a dry smirk. "I wish you would have been thereto beat the daylights out of that fat ass Mexican for shooting me. I think I blacked his daughter's eye. They left right before you pulled up. Alexus made them leave."

Blake kept quiet. Kept smoking and coughing. His mind was on other things, like the three Louis Vuitton duffle bags in the trunk of his Phantom. Two of them contained Ak-47s and 100-round drum clips, and

$450,000 in hundreds filled the third duffle.

"Why are we going to Michigan City?" Nona asked.

"I gotta take care of somethin'. I'll get you a hotel room.""Your ass better be there with me."

"I will. I'm thinking about flyin' us out to New York tomorrow, fuck wit' Jay and Kanye for a li'l bit. I need to get in the studio wit' them anyway. I'm done wit' the streets for a while after tonight. Them niggas almost hit me like Pac and Biggie got hit." He adjusted the rearview mirror and checked to make sure the Ferrari and Range Rover were still trailing hisPhantom. They were. "Jay said it ain't no use in me havin' all this money ifI'm just gon' keep doin' the same shit I was doin' before I got it."

"He's right. Hell, you're almost a billionaire. Boss up and lean back. Put a ring on my finger"—she giggled softly—"and let me upgrade you."

Blake shook his head. "A wise woman once told me, 'You're only nineteen, Bulletface. I'm twenty-six, and I'm not even ready to get married yet.' I think I'll just take her advice."

"Things were different then." Nona smiled then grimaced in pain. She touched the side of her head where the bullet had struck. "JesusChrist. Feels like somebody hit me with a bowling ball."

The smartphone on Blake's hip began singing the chorus to Tupac's "Dear Mama." He answered the call and immediately heard thepanic in his mother Carolynn's voice.

"Blake?"

"Yeah, what's up, Ma?"

Carolynn breathed a sigh of relief. "Boy, you almost gave me a heart attack. Your uncle Noble just called saying he'd heard something about your car being shot up in Chicago."

"I'm cool, Ma. They did shoot my Bugatti up, but they didn't hitme. You can go to bed. I'll call you in the mornin'."

"Have you talked to Alexus? I know she's got be shaken up about what's happened at the MTN Tower."

"What? What happened?"

"It's all over the news. Mass shooting at MTN Tower. Eighteen confirmed dead."

Blake could not believe it.

"I'ma call you tomorrow, Ma. Kiss Vari good night for me."

"Getcho butt somewhere and sit down, Blake. You hear me?""Love you, Ma."

"I love you, too."

*****

Zipping down Interstate-94 in Squirms' blue Dodge Magnum, twenty-four-year-old Reggie Freeman was feeling good, rocking back and forth in the driver's seat and listening to the Freddie Gibbs song that was blasting from the four fifteen-inch speakers in back. This was the first time he'd been able to smile since his girlfriend and son were killed by whoever it was that had rescued Alexus's kidnapped son from his girlfriend's Gary apartment. Getting some payback felt good. Real good. And now he and hispartner in crime, Lil' Ant, were going to get forty kilos of cocaine to split for killing Bulletface.

Yeah, he definitely felt good.

The eight TVs inside the Magnum were playing a Pinky XXX porn, and Lil' Ant was in the backseat getting head from the thick

232

redbonethey'd picked up before leaving Chicago. Her friend, a dark-skinned chickwith a tight ponytail, was asleep with her head against the window next toReggie. But he didn't give a fuck. He was thinking about the twenty kilos.

"Sell dem muhfuckas for thirty bands apiece," he mumbled to himself as he clicked on the turning signal to switch lanes. "Make that quick six hun'ed thousand, prob'ly cop me a Benz or a—" He looked at theRange Rover he was passing, and the gray Ferrari in front of it. Then he spotted a black Rolls-Royce cruising ahead of the Ferrari. "Shit, I might even lease me a Phantom," he said thoughtfully. "Yeah, dat's what I'ma do.I'ma get me a Phantom."

*****

Blake's breathing stopped the moment he noticed the Magnum pulling up alongside his Phantom. A few weeks ago, he had watched two Vh-1 documentaries detailing the murders of Tupac Shakur and Christopher"Biggie" Wallace. Now those images were flashing through his mind.

Simultaneously, he lifted the gold-plated .50-caliber from hislap and rolled his window. Then he stuck his arm out the window and opened fire.

BOOM BOOM BOOM BOOM BOOM

The Magnum's driver window collapsed. Bullet holes the size of fifty cent pieces appeared in its door and the glossy blue Dodge fishtailedwildly before turning sideways and flipping up into the air. It rolled several times and then landed harshly and rolled eight or nine more times. One of its chrome thirty-inch rims divorced the Magnum and flew straight toward Blake's windshield. Nona somehow managed to swerve out of the tire's path, and it smashed into the right headlight of Streets' quarter-million- dollar Ferrari.

Nona screamed, "Blake! What the fuck, man, are you nuts?!" She sped up, reaching a hundred miles an hour in no time.

"Just drive, baby," Blake said, looking back at the flaming wreckage. "The Michigan City exit is right up here. Slow down 'fore wefuck around and get pulled over."

Too late.

An Indiana State Trooper vehicle popped up out of nowhere and hit its flashing lights. It veered around the upside down Dodge. Sped past Lil Meach's black Range Rover.

Blake's IPhone5 chimed. It was Streets.

"Damn, li'l bruh," Streets said as the squad car got behind his Ferrari. "Was that them niggas who--"

"Yeah, that was them." Blake checked his rearview mirror.

Streets was pulling over to the side of the highway, and the cop was, too."Bruh, just play it cool, a'ight? Shit. Shit, they might think the gunshot came from yo' car."

Blake heard the cop shout. "Turn off your engine and put your hands out the window! NOW!"

"Damn," said Blake."Fuck," said Streets.

Chapter 44

Even though T-Walk had forced his ex-girlfriend, Ashley "Thunder" Hunter to get an abortion a few months ago, she still clung to him like white on rice, texting and calling him incessantly asking for this and that. A Birkin bag here. A pair of Louboutins there. So he was not at allsurprised to see her beautiful Nigerian face when he answered the knock at his office door.

She sashayed in wearing a backless red Valentino mini-dress (T-Walk remembered paying $30,000 for it) that thoroughly accentuated her stallion-esque lower half. Red diamond earrings ($85,000 out of T-Walk's wallet) blinged in her ears.

"I was looking for you in the VIP section," she said, pressing her fluffy lips against his as he filled his hands with her huge ass. "Your guySquirm said you came up here to grab something."

"I'm grabbing all I want to grab right now," T-Walk said."Oh yeah?"

"Hell yeah. How'd you know I was here?"

"I followed you." She smiled as he pushed the door shut. "What's wrong with Tasia? She looked like she was pissed."

T-Walk shrugged his shoulders, and pulled Thunder down to the sumptuous black carpet. He had come up to his old office to get the Glock- 27 he kept in his safe, and to watch the clique of Dub Life niggas that had entered his nightclub less than fifteen minutes ago. He'd been watching them from his second-floor office's mirrored windows when Thunder's softknock had sounded.

He got on top of her and started kissing and sucking on her neck. His head was a merry-go-round, no thanks to the bottle of Ciroc he'dfinished, and now his mouth was watering as he anticipated the taste of Thunder's sweet pussy.

As soon as she took off her panties, he moved his mouth down to her inner thighs and began kissing them in the same passionate way he'd kissed her neck. When the scrumptious scent of her warm pussy became toomuch to bear, he swiped his tongue up and down its juicy lips, squeezing her meaty black thighs in his palms. Then he applied his flickering tongueto her clitoris and watched her shudder.

"Oooh, yeah," she moaned, playing with T-Walk's ears. "I almost forget how talented you were with that tongue. Mmm… mmm, keepdoing that."

But no urging was needed. He would have continued anyway. The feast between her thighs was too irresistible to leave uneaten.

So he ate until she started shaking and gushing her sugary juices onto his eagerly fluctuating tongue. Then he told her to turn over while he took off his clothes.

"You know the drill," he said, slapping his dick on herenormous ass cheeks. "Face down, and lift that fat ass up."

She glanced over her shoulder at him, then squeezed her eyes shut and bit down on her bottom lip as he sank his thick pole deep into her sopping-wet pussy. He pushed her dress up so that it covered her head and pounded in and out of her dripping hole, ogling her wobbling butt cheeks. Thunder had ass for days. In fact, she'd gotten her nickname during a UGKvideo shoot when she had been twerking and making her ass clap. Fucking her was one of the few things in life that T-Walk knew he would never tire of doing. Especially since she was the most popular cast member of his hit reality TV show, Brick House of Jupiter Island.

Within ten minutes her snug juicebox became too much for him to endure. He snatched his dick out, intent on striping her jiggling cheeks with his semen, but she turned around and sucked the head into her mouth just as the first warm spurt of cum shot out of it.

Her sexy dark face twisted into an expression like that of a person who'd just bitten into a sour lemon, and her throat muscles contracted several times as she swallowed his cum. Her wet lips bobbed slowly on the tip of his deflating muscle until it was limp in her mouth. Then she stood up and fixed her dress.

T-Walk got dressed and, lighting a Newport, plopped down in the chair behind his desk. He picked up his smartphone and saw that Squirm had sent him a text with a link to CNN.com. He clicked on it and read:

'Rapper Bulletface's car riddled with bullets outside Chicago nightclub; no suspects in custody' T-Walk smiled.

"What are you smiling at?" Thunder asked, sauntering over to the mirrored floor-to-ceiling windows that overlooked the clubs'

The Cocaine Princess 3

jam- packed first floor. "Was I that good? You miss this pussy that much?"

"You know I do." T-Walk leaned back in his chair, gazing at the Nigerian goddess. "I'm telling you baby, as soon as my five-year contract with Costilla Corporation expires, I'm moving us to Malibu, get us a nice house overlooking the Pacific Ocean, matching Phantoms—the whole nine.might even get us a reality show like Ice and Coco. I already discussed it with Seacrest."

"Ryan Seacrest?""Yep."

Thunder looked back at him, rolling her eyes skeptically. "I'll believe it when it happens. You were supposed to stay with me last time andyou didn't. I got left behind for Alexus."

"Are you telling me you wouldn't leave me for a billionaire?"

"I'm not like you."

"You didn't answer the question."

She hesitated. "Not for good. I mean, I'd take care of you without him knowing. I'd probably marry him for couple of months, set him up to cheat on me with one of my friends, then divorce his ass, takehalf of his money, and spend it all with you."

"Well, what do you think I'm doing? I'll walk off with somewhere around thirty billion if I do this right. We'll be rich forever withthat kind of money. And even if I don't marry her, I'll still have at least twohundred and fifty million in five years."

"Who are you kidding, Trintino? You're never gonna leave her. I'll be chasing behind your raggedy ass forever." Rubbing the front of her neck, she cleared her throat and flicked her eyes at the small refrigerator that stood next to the safe behind T-Walk's desk. "You got something to drink in there? I think some of your kids are growing in my throat." T-Walk gave her a disgusted look. *'Nasty-ass bitch,'* he thought ashe opened the mini fridge and tossed her a bottle of water.

"Don't look at me like that," Thunder said. "I wasn't about to letyou cum on this thirty-thousand-dollar Valentino."

A witty retort was on the tip of T-Walks' tongue.But then his office door opened.

And in walked Alexus Costilla.

237

King Rio

Chapter 45

Her hair was unkempt; it spilled out from beneath her white furhat like a tangled black mop. The tears she'd cried out over the past hour had caused her mascara to streak down her perfect face, and she hadn't bothered to wipe away the sad black lines. Her full-length white fur was buttoned shut to conceal her bloodied dress. To avoid being seen she had made Enrique park the million-dollar limo behind the club. Then he'd escorted her up the rear stairs to the hallway that led to T-Walk's office, leaving Mercedes and Papi to work out their issues inside the stretch Phantom.

And now she stood in T-Walk's sex-scented office, studying his flabbergasted expression. Thunder wore an identical mask of surprise.

Alexus grabbed her hips and stared at her boyfriend. "Are you fucking serious, T-Walk?" She murmured, growing angrier by the second.

"Baby, I can explain," he said.

"Explain what? Why you didn't cum on her dress? Why you're here fucking this broke bitch while your woman is going through hell?"

"Bitch, I'm far from broke," Thunder quipped, rolling her neck.

There were two gold-plated .44 revolvers tucked away in the deep side packets of Alexus's coat; she drew one out of her right pocket andaimed it at Thunder's forehead.

"I don't want to hear another peep out of you, comprende?" she said to Thunder. "One more word and your head goes out that window.

What are we paying you bum bitches, anyway? Forty grand an episode? Fortwelve lousy episodes? Let' see, four hundred and eighty grand before taxes, about three hundred grand after taxes—you're a broke bitch in my book."

Alexus turned her attention back to T-Walk, stepping aside as Enrique walked in and rested his back against the oak-paneled wall besideher.

T-Walk stood up. "Lexi, I'm—I'm sorry, okay? I'm really, truly sorry, baby. I don't know what I was thinking—"

"Oh, no, it's cool," Alexus calmly replied, lining up the revolver's sights with T-Walk's chest. "I might as well make your heart bleed, too." She threw a diabolic smirk. "King Neal isn't yours."

"What?" He dropped his head back for a brief chuckle. "You don't have to lie to try and hurt my feelings. I said I'm sorry, baby."

"Do I look like I'm lying?"

"Come on, now, baby. I read the same paternity test results that you read."

"You read what I e-mailed you. I had the original results changed before I sent them to you. King Neal's father is Blake King."

Alexus was widening her smirk to a full-on grin and lowering the .44 when suddenly a crippling blow was introduced to the back of her head. She fell to the floor and blacked out.

*****

By the time Squirm-G had landed the first punch to the back of Alexus's head, Gusto's mammoth fists were already colliding with Enrique's face. Four sharp jabs and a brutal uppercut was all it took to render the brawny bodyguard unconscious. He slid down the wall and slumped over, his nose and jaw broken, blood pouring out the side of his mouth.

"You got bitches pointin' guns atchoo an' shit," Squirm said bending to pick up the golden revolver. "Fuck was she on?"

"Some bullshit." Tucking his Glock in the waistline of his Pelle Pelle jeans, T-Walk stepped around the desk and stood over Alexus.

"Ay, folks," Squirm said, "I need them blocks to lay on Reg and Ant for handlin' that business."

"They gotta wait until I can verify that."

"Nigga, what the fuck you think this is, Burger King? You can't always have it your way," replied Squirm.

Those were his last and final words.

*****

As Alexus slowly regained consciousness, she heard Squirms' voice, the voice that had always for some reason made her skin crawl.

Now the reason was clear.

Squirm was the guy who had demanded a billion dollars for King Neal's ransom. "Bitch, what the fuck you think this is, Burger King?"He'd said, and now he had just practically repeated the same question.

'I have to get out of here and find my momma,' Alexus thought, slowly pushing her hand down into the left pocket of her coat. She took a deep breath. Fought through the foggy pain that was pounding at the rear ofher skull.

Then, drawing the revolver, she rolled over onto her back and buried a bullet beneath Squirm's chin, sending the top of his head and everything inside it to the ceiling. Before his brainless body could even hitthe floor, Alexus turned the gun on his bear-sized comrade and blasted himtwice in the chest. She considered putting a hole in T-Walk's ass as he fledthe office, but her attention shifted to Thunder, who had just crawled underT-Walk's desk.

"Nuh-uh, bitch," Alexus said, walking around the desk. She grabbed a handful of Thunder's hair and dragged her out of the impromptuhiding spot. She pressed the.44's smoking barrel into the reality star's left eyelid. "Did you by any chance see what happened to these men?"

"I didn't see anything," Thunder cried."Are you sure about that?"

"Yes. Yes, I'm sure. I didn't see a thing. I was in the restroom."

Alexus felt compelled to slap the revolver across Thunder's face. But what was the use? And she had to hurry up and get to the churchbefore it was too late.

So she let go of Thunder's hair and, through clenched teeth, said, "Don't you *ever* touch my man again. Don't call him, don't text him—don'teven look at him. Remember Nat Turner? The MTN News anchorman my mother used to date? Do you remember how he died in Southampton County, Virginia? They found him hanging from the same tree that his sisterhad been lynched from. You remember that, don't you? It happened on November eleventh of last year." She kicked the sharp toe of her Louboutinheel into Thunder's exposed ribcage and stepped back as the equally thick- bottomed reality star curled up into an aching fetal position. Then she turned and walked away, stopping to pry her otherrevolver from Squirm's flaccid grip.

"Broke-ass hood rat," she said, leaving the office. "*I'm thee* boss bitch. I'm the cocaine *princess*. Pablo Escobar ain't got *shit* on me."

Chapter 46

Parked behind the white Rolls-Royce limo was Blake's matte black two-door Phantom. Its suicide doors were wide open, and Blake was sitting with his legs outside the driver's door, rolling yet another blunt of Kush and staring at The Swagger's rear exit door. His twin Desert Eagles were resting on his lap, and between them was his iPhone5; he was on the phone with Lil Meach, his rap protégé.

Lil' Meach and the other three MBM rap stars who had accompanied him in the Range Rover were in front of the club, waiting on T-Walk to make his exit.

"Bruh, we' ready," Meach said. "Dub Life twenty cars deep out here. That nigga finna get it."

"You say everybody leavin'?"

"Man, they rushin' out this muhfucka. Somebody said they heard some gunshots comin' from upstairs."

"They 'bout to hear some more," Blake said. He looked at Nona, who was standing beside Mercedes near the trunk of the limo. She was massaging Mercedes' shoulders. Mercedes was crying, and Blake figured it was because she felt she'd betrayed him by letting Duke get ahold of her backstage pass.

But that situation was already out of Blake's head. He'd gotten a text message from Reesie Cup a few minutes ago. Duke and another Four Corner Hustler had just been shot to death outside of a Chicago hospital.

Blake owed Cup $100,000 for the hit.

"We gon' catch this nigga drivin' out the parkin' lot," said Meach.

"Just make sure y'all leave his ass stankin'. I can't accept no fuck ups. Not this time. Not after that highway stunt they just pulled." His phone vibrated with a call from Cup. "Make sure Alexus ain't with him before y'all start shootin'. I got another call, bruh."

Lighting his blunt, Blake clicked over to speak with Reesie Cup, nodding his head to the distant beat of a Mary J. Blige ringtone as it blared from Mercedes' smartphone.

He wondered if it was someone calling her with the news of her baby's daddy's unfortunate demise.

He kept an eye on her.

"You're at The Swagger, right?" Cup asked.

"Ain't that what I told you five minutes ago?" Blake retorted sharply. He was still upset about Reesie Cup's involvement in his daughter's kidnapping two years prior. "I'm parked in the alley behind theclub. Why you out here?"

"Yeah. I'm pulling around now."The next minute or so was a blur.

Just as he ended the call, Mercedes came running at him,slinging her phone at him as she ran.

Blake jumped to his feet and grabbed Mercedes' arms before she got a chance to swing. His Desert Eagles fell to the alley's gravel floor.

"You killed my—Motherfucka, you killed *Duke*!" Mercedes screamed, kicking at his legs.

He picked her up and quickly carried her across the alleyway, slamming her back against the club's rear door just as two black Bentley coupes turned into the alley.

"What the fuck is you talkin' about?!" he shouted at her snarling face. "I ain't killed nobody! Stop trippin'!"

"Bitch-ass nigga, I know you did it! You paid somebody to kill him!" She was sobbing hysterically and fighting against his strong hands. "Nigga, you goin' to jail! I hope you never get out!"

She spit in Blake's face, and as he was pulling his arm back to slap the taste out of her mouth, the door swung open, cracking against theback of her head.

Mercedes dropped to the ground.

A black steel Glock skidded out the half-open door.And out fell T-Walk.

Chapter 47

Blake did not hesitate.

He turned and tried to kick a hole in T-Walk's face, but T-Walk dodged the kick with his forearms, rolled away from Blake, then rushed tohis feet.

The two rivals threw icy stares at each other for a half a second. In Blake's periphery he saw Papi step out of the limo.

Then he and T-Walk traded in their icy stares for balled-up fists.

T-Walk landed the first punch, but after that swift jab, a fight worthy of a UFC championship match followed. They pounded each other'sfaces. Slammed each other around. Bake tasted warm blood in his mouth.

While still throwing punches at T-Walk he glanced at the two Bentleys thathad just parked behind his Phantom and wondered why Reesie Cup was notrushing to his aid.

Mercedes jumped on Blake's back and dug her fingernails into his face. "Bitch, get off me!" He said, and flung her against the funky- smelling dumpster behind him.

T-Walk was getting back to his feet when Blake caught him with the next punch, a vicious right hook that knocked T-Walk onto his back.

Blake picked up the Glock and aimed it at Trintino's face.

"Yeah, fuck nigga, you know what time it is" Blake said, getting ready to pull the trigger. "See you at the crossroads, nigga."

Mercedes was replete with rage as she swung an empty Remy Martin bottle at the back of Blake's head. The bottle shattered on impact, cutting open Mercedes' hand and sending Blake to the ground just as the gun he was holding fired. She pounced on him like a ravenous lioness, punching the upward-facing side of his face. Papi shouted for her to stop,but she kept pounding on Blake... until her sister emerged from the door behind her and pushed her off of him.

"Mercedes, we have to get out of here right now! Come on!" Alexus reached for her sister's elbow, but Mercedes snatched away and stood up.

"Do you *really* think I'd go *anywhere* with *you*?!" Mercedes shouted, casting a tear-filled scowl at Alexus. "My mother is *dead* because of you! And now my kids' daddy is dead because of *him*!" She looked down at Blake, who was on his hands and knees, struggling to regain hisbalance, and T-Walk was attempting to do the same.

"Oh, my God!" Alexus suddenly screamed; her eyes, wide and shocked, were directed toward the limo. "Papi!"

Mercedes turned around… and gasped.

Their father was lying supine on the trash-littered gravel, right next to the Rolls-Royce limousine's rear driver's side tire. Nona had her hands on his chest, corking the gushing bullet hole.

Alexus ran over and dropped to her knees beside him, and Mercedes followed timidly, her anger momentarily forgotten. She stoppedat the other side of him. Watched Alexus cradle his head in her lap.

"Call nine-one-one!" Alexus shouted out in panic. "Somebody call nine-one-one! Help me get him in the car!"

"Calm down," Papi muttered weakly. He coughed, and a bloody mist sprayed from his mouth. His eyelids fluttered rapidly. "I'll be okay here. Just go and… get Rita. Save her. And no"—he grimaced—"no snitching. Leave the CIA, the FBI"—another bloody cough—"leave them out of it. And take care of Mercedes. You're the boss now Alexus. Be a great one. Be a…" His words faded.

Mercedes watched her father pass away in Alexus's arms, and the sight of it stunned her so deeply that she did not move until Enrique appeared beside her, his face bruised, broken and bloated. He helped her usher Alexus into the limo, then he got in the driver's seat as she slipped innext to her distraught sister.

The limo was already out of the alley when Mercedes looked back and saw Reesie Cup's Bentley following behind them.

Chapter 48

Stumbling toward the Glock, with blood pouring from his head and his thoughts churning in a blender of dizziness, Blake tried to focus on the task at hand: defending himself against his long-time enemy.

Nona grabbed him before he could get to T-Walk's gun. "Let's go Blake. Let's go home," she said, pulling him toward the open driver's door of his Phantom.

He felt the bullet hit the back of his neck before he heard the gunshot.

Falling to the ground next to his Phantom, he picked up one of his .50-calibers, turned so that his back would meet the ground first, aimedthe heavy gun at T-Walk's chest, and squeezed off two shots... just as T- Walk sent another round his way.

The bullet ripped through Blake's right cheek and exited the back of his head. Images of his life experiences flashed cross his mind; images of his daughter, his parents, King Neal, and Alexus.

Then the darkness took him.

King Rio

Chapter 49

"I'll help you get Rita out of there safely, but don't think for one minute that I'm over what you had done to my mother," Mercedes muttered, staring out the tinted side window as the limo stopped in front of the church on the corner of 8th and Willard.

Alexus was crying into the palms of her blood-covered hands. *'NotPapi!'* She kept thinking. *'Please, God, not Papi. Not my Papi!'*

"This is not the time to be breaking down," Mercedes advised. "We need to get in there as soon as possible."

Reluctantly, Alexus lifted her hands. She looked at the splotches of her father's blood that had soaked into her long fur coat. Eyed a group of drug-dealers who were gathered beside Blake's convenience store two blocks down. Then, thumbing away her tears, she mumbled, "Come on," and pushed open her door, wondering if she and her sister would survive whatever it was Aunt Jenny had planned for them.

To Be Continued...
The Cocaine Princess 4
Coming Soon

Lock Down Publications and Ca$h Presents assisted
publishing packages.

BASIC PACKAGE $499
Editing
Cover Design
Formatting

UPGRADED PACKAGE $800
Typing
Editing
Cover Design
Formatting

ADVANCE PACKAGE $1,200
Typing
Editing
Cover Design
Formatting
Copyright registration
Proofreading
Upload book to Amazon

LDP SUPREME PACKAGE $1,500
Typing
Editing
Cover Design
Formatting
Copyright registration
Proofreading
Set up Amazon account
Upload book to Amazon
Advertise on LDP Amazon and Facebook page

***Other services available upon request. Additional
charges may apply
Lock Down Publications

P.O. Box 944
Stockbridge, GA 30281-9998
Phone # 470 303-9761

Submission Guideline

Submit the first three chapters of your completed manuscript to ldpsubmissions@gmail.com, subject line: Your book's title. The manuscript must be in a .doc file and sent as an attachment. Document should be in Times New Roman, double spaced and in size 12 font. Also, provide your synopsis and full contact information. If sending multiple submissions, they must each be in a separate email.

Have a story but no way to send it electronically? You can still submit to LDP/Ca$h Presents. Send in the first three chapters, written or typed, of your completed manuscript to:

**LDP: Submissions Dept
Po Box 944
Stockbridge, Ga 30281**

DO NOT send original manuscript. Must be a duplicate.

Provide your synopsis and a cover letter containing your full contact information.

Thanks for considering LDP and Ca$h Presents.

NEW RELEASES

THE STREETS WILL NEVER CLOSE by K'AJJI
MONEY IN THE GRAVE 3 by MARTELL "TROUBLESOME"
BOLDEN
BETRAYAL OF A THUG by FRE$H
THE STREETS WILL TALK by YOLANDA MOORE
THE COCAINE PRINCESS by KING RIO

Coming Soon from Lock Down Publications/Ca$h Presents
BLOOD OF A BOSS **VI**
SHADOWS OF THE GAME II
TRAP BASTARD II
By **Askari**
LOYAL TO THE GAME **IV**
By **T.J. & Jelissa**
IF TRUE SAVAGE **VIII**
MIDNIGHT CARTEL IV
DOPE BOY MAGIC IV
CITY OF KINGZ III
NIGHTMARE ON SILENT AVE II
THE PLUG OF LIL MEXICO II
By **Chris Green**
BLAST FOR ME **III**
A SAVAGE DOPEBOY III
CUTTHROAT MAFIA III
DUFFLE BAG CARTEL VII
HEARTLESS GOON VI
By **Ghost**
A HUSTLER'S DECEIT III
KILL ZONE II
BAE BELONGS TO ME III
By **Aryanna**
KING OF THE TRAP III
By **T.J. Edwards**
GORILLAZ IN THE BAY V
3X KRAZY III
STRAIGHT BEAST MODE II
De'Kari
KINGPIN KILLAZ IV

The Cocaine Princess 3

STREET KINGS III

PAID IN BLOOD III

CARTEL KILLAZ IV

DOPE GODS III

Hood Rich

SINS OF A HUSTLA II

ASAD

RICH $AVAGE II

By Martell Troublesome Bolden

YAYO V

Bred In The Game 2

S. Allen

CREAM III

THE STREETS WILL TALK II

By Yolanda Moore

SON OF A DOPE FIEND III

HEAVEN GOT A GHETTO II

By Renta

LOYALTY AIN'T PROMISED III

By Keith Williams

I'M NOTHING WITHOUT HIS LOVE II

SINS OF A THUG II

TO THE THUG I LOVED BEFORE II

IN A HUSTLER I TRUST II

By Monet Dragun

QUIET MONEY IV

EXTENDED CLIP III

THUG LIFE IV

By **Trai'Quan**

THE STREETS MADE ME IV

By **Larry D. Wright**

255

King Rio

IF YOU CROSS ME ONCE II
By **Anthony Fields**
THE STREETS WILL NEVER CLOSE III
By K'ajji
HARD AND RUTHLESS III
THE BILLIONAIRE BENTLEYS III
Von Diesel
KILLA KOUNTY III
By Khufu
MONEY GAME III
By Smoove Dolla
JACK BOYS VS DOPE BOYS II
A GANGSTA'S QUR'AN V
By Romell Tukes
MURDA WAS THE CASE II
Elijah R. Freeman
THE STREETS NEVER LET GO II
By Robert Baptiste
AN UNFORESEEN LOVE III
By **Meesha**
KING OF THE TRENCHES III
by **GHOST & TRANAY ADAMS**

MONEY MAFIA II
LOYAL TO THE SOIL III
By **Jibril Williams**
QUEEN OF THE ZOO II
By **Black Migo**
THE BRICK MAN IV
THE COCAINE PRINCESS IV
By King Rio
VICIOUS LOYALTY II

By Kingpen
A GANGSTA'S PAIN II
By J-Blunt
CONFESSIONS OF A JACKBOY III
By Nicholas Lock
GRIMEY WAYS II
By Ray Vinci
KING KILLA II
By Vincent "Vitto" Holloway
BETRAYAL OF A THUG II
By Fre$h

<u>**Available Now**</u>

RESTRAINING ORDER **I & II**
By **CA$H & Coffee**
LOVE KNOWS NO BOUNDARIES **I II & III**
By **Coffee**
RAISED AS A GOON I, II, III & IV
BRED BY THE SLUMS I, II, III
BLAST FOR ME I & II
ROTTEN TO THE CORE I II III
A BRONX TALE I, II, III
DUFFLE BAG CARTEL I II III IV V VI
HEARTLESS GOON I II III IV V

King Rio

A SAVAGE DOPEBOY I II
DRUG LORDS I II III
CUTTHROAT MAFIA I II
KING OF THE TRENCHES
By **Ghost**
LAY IT DOWN **I & II**
LAST OF A DYING BREED I II
BLOOD STAINS OF A SHOTTA I & II III
By **Jamaica**
LOYAL TO THE GAME I II III
LIFE OF SIN I, II III
By **TJ & Jelissa**
BLOODY COMMAS I & II
SKI MASK CARTEL I II & III
KING OF NEW YORK I II,III IV V
RISE TO POWER I II III
COKE KINGS I II III IV V
BORN HEARTLESS I II III IV
KING OF THE TRAP I II
By **T.J. Edwards**
IF LOVING HIM IS WRONG…I & II
LOVE ME EVEN WHEN IT HURTS I II III
By **Jelissa**
WHEN THE STREETS CLAP BACK I & II III
THE HEART OF A SAVAGE I II III
MONEY MAFIA
LOYAL TO THE SOIL I II
By **Jibril Williams**
A DISTINGUISHED THUG STOLE MY HEART I II & III
LOVE SHOULDN'T HURT I II III IV
RENEGADE BOYS I II III IV

258

The Cocaine Princess 3

PAID IN KARMA I II III

SAVAGE STORMS I II III

AN UNFORESEEN LOVE I II

By **Meesha**

A GANGSTER'S CODE I &, II III

A GANGSTER'S SYN I II III

THE SAVAGE LIFE I II III

CHAINED TO THE STREETS I II III

BLOOD ON THE MONEY I II III

A GANGSTA'S PAIN

By J-Blunt

PUSH IT TO THE LIMIT

By **Bre' Hayes**

BLOOD OF A BOSS **I, II, III, IV, V**

SHADOWS OF THE GAME

TRAP BASTARD

By **Askari**

THE STREETS BLEED MURDER **I, II & III**

THE HEART OF A GANGSTA I II& III

By **Jerry Jackson**

CUM FOR ME I II III IV V VI VII VIII

An **LDP Erotica Collaboration**

BRIDE OF A HUSTLA **I II & II**

THE FETTI GIRLS **I, II& III**

CORRUPTED BY A GANGSTA I, II III, IV

BLINDED BY HIS LOVE

THE PRICE YOU PAY FOR LOVE I, II ,III

DOPE GIRL MAGIC I II III

By **Destiny Skai**

WHEN A GOOD GIRL GOES BAD

By **Adrienne**

King Rio

THE COST OF LOYALTY I II III
By Kweli
A GANGSTER'S REVENGE **I II III & IV**
THE BOSS MAN'S DAUGHTERS I II III IV V
A SAVAGE LOVE **I & II**
BAE BELONGS TO ME I II
A HUSTLER'S DECEIT I, II, III
WHAT BAD BITCHES DO I, II, III
SOUL OF A MONSTER I II III
KILL ZONE
A DOPE BOY'S QUEEN I II III
By **Aryanna**
A KINGPIN'S AMBITON
A KINGPIN'S AMBITION **II**
I MURDER FOR THE DOUGH
By **Ambitious**
TRUE SAVAGE I II III IV V VI VII
DOPE BOY MAGIC I, II, III
MIDNIGHT CARTEL I II III
CITY OF KINGZ I II
NIGHTMARE ON SILENT AVE
THE PLUG OF LIL MEXICO II

By **Chris Green**
A DOPEBOY'S PRAYER
By **Eddie "Wolf" Lee**
THE KING CARTEL **I, II & III**
By **Frank Gresham**
THESE NIGGAS AIN'T LOYAL **I, II & III**
By **Nikki Tee**
GANGSTA SHYT **I II &III**

260

By **CATO**

THE ULTIMATE BETRAYAL

By **Phoenix**

BOSS'N UP **I , II & III**

By **Royal Nicole**

I LOVE YOU TO DEATH

By **Destiny J**

I RIDE FOR MY HITTA

I STILL RIDE FOR MY HITTA

By **Misty Holt**

LOVE & CHASIN' PAPER

By **Qay Crockett**

TO DIE IN VAIN

SINS OF A HUSTLA

By **ASAD**

BROOKLYN HUSTLAZ

By **Boogsy Morina**

BROOKLYN ON LOCK I & II

By **Sonovia**

GANGSTA CITY

By **Teddy Duke**

A DRUG KING AND HIS DIAMOND I & II III

A DOPEMAN'S RICHES

HER MAN, MINE'S TOO I, II

CASH MONEY HO'S

THE WIFEY I USED TO BE I II

By Nicole Goosby

TRAPHOUSE KING **I II & III**

KINGPIN KILLAZ I II III

STREET KINGS I II

PAID IN BLOOD **I II**

King Rio

CARTEL KILLAZ I II III
DOPE GODS I II
By **Hood Rich**
LIPSTICK KILLAH **I, II, III**
CRIME OF PASSION I II & III
FRIEND OR FOE I II III
By **Mimi**
STEADY MOBBN' **I, II, III**
THE STREETS STAINED MY SOUL I II III
By **Marcellus Allen**
WHO SHOT YA **I, II, III**
SON OF A DOPE FIEND I II
HEAVEN GOT A GHETTO
Renta
GORILLAZ IN THE BAY **I II III IV**
TEARS OF A GANGSTA I II
3X KRAZY I II
STRAIGHT BEAST MODE
DE'KARI
TRIGGADALE I II III
MURDAROBER WAS THE CASE
Elijah R. Freeman
GOD BLESS THE TRAPPERS I, II, III
THESE SCANDALOUS STREETS I, II, III
FEAR MY GANGSTA I, II, III IV, V
THESE STREETS DON'T LOVE NOBODY I, II
BURY ME A G I, II, III, IV, V
A GANGSTA'S EMPIRE I, II, III, IV
THE DOPEMAN'S BODYGAURD I II
THE REALEST KILLAZ I II III
THE LAST OF THE OGS I II III

Tranay Adams
THE STREETS ARE CALLING
Duquie Wilson
MARRIED TO A BOSS I II III
By Destiny Skai & Chris Green
KINGZ OF THE GAME I II III IV V VI
Playa Ray
SLAUGHTER GANG I II III
RUTHLESS HEART I II III
By Willie Slaughter
FUK SHYT
By Blakk Diamond
DON'T F#CK WITH MY HEART I II
By Linnea
ADDICTED TO THE DRAMA I II III
IN THE ARM OF HIS BOSS II
By Jamila
YAYO I II III IV
A SHOOTER'S AMBITION I II
BRED IN THE GAME
By S. Allen
TRAP GOD I II III
RICH $AVAGE
MONEY IN THE GRAVE I II III
By Martell Troublesome Bolden
FOREVER GANGSTA
GLOCKS ON SATIN SHEETS I II
By Adrian Dulan
TOE TAGZ I II III IV
LEVELS TO THIS SHYT I II
By Ah'Million

King Rio

KINGPIN DREAMS I II III
By Paper Boi Rari
CONFESSIONS OF A GANGSTA I II III IV
CONFESSIONS OF A JACKBOY I II
By Nicholas Lock
I'M NOTHING WITHOUT HIS LOVE
SINS OF A THUG
TO THE THUG I LOVED BEFORE
A GANGSTA SAVED XMAS
IN A HUSTLER I TRUST
By Monet Dragun
CAUGHT UP IN THE LIFE I II III
THE STREETS NEVER LET GO
By Robert Baptiste
NEW TO THE GAME I II III
MONEY, MURDER & MEMORIES I II III
By **Malik D. Rice**
LIFE OF A SAVAGE I II III
A GANGSTA'S QUR'AN I II III IV
MURDA SEASON I II III
GANGLAND CARTEL I II III
CHI'RAQ GANGSTAS I II III
KILLERS ON ELM STREET I II III
JACK BOYZ N DA BRONX I II III
A DOPEBOY'S DREAM I II III
JACK BOYS VS DOPE BOYS
By **Romell Tukes**
LOYALTY AIN'T PROMISED I II
By Keith Williams
QUIET MONEY I II III
THUG LIFE I II III

EXTENDED CLIP I II

By **Trai'Quan**

THE STREETS MADE ME I II III

By **Larry D. Wright**

THE ULTIMATE SACRIFICE I, II, III, IV, V, VI

KHADIFI

IF YOU CROSS ME ONCE

ANGEL I II

IN THE BLINK OF AN EYE

By **Anthony Fields**

THE LIFE OF A HOOD STAR

By **Ca$h & Rashia Wilson**

THE STREETS WILL NEVER CLOSE I II

By **K'ajji**

CREAM I II

THE STREETS WILL TALK

By **Yolanda Moore**

NIGHTMARES OF A HUSTLA I II III

By **King Dream**

CONCRETE KILLA I II

VICIOUS LOYALTY

By **Kingpen**

HARD AND RUTHLESS I II

MOB TOWN 251

THE BILLIONAIRE BENTLEYS I II

By **Von Diesel**

GHOST MOB

Stilloan Robinson

MOB TIES I II III IV V

By **SayNoMore**

BODYMORE MURDERLAND I II III

King Rio

By Delmont Player

FOR THE LOVE OF A BOSS

By C. D. Blue

MOBBED UP I II III IV

THE BRICK MAN I II III

THE COCAINE PRINCESS I II

By King Rio

KILLA KOUNTY I II III

By Khufu

MONEY GAME I II

By Smoove Dolla

A GANGSTA'S KARMA I II

By FLAME

KING OF THE TRENCHES I II

by **GHOST & TRANAY ADAMS**

QUEEN OF THE ZOO

By **Black Migo**

GRIMEY WAYS

By Ray Vinci

XMAS WITH AN ATL SHOOTER

By Ca$h & Destiny Skai

KING KILLA

By Vincent "Vitto" Holloway

BETRAYAL OF A THUG

By Fre$h

BOOKS BY LDP'S CEO, CA$H

TRUST IN NO MAN

TRUST IN NO MAN 2

TRUST IN NO MAN 3

BONDED BY BLOOD

SHORTY GOT A THUG

THUGS CRY

THUGS CRY 2

THUGS CRY 3

TRUST NO BITCH

TRUST NO BITCH 2

TRUST NO BITCH 3

TIL MY CASKET DROPS

RESTRAINING ORDER

RESTRAINING ORDER 2

IN LOVE WITH A CONVICT

LIFE OF A HOOD STAR

XMAS WITH AN ATL SHOOTER

King Rio